Poet in the Gutter

Poet in the Gutter

John Baker

VICTOR GOLLANCZ

LONDON

First published in Great Britain 1995
by Victor Gollancz
An imprint of the Cassell Group
Wellington House, 125 Strand, London WC2R 0BB

A catalogue record for this book is
available from the British Library.

ISBN 0 575 06039 5

Typeset by CentraCet Ltd, Cambridge
Printed in Great Britain by
St Edmundsbury Press Ltd, Bury St Edmunds, Suffolk

Heard the song of a poet who died in the gutter

Bob Dylan

Chapter 1

There was this freak in the men's group. Well, Jesus, they were all freaks, including Sam Turner, but there was this one who stood out. Terry Deacon, he was called, and he stood out from the rest because he didn't wear an ear-ring. He'd just turned forty. The time when all the guys who were younger than him were just going out and having it done, he'd been wondering if it was too effeminate. Then a few years later, after he'd missed the boat, he was thinking he'd really like to wear an ear-ring but if he had it done now people'd think he was trying to be younger. Sensitive sort, that was Deacon. He was also rich. And that made him stand out.

Anyway, it was him told Sam Turner about Hemingway and the first true sentence which got Sam reading again. And after Hemingway he read Chandler, and they became his favourite dead writers. His favourite living writer was Elmore Leonard. He was only interested in class stuff.

Sam went to the men's group because it was winter and cold in the flat, and because he was off the booze, and because another marriage had gone bust. There's this place runs groups of all kinds, every night of the week. It cost ninety pence to get in, and that particular night Sam had the choice of Esperanto or the men's group or going back on the booze. He walked in on them and sat down in the circle.

They were talking about fairy stories and *Iron John* and about how women were in touch with the earth and men in the twentieth century were alienated. Sam thought about switching

7

to Esperanto or walking fifty yards down the road for a beer and chaser. But he stayed put.

Two of them were gay, or playing with the idea, and bought their ear-rings together. That night they were wearing tiny silver and black guitars, but other nights they would wear large hoops or love hearts or a couple of Js. They were called John and Jeffrey. Most of the others wore small gold rings, except for Deacon, who didn't wear anything, and a guy called Bock, who had nine rings in one ear, three in the other, and two up his nose. The guy looked like a Christmas tree.

Before they started they all said their name and what they did for a living. When it came to him Sam said he was called Sam Turner and he was a private detective, and they all said that was really *interesting*. What Sam thought was interesting was where the name came from, because he'd just plucked it out of the air some years before, while travelling round California. The bit about being a private detective was nearly true. He'd been thinking about it all his life. It was a song he knew well, no reason not to sing it.

The only Iron John Sam'd ever known had been in Hull Prison, serving twenty years of a life sentence for a cop killing. When Sam told them this they stopped talking about fairy stories and turned their ear-rings to him. This was *really* interesting, they thought. Their little eyes lit up like sparklers. What was he like? Did he show remorse? And the Hull Prison, what were the conditions like? Jesus Christ, these guys were unbelievable. Forty-five minutes and Sam had them eating out of his hand.

Like the man said, you've got to serve somebody.

He went to that place nearly every night. Monday he went to AA. Tuesday was a solo club. Wednesday the men's group. Thursday another solo club. And Friday an electronics user group. When you're on the waggon you can't afford to stop.

Sam thought the solo clubs would help him keep up his sex life without much effort, but they were really hard-going. People frightened of getting hurt again. Jesus, where've they been?

Brenda, his last wife, she used to say, If it don't hurt a bit, it's not worth having. She found a guy running a Merc and three houses and it was love at first sight. Sam told her he wouldn't stand in her way, and she said: 'Who's asking *you*?' and went. He still couldn't remember all the best things she said. Living in Tadcaster with the Merc guy. But he didn't mind too much. Life soon went back to normal. He drove to Sainsbury's and spent £170 on their good whisky. He packed a tent in the car and drove up to the moors, pitching about a mile and a half above the Blakey Head pub. Then he drank himself unconscious.

Next day he walked to the Blakey and got a beer with a chaser. He stayed there until closing time and went back to the juice in the tent. It took about three weeks altogether. He lost twenty pounds, and stopped dreaming about Brenda.

Back in York he was dry for a month, then three weeks on the hard stuff. He was dry again. Hitting it again. Still managed to get a flat together, ground-floor job, of course, save himself breaking bones when he was on the juice. He'd go dry, feed himself up, take all his clothes to the launderette. He'd stock the cupboards with food, clean the carpets, do a month's washing up, start shaving again. Then he'd be in a bar with a glass in front of him and he might sit there all night and not touch it until closing time. The next time he looked in a mirror he'd have lost several weeks. After a year he woke up one afternoon in a pool of spew and said to himself: You're worth more than this.

That's when he went to the AA and the men's group and . . .

Chapter 2

Deacon rang him one night as he was going out to the solo club.

'I think I'm going to need your services,' he said. Deacon spoke quietly, rhythmically. He was a composer and a Buddhist as well as a very successful businessman.

'What?' said Sam. He didn't have a clue what the guy meant.

'It's my wife,' Deacon explained. 'I think she's having an affair.'

'Dump her,' Sam told him. 'A woman starts an affair, she's finished with you.'

'I don't know for sure,' Deacon said. 'I'd like you to check it out.'

'Oh, I see.' Sam did a double take into the telephone. He sat down and reached into his pocket for tobacco, papers. 'Detective work.'

'Yes. I know you do commercial work. But I thought you might be able to help out.'

'Sure, Terry,' said Sam, rolling with one hand, lighting up, thinking fast. 'I'm a bit tied up at the moment, but I think I can fit you in. When were you thinking?'

'Now,' said Deacon. 'It's happening now. Can I come see you?'

'I'm doing a surveillance job at the moment,' Sam said, still thinking. 'I could meet you tomorrow. I'll be in Betty's about two. And, Terry?'

'Yes?'

'This isn't going to be cheap.'

'Oh, I know,' said Deacon, eager to smooth over any misunderstanding. 'I didn't mean . . . I hope you didn't think I was asking . . .'

10

'Don't worry,' said Sam. 'I won't break you. But I have to make a living.'

'I really wasn't . . .' Deacon continued, 'I really wasn't expecting you to work for nothing. I'm very happy to pay the going rate. I hope you don't think . . .'

'It's OK, Terry. Don't worry about it. Betty's at two. Don't be late.' Sam rang off and stubbed his cigarette in the ashtray. He looked at the phone.

He'd been great. He'd handled it smoothly. Betty's was a nice touch. Betty's was a *wonderful* touch. Just the sort of place Deacon would fall for. Quiet, mirrors everywhere, waitress service, good strong coffee. And it would be money for old rope. Just following some woman about all day. Sam reckoned Deacon must be good for forty a day. Plus expenses, of course. You have to be professional about these things. He'd always known that life was ups and downs. This was the beginning of an up.

At the solo club Sam concentrated on Wanda. He couldn't *believe* her name, had real difficulty disassociating it from the fish film. But she'd shown some interest over the last couple of weeks, enough to make it worth pursuing. She was a redhead, like Brenda. That didn't put Sam off. He wasn't superstitious. Wanda had been divorced for two years. She had two kids, both girls; the youngest was two and the eldest four. She drove her own car, a two-year-old Rover with leather upholstery, and she had her own house somewhere on the outskirts of town. This woman was not going to be any kind of *drag*. She wasn't looking for someone to support her. She was doing very nicely as it was. And tonight she was coming on strong.

Sam had spent several years in California when he was younger, and Wanda had been quizzing him about LA. She'd been there herself with her ex-husband, shortly after they were married. Sam had spent most of his time there in Santa Monica, which Wanda had never visited, and she'd stayed in Corona del Mar, which Sam had only driven through once. So they talked about vegetation

11

instead: towering eucalyptus, graceful pepper trees, tropic palms, rubber trees, giant bananas, yuccas, and the wonderful growth of roses, heliotrope, calla lilies in hedges, orange trees, jasmine, and giant geraniums.

'Christ, stop,' said Sam. 'It just makes me want to go back.'

'Me too,' said Wanda.

They smiled at each other. Wanda looked away, then looked back at him again. She lowered her voice and said something he didn't catch. 'Say it again,' he said.

'The children are away this weekend,' she told him.

'So you'll be out on the town. Living it up a little?'

Wanda smiled. She smiled a lot, but usually the smile was a stick-on job. This smile was different, it came from inside. 'No. I don't go out much in the town.'

'What'll you do, then?' asked Sam. 'Sit at home and watch the box?'

'Nothing on Saturday night,' Wanda said. 'Sunday I'm going on the walk.' The club had organized a hike in the dales on Sunday.

'We could go together,' Sam tried. 'If we go in one car, we'll save petrol.'

'OK. I'll drive. Get to my place about ten, I'll be ready.'

Sam wanted to fix her up for Saturday night. But he needed more encouragement. Wanda wasn't the kind of woman you could rush. Well, maybe it would work, but Sam liked things better when they were on the edge.

'I'll give you a ring on Saturday night,' he said. 'I think I'm tied up, but I'll give you a ring. Make sure everything's OK for Sunday.' He wasn't doing anything Saturday night, but it wouldn't harm to let her sweat a little. Wondering what he was up to.

Chapter 3

Sam took his camera along to Betty's, bought a pocket book and a pen from Smith's on the way, and installed himself with a cup of coffee by the window. Watched the tourists going by, Americans and Japanese, groups of Scandinavian teenagers with enough Nikon cameras to fill a truck.

Deacon arrived ten minutes later, waving as he passed the window. He joined Sam and pushed his briefcase under the table. Nice leather job.

'Hope you haven't been waiting long,' he said.

'Don't worry,' Sam told him. 'I'm on a job. Been here an hour.' Sam glanced at a table across the room from them. Deacon followed his gaze, and took in two women, obviously a mother and daughter, and a young man who could have been the brother of the younger woman or her lover. 'Don't make it obvious,' said Sam.

'Oh, sorry,' said Deacon, quickly looking away. 'I didn't mean . . .'

'No damage done,' said Sam. 'I have to keep my eye on them, but you've got my full attention.'

The waitress took their order for coffee Sam ordered a big one with cream, Deacon settled for a small one with milk.

'Where do I start?' asked Deacon.

Sam picked up his pen and opened the notebook towards the end. 'I need personal details,' he said. 'Name, address, date of birth, and a photograph would be useful.'

She was called Jane Deacon, and they lived together in a large house in Bishophill. They had been married twelve years.

Recently Jane had been going out twice a week, Tuesday and Thursday, ostensibly to her friend's or sister's house. But Deacon knew she didn't go to either. He didn't know where she went. He thought she had a boyfriend.

From the photograph Sam thought it would be very nice for the boyfriend, whoever he was. Jane Deacon wasn't in the first flush of youth, but she was a looker nevertheless. If she was on the menu, he would've skipped the soup, got to the main course quick. Sad-eyed lady . . .

'Why would it be a boyfriend?' he asked.

'Because she dresses up,' Deacon explained. 'I bought her a suit. It's blue, cashmere. She looks really good in it. She always wears that, and she fixes her hair, wears make-up. She makes a real effort. Why would she do that if it wasn't a man?'

'You a detective, or what?' said Sam.

Deacon didn't get the joke. 'I can't cope with the uncertainty,' he said. 'I can't do my meditation any more. My work is suffering. I'm short with people.'

'Forty pounds a day,' Sam told him. 'Plus expenses.'

'Yes. Whatever. I want to get it sorted.'

Sam waited. Thought maybe he was too cheap, should have asked for fifty a day, maybe sixty. He glanced across at the other table. The young woman got up and went to the ladies. 'I'll need something up front,' he said.

'Oh, of course.' Deacon reached for his wallet.

'Say two hundred,' said Sam. 'I'll keep records. Give you a detailed invoice.'

'I don't carry that much around. Will a cheque be all right?'

Sam bit his lip. 'I could use *some* cash,' he said.

Deacon inspected the contents of his wallet. He gave Sam sixty in cash and a cheque for a hundred and forty.

The younger woman returned from the ladies and her mother and brother stood to leave. Sam closed his notebook and reached for his camera. 'I've got to go,' he said.

'When will I hear?' Deacon asked him.

'Give me a week,' said Sam. He pointed at the empty cups. 'Pick up the tab for this, will you?'

Chapter 4

Frances went to the supermarket. She bought one of those Kellogg's variety packs, a mixture of individual boxes of breakfast cereals. Some cartons of yoghurt. Ten eggs, and a pack of bacon. She bought a small cake. A treat.

Her house in Clifton was small, but warm, being in the middle of a terrace. In the kitchen she put her purchases on the shelf neatly. Yoghurt, eggs and bacon in the fridge. There was also an onion in there, on a plate; and some left-over lasagna.

The neighbours were nosey, but she ignored them. Frances kept herself to herself. She didn't need neighbours poking around. Frances didn't need anybody. She had work to do.

She was a big woman, thickly set. Thirty-four years old. There was a smell in the house, somewhere in the kitchen. Frances put an apron on and filled a blue plastic bucket with hot water from the tap. She got on her hands and knees and scrubbed the floor, going over it twice, putting all her strength into each sweep of the brush. Then she refilled the bucket with clear water, and went over the floor again, rinsing it until it gleamed.

In the sitting room she took down Graham's loose-leaf folder of poems, opened it at random, and began to read. She could hear Graham's voice in her head. That slight New Zealand twang he'd never lost. She looked at the words and Graham's voice spoke in her head. That's how it worked.

Half of the poems were about her. Love poems. Poems Graham had stayed up nights with, he beavered away at them, bringing

them to her in the morning. She liked those poems. They were a
fitting memorial to Graham. To her as well. To their *relationship*.

The other half of the poems were about other people. People
she didn't know, or hardly knew. They were about bastards and
tarts. People who'd used and tormented Graham. People who'd
ruined his life before she met him.

Frances still sent some of Graham's poems to magazines. They
usually came back with a rejection slip. But occasionally one
would be published. Some day she would arrange for the whole
collection to be published in a book. That's what Graham would
have done. That's what Graham wanted above everything else.

The thought made Frances smile. She listened to Graham's
voice inside her head, and at the same time she felt the smile
breaking out over her face. It didn't come often these days, that
smile, but when it did come, at times like these, when she was
alone with Graham, it was the same old big, big smile he used to
love.

Chapter 5

He rang Wanda at five on Saturday afternoon. He had *Desire* on
his tape deck, and let it play while he punched the numbers. She
picked up the phone and repeated the number he'd just dialled.
Her voice was not unlike Brenda's. She didn't waste words.

Sam waited a few seconds before speaking. He could feel her at
the other end of the line, getting tense. 'How're you doing?' he
said.

'Sam?' she said. 'Goodness, I thought it was a breather for a
minute.'

'Do you get them?' he asked.

'No. I never have. But you hear about them.'

'I could breathe for a while if you like. Talk dirty? Whatever you fancy.'

Wanda laughed. A high-pitched laugh, embarrassed but interested, a little frightened maybe. 'That's no way to speak to a lady,' she said.

'Really? I must've met the wrong ones.'

'You probably do, in your line of work.'

'Yeah,' he said. 'I meet all sorts. Have your kids, I mean your *children*, have they gone?'

Wanda laughed again. 'About an hour ago.'

'So what you doing now?'

'Nothing. Talking to you. I had a bath.'

'What you wearing?'

The laugh came down the line.

'What you wearing?' Sam asked again, getting into the spirit of it.

'Do you mean it?' she said.

'I've asked you twice.'

'It's a kind of robe,' she said.

'A bath robe? What colour?'

'No. It's silk. It's a red silk dressing gown.'

'Short?'

'Long. Down to my ankles.'

'Sounds nice,' he said. 'Wish I was there.'

'Yes.' Her voice turned the corner into wistfulness. 'If you weren't such a busy man . . .'

'Shall I come now?' he asked.

'No. Later,' she said. 'I'll cook some food. Come about eight.'

'Just don't change your clothes,' he said, and hung up. He slapped the wall with his open hand. 'Yes,' he said. 'Yes. Yes. Yes.'

Sam drove a very old Cortina. It reminded him of Brenda every time he looked at it. Like her, it succeeded in screwing up his day every morning. He had to pet it, tread around it warily, feel out what kind of mood it was in. He took comfort from the fact that, like Brenda, it wouldn't last the rest of his life. Words in his head . . . *And she was once a true love of mine.*

He threw his parka and hiking boots in the back of the beast. It sounded like Wanda would want him to stay the night, and he might as well be ready for the walk tomorrow.

He drove round to Bishophill and parked fifty yards up from the Deacon house. It was a cul-de-sac, cars parked on both sides. Sam would have to reverse out. He adjusted the mirror so that he could see the gate, rolled up a cigarette and waited. Just after six Jane Deacon turned the corner in front of him, loaded down with parcels and plastic carrier bags.

She was a real looker, better than the photograph. Short blond hair and blue eyes. A mean little mouth to add some excitement to the face. And legs going all the way up to her bum. If she *had* found herself a new boyfriend, Deacon was really going to miss her one of these days.

She passed the car and Sam watched her rear view through the mirror. She was good to watch. She was very good to watch. 'I'll see you on Tuesday,' he said to himself as she turned into the gate of the big house. *Very* big house, like in the magazines at the doctor's.

Wanda opened the door in a little black number with a single thread of pearls at her throat. 'You've changed,' he said.

'I was cold.' She led him into a spacious living room. At the far end the dining table was set for two. Candles. Wine glasses.

'You look like a million dollars,' he said.

'A girl has to try.'

'Some harder than others. *You* don't have to do much.'

She served up a roast and poured wine into his glass. 'Say when?' she said.

Sam said nothing. Burgundy's OK; in his time he'd hit harder stuff. Only you *can* manage wine if you try – believe you're the strongest man in the world. The trick is not to have more than one glass, never let her fill it up again, and never let it get empty. Never worry about it. Sip it. Let her have the rest of the bottle if she wants.

He picked up the glass and caught her eye. 'To us,' he said.

'I'll drink to that,' said Wanda.

After the cheesecake she made coffee and they sat at the table for an hour while she told him her life story. It was an average story for a redhead. Lower-middle-class beginnings in the West Midlands, secretarial college, married the boss, moved to York, got pregnant twice in succession, divorced him and came out of it with a house and a car and a settlement that kept her comfortable. Fascinating stuff. Sam couldn't help it if he was lucky.

She suggested they move to more comfortable chairs, and they left the table, went to the other end of the room, where Sam stood with his back to the fire. She stood closer than she'd ever been before.

'You've led such an interesting life,' he told her.

She smiled. She didn't think so. She said, 'Are you going to stay?'

Sam said, 'If you want me to, yeah.'

She moved towards him and he reached for the long zipper at the back of the black dress. Over her shoulder he noticed there was still half an inch of red wine in his glass.

Chapter 6

Frances washed her breakfast bowl and scoured the sink and draining board. As a child she had been the youngest and the apple of her father's eye. No one had expected Frances to do mundane or domestic chores. She had been cared for, loved by her father. 'My princess,' he would call her. 'My cuddly little princess.'

Those had been secure days, when she was the baby, letting everyone else take on the responsibility. Frances had known then that life would not be simple when she grew up. She always said that she didn't want to grow up, that she wanted to remain a child for ever. But they wouldn't let her. No matter how passively she acted, slowly, inevitably, her body grew. Frances remained a child inside that body, somewhere inside her she was still her father's princess. But she didn't talk about that to anyone. She kept it inside.

She sat at the empty kitchen table and took out the butcher's knife from the drawer. She placed it on the table in front of her and watched the blade gleam in the sunlight from the window.

She took an A4 sheet of paper from Graham's folder, holding it with her nails, and read the message on it. Then she placed it back in the folder, and put the folder neatly on the shelf.

She took her coat from the peg and draped it round her shoulders. She opened her handbag to check the car keys were inside, and walked through the kitchen to the door. As she passed it, she patted the knife, and she said: 'Soon. Soon.'

Frances drove the black Panda to Bishophill and left it by the side of the road. She walked to the cul-de-sac, and then walked down it on one side, and up again on the other. The Deacon's house looked quiet at this time of day.

She walked back down the cul-de-sac again, but this time took a footpath at the blind end and followed it into town.

During the course of the day she returned four times. The second time she saw Jane Deacon coming out of the house. She followed her for a while, but gave up when Jane Deacon met another woman and stood gossiping on the pavement.

The fourth time Frances returned to the cul-de-sac she saw Terry Deacon. His car was filthy. He didn't care for anything. He didn't *take* care of anything.

20

'I've seen him,' Frances told the knife when she got home. 'He's disgusting.'

Chapter 7

On Monday, during the AA meeting, Sam took stock. Life was really looking up. He had money and a woman, and he was a private detective. He didn't have to bullshit any more.

The evening of Tuesday he was waiting for half an hour before Jane Deacon came out of the gate in her little blue cashmere suit, got into her white Peugeot, and drove slowly along the street, over the sleeping policemen. Sam put the Cortina in gear and followed at a reasonable distance.

It was not a long journey. She drove out on the Hull road and pulled in the driveway of a house with a double-bay front, 386a. The house was detached. and not as old as its neighbours. Sam thought maybe a couple of the older houses had been pulled down, and this one built in the space left behind. He drove on past, turned around and came back, stopping on the opposite side of the road. All rooms on the ground floor were lit. Only one of the upper rooms. Sam waited nearly two hours.

It would be nice, if the cash keeps coming in, to trash this car and get something a little better. Nothing ostentatious, though. Something people wouldn't notice, but with more oomph. And maybe a stereo system, to pass the time. Play all his Dylan tapes. No, maybe not. Some bastard'd steal it.

The surprising thing was, when she came out, she was shown out by a *woman*. A middle-aged woman, no distinguishing characteristics. White Anglo-Saxon Protestant.

And, surprise, surprise, Jane Deacon got into her white car and drove straight home to her Buddhist husband.

A mystery, Sam wrote in his notebook. A real mystery. Somebody better investigate.

Wednesday he checked out the electoral register in the library. Number 386a, Hull Road, was occupied by David and Ellen Watson.

He knocked on the door of 386a, but there was no answer. At 387 a woman came to the door and opened it before he had time to knock. She looked like the lady who knew everyone in the neighbourhood, the one they all avoided.

'Mrs Watson?' said Sam.

'No. You want to be next door,' said the woman. 'She'll be at work, though. *He* might be in. But he doesn't always answer the door.'

'Oh, dear,' said Sam. 'I wanted Mrs Watson. When will I get her?'

'She's usually back about six,' said the woman.

Sam put on his worried look. 'It's rather urgent,' he said. 'Does Mr Watson work at home?'

'He's usually there,' said the woman. 'His studio's upstairs. I don't know if he can't hear the door, or if he doesn't want to.'

'Studio?'

'Yes. He's a painter. Paints portraits.'

'That's right,' said Sam. 'Yeah, I'd heard that. He's a painter.'

There was an ad in the *Yellow Pages*:

> *David Watson*
> *Portraits in Oils*
> *Sittings by Appointment*
> *386a Hull Road*

'Jesus,' said Sam. 'She's having her fuckin' picture painted.'

Chapter 8

Jane Deacon had driven fairly slowly on Tuesday evening, aware that the red Cortina with Sam Turner was still behind her. She didn't want to lose him. That would be impossible. He acted like a professional tail, keeping his distance at all times, sometimes three or four cars between him and her.

Jane was happiest when she was in control. Things were beginning to happen now, she was making them happen, not just leaving them to chance. When Jane was a child, a small child of six years, her mother had died. Just like that. One day she had been there, mothering, the next day she was gone. That was chance, that was what chance did, took the world away from under your feet. Since then Jane had been working at being in control of her world. Not letting it get away.

The car was a liability though, the Cortina. It was so old you had to notice it. Hope it's reliable. Don't want it to break down. After all, Sam Turner was her alibi.

Jane felt good tonight. She'd had a bath, fixed her hair, and she knew she looked fine in this suit. You could look for clothes for ever and not find something like this. Fits everywhere, expensive material that takes the strain exactly where it's needed, and the colour was perfect for Jane's complexion, her hair, her eyes. She glanced in the mirror to check he was still there. Yes, two cars back.

It was a pity she didn't know what he looked like. If he was anything like his car, he wouldn't be up to much. She had a picture of him as a grubby little man, maybe someone who rolled his own cigarettes, nicotine stains on his fingers. She knew he wouldn't be like that in reality, because Terry wouldn't know anyone like that. But he's like that inside, she thought. Nicotine stains on his *mind*.

After the sitting he was still there, doing his job really well. He didn't pull away from the kerb straight after her. If she hadn't known what he was up to, there would be no way of suspecting it. Probably had a little notebook or a tape recorder, was speaking into it now, saying something like: 'Suspect left the house at nine-thirty p.m. Am now in pursuit.'

Get it right, Mr Turner. We don't want you making any mistakes.

He stayed behind her all the way home. Parked his junkie Cortina and watched her go into the house.

Terry was waiting when she got inside. 'You all right?' he asked, kissing her on the cheek.

'Yes, your detective friend was with me all the way.'

Chapter 9

Sam didn't go to the men's group on Wednesday. He sat at home brooding. His ground-floor flat consisted of three rooms, sitting room and kitchen combined, with separate bedroom and bathroom. Apart from the table where Sam sat to eat, there was a battered sofa and an arm chair which had once been part of a suite, several bookcases and a black metal rack which housed his stereo equipment. He had lived there so long now it felt like home, and one day he was going to fix it up good. Needed something on the walls, pictures. He'd never got round to the walls, not liking posters, and being unable to afford a really good picture.

Tonight, even *Blonde on Blonde* didn't work. Everything had been going right. For a few days things were coming together. Now there was no case. He didn't want to go to Deacon and tell him his wife was sitting for a portrait, probably for his – Deacon's – birthday.

Hell, matrimonial cases were the pits, everyone knew that. You followed a broad around for a week or two, took photographs of her and her lover in compromising situations. You spent most of the time sitting in a car waiting. And all for peanuts.

But on your first case in the whole universe, to end up with no guilty party, after only one night's work. That was bad luck. That was enough to make a man drink.

Sam wanted the case to be solid. OK, he could go out and buy a bottle. It was easy. He'd done it before, a thousand times. By tomorrow Deacon and his beautiful wife could be a hazy memory. Not even that. They could be *blotted out*.

Only one thing kept him away from the bottle. One tiny possibility. Jane Deacon *could* be screwing the painter. OK, it was not probable. But it was ever so faintly possible.

Sam slept badly, and on Thursday he spent the afternoon in the snooker hall at the Stonebow. He hustled a couple of games with Gus, an old friend, now working there as the barman. Sam won one and lost one. He read no significance in the scores.

It looked more and more like Jane Deacon led a blameless life. Tuesday and Thursday evenings at the painter's house was the only time she had to play around. During the day she worked in the same office as her husband, running the family business, manufacturing and marketing children's toys. They both put in an average of around fifty hours a week. Getting richer all the time. Still, Sam felt something was going on. He didn't know what it was, but when he sat still there was something nagging away inside him. Something that wouldn't go away.

By the early evening he sat in his car outside the Deacons' house and waited for the blonde lady to make her move.

It was exactly the same procedure as Tuesday. She drove out to 386a, parked in the drive and went inside. Two hours later the middle-aged WASP woman saw her out, and she got back into her white Peugeot and drove home.

Sam drove into the cul-de-sac behind her and parked on the opposite side of the road. He watched her lock the car and turn into the gate. She seemed to hesitate a moment, then carried on towards the door of the house.

Sam felt for his keys in the ignition, glanced in his rear-view to make sure the way was clear to reverse. Fuckin' cul-de-sacs; fuckin' portrait painters.

The starter motor turned over and died. He tried again and the engine coughed but struggled on. He gave it a little burst of revs, which it seemed to like, and eased the choke out about a quarter of an inch. It purred like a cat. 'I've got your number,' Sam told it, swinging the wheel round to miss the bumper of the car in front.

Jane Deacon appeared in front of him in the middle of the road. Her blue cashmere jacket was open, showing a high-necked white blouse, brilliant in the lights of his Cortina, fastened at the neck with a brooch the size of a fist. Get tangled up in blue cashmere. Good way to lose your first customer.

Sam turned the engine off, and let the car slide backwards into the kerb. He hit the light switch and wound down the window as the blonde came around the car.

'Mr Turner?' she asked through her little mouth.

'Yeah,' said Sam, wondering how she'd rumbled him. 'Call me Sam.'

'The door's open,' she said, motioning towards the house. 'I didn't go in. I called, but I think somebody might be inside.' Her hand was shaking. She gripped the side of the door, and her knuckles were blue.

Sam opened the door and got out. 'Wait here, he said. 'I'll take a look.' He walked towards the house and looked back at Jane Deacon standing by his car. 'Get in,' he called. 'Sit down for a minute.'

Mr Turner! She even knew his name. OK, Sam wasn't a trained surveillance operator, but he'd kept a fair distance between the cars. If this woman was really bright, she might have twigged someone was following her, but how did she know his surname? No one called him Mr Turner.

The door to the house was ajar. Sam stood inside the hallway and listened. Nothing. No movement. 'Terry,' he called. And then again: 'Terry.' There was no reply.

What the hell was this? The guy says he wants his wife tailed, then when Sam's out tailing her the guy does a bunk and leaves the house open. Was Terry Deacon supposed to be here? Jane Deacon hadn't said, just: 'I think somebody might be inside.' What're you looking at here, Sammy boy, a burglary or what?

Terry Deacon was in the front room. There was a piano behind the door. There was one of those plushy sofas like Wanda's. And Deacon was in the space between the piano and the sofa. He might have been pissed, but the blood seemed to indicate something more radical. The first client and, by default, one of the founding fathers of the Sam Turner Detective Agency had been stabbed repeatedly in the upper chest, neck and face. There was a real look of surprise on his face. He was lying on his back with his arms and legs akimbo, and carefully placed on his stomach was a sheet of A4 paper with a message:

> **Terry**
> **Deacon**
> **Deserves**
> **to**
> **Die**

The corpse had slippers on and looked very lonely. Correction, the corpse had one slipper on. The left slipper was on the other side of the room, by the curtains. Over in a corner the television was on, the sound turned down. Sam watched the newscaster smiling as he introduced the weatherman. But it was patently obvious which way the wind was blowing.

Chapter 10

Sam checked the other rooms in the house, all of them empty. He returned to the car and got in the front passenger seat next to the blonde.

'What did you expect to find in there?' he asked.

'Terry.' A note of hysteria had taken possession of her.

'Look,' he said, taking her hand. 'I'm not good at this. I don't want you to go in the house. Terry is ... well, he's had an accident.'

She moved to get out of the car, but Sam kept a grip of her. 'What?' she said. 'Tell me what's happened.'

'He's dead,' said Sam. 'He's been murdered.'

She was very still. She didn't move for almost a minute. Sam felt like something inside her was curling up or fading away. He squeezed her hand, something to reassure her or himself, or maybe to provoke some kind of response from her.

She said in a quiet voice, almost a whisper: 'With a knife? And a note?'

'Yeah. How did you know ...?' But Jane Deacon passed out while he was talking. She slumped forward over the steering wheel, cracking her forehead.

Sam pulled her back. She was out of it. He left the car and

dialled 999 in the phone box on the corner. Then he went back to the car and held her hand until the cops arrived.

She came around just before the police car turned into the street. 'Don't leave me,' she said.

'OK. Sit tight.'

'No,' she gripped his hand. 'I want you to promise. Don't leave me.'

Sam sat in the car and watched the police operation. By midnight they had taken Jane Deacon some place. Chief Inspector Delany had spent one minute with him.

'Did you make the call?' he asked.

'Yeah.'

'Were you in the house?'

'Yeah.'

'Did you touch anything?'

'No.'

'Stick around. I'll need to talk to you.'

Delany had been in the house nearly three hours. The forensic boys had been and gone. A police surgeon or doctor or whatever they call them had been and gone. An ambulance arrived and took the body away. One of Delany's henchmen had taken a statement from Sam. He told it straight. Everything he knew. How he had found the body.

At two a.m. Delany asked Sam to go to the police station with him. 'I want my car,' Sam told him. 'I'll follow you.'

Delany came into the interview room with Sam's file. He threw it on the desk. 'Is this true?' he asked.

Sam nodded. It was getting late. He'd had a full day.

'Did you kill him?'

'No. You've got the statement. That's all I know.'

'You've done time.'

'For dealing pot,' said Sam. 'And you buggers planted that on me. I hardly even used it before I went inside.'

'Did *she* kill him?'

'I don't think so,' said Sam. 'When did he die?'

'About an hour before you rang in.'

'She can't have,' said Sam. 'She was having her picture painted. But you must know that by now.'

Delany smiled. 'Just checking,' he said. 'What was to stop you leaving her at the painter's house and driving back to top her husband?'

'I'd have to be crazy,' said Sam. 'The guy was *paying* me.'

Delany picked up the file. 'OK,' he said. 'You can go. But don't leave town. I'll need to talk to you again.'

Sam stood. 'Is that all?' he said. 'I wait three fuckin' hours, and you want the answer to a question you already know?'

Delany turned at the door. 'There is one other thing,' he said. 'Have you ever been to Sweden?'

'No,' Sam told him. 'I went to Paris once. Real nice town. And wandered through rubble in the streets of Rome. You ever been to Amsterdam?'

Chapter 11

It was easy. Frances had seen Jane leave the house on Thursday evening just like she did every Thursday evening. Poncing off in her little blue suit in her little white car. Earlier she had seen Terry Deacon come home from work. He wouldn't leave the house again, and Jane wouldn't return for a couple of hours. Frances had all the time in the world.

Only one thing different. The Cortina, and the man in the Cortina. He had arrived fifteen minutes before Jane was due to leave. He had sat in the car, and then when Jane's little white car had pulled out of the cul-de-sac, the Cortina had taken off after her.

Graham's voice calmed her. 'Do the job,' it said. 'Do the job for Graham.'

When the street was quiet she walked up to the house, and knocked on the door. There was the sound of a piano playing inside.

Deacon answered the door in his slippers. So cosy. 'Yes?' he said.

Frances smiled. 'You don't remember me?' she said. 'It's Frances.'

'Oh, my goodness.' Recognition on his face. 'Come in. It's been such a long time.' He showed her into the sitting room. 'Graham's not with you?'

'No,' Francis said. 'Is Jane at home?'

'Out, I'm afraid,' said Deacon. 'You missed her by about half an hour.'

'Never mind,' said Frances. 'I'll catch her another time.'

Deacon was embarrassed. He'd never liked Frances. Always thought she was bad news. The feeling was mutual. Frances had never liked him.

There was a silence. Deacon didn't know why she was there. Why should he? Frances let him stew. She wasn't there to cheer him up.

'What can we do for you?' he asked eventually, rubbing his hands together. He always did that when he was embarrassed, rubbed his hands together. 'Or was it just a social call?'

'No. Not at all,' said Frances. 'I've got something for you.' She opened her handbag and took out the knife. Deacon looked at it. He looked at Frances. He looked at the knife again. Like it was a present, a gift, or maybe something she'd borrowed once, and was now returning. It was when he looked back at Frances for the second time that she stabbed him in the face.

He said something. He didn't call out. He said something

indistinct, then he moved his hand up to his face and away again. He looked at the blood on his hand.

Frances stabbed him again. In the throat, and then twice in the chest. He fell to the floor and she knelt beside him, giving him the point of the knife until he stopped breathing, made that gurgling sound she'd heard before.

She took the note from her bag and placed it on his stomach. She checked her watch. She still had an hour to wait until Jane came back.

Frances sat on a chair and waited. She could do that, simply block the body out, even though it was there in front of her. She could do that because she had been loved, by her father, and by Graham. Frances's father had always let her win when she was a child. They played Monopoly, or card games; whatever it was, he would let her win. He couldn't help himself, he loved her so much.

She heard the car arrive outside, the car door slam. Jane Deacon didn't come in. Instead she stood in the doorway and shouted: 'Terry?'

The front door was open. Jane shouted a couple more times.

Frances went to the front door. Jane Deacon had already gone. Frances saw her running along the cul-de-sac. And there it was again. The old Cortina with the man. He had followed her back.

Frances left the house and took the footpath at the blind end of the cul-de-sac. Life was like that. Frances was patient. She would take them one at a time. She would not be tempted to rush anything. Patience was its own reward.

Chapter 12

The blonde rang him Saturday morning. 'Is it Mr Turner?'

'I don't relate to that name,' he said.

'It's Mrs Deacon.'

Didn't she know he was a detective? 'How're you doing?'

'I need to see you,' she said. 'Is it possible?'

'At your place?'

'No. I'm staying at Terry's brother's.'

'I could come this afternoon.'

'No, Not here,' Jane Deacon said. 'The whole family'll be here, and . . .'

'Betty's,' Sam told her. 'At two. Real nice coffee there.'

She arrived in the blue cashmere suit, something black and shiny under the jacket. Her eyes were swollen, but she had hold of herself. Sam called the waitress and got her a coffee.

'I need help,' she said.

Sam looked straight into her eyes. 'You're calling the shots,' he said. 'I'm unemployed.'

'Terry's . . . death. I think it was supposed to be me.'

'Terry gave me the story about you having an affair because he wanted me to keep an eye on you?'

'Yes.'

'He knew about the portrait?'

'Yes.'

'Why? If you need a bodyguard, hire a bodyguard. Tell the man what the job is, then he can do it. If I'd known I was a bodyguard, I'd have been prepared. I might've got someone else to watch the house. Kept you both covered. Maybe you'd still have a husband.'

She looked down at the table. Took a handkerchief out of her sleeve and dabbed her eyes, though there was nothing coming out of them. Sam touched her arm. 'I don't want to be hard,' he said. 'But you've been giving me the run-around.'

Jane Deacon took a breath and pursed her little mouth. 'I'll tell you the whole story,' she said. 'Everything.'

'Somebody better,' said Sam. 'I'm on the dark side of the road. At the moment I don't know fuck.'

'I had a friend,' said Jane. 'A Swedish girl, called Lotta Jensen. It's a long story, you'll have to bear with me.'

'I'm not going anywhere,' Sam told her.

'Before we were married we lived in a communal house. There were six or seven of us, mainly young professionals. There was this young New Zealander called Graham, Graham East. He was OK at first. He didn't have any qualifications, and I suppose we all thought he was simple-minded. We patronized him, but he did a lot of work in the house, and he became part of the fixtures. He seemed to be good-hearted.'

Sam rolled a cigarette and offered one to Jane. She shook her head and reached into her handbag for a packet of straights. 'God, I knew there was something I needed,' she said. He lit his own and passed the flame over.

'Most people had paired off before Graham arrived. I wasn't with Terry then, I shared a room with someone called Steve. And Terry, he lived with another girl. Everything was fairly harmonious.

'When Lotta arrived things started to go wrong. It wasn't her fault. The main reason she came was to learn English, she hardly spoke a word. Graham suggested he give her lessons in English, and she teach him Swedish. That seemed fine, except about ten days after she arrived, Graham announced he was in love with her.

'Lotta didn't want to know. She already had a boyfriend in Sweden who was giving her a hard time. Graham was just an extra burden. He was hopeless. Mooning around all the time. Big eyes. He would knock on the door of her room, and when Lotta opened it he would just stand there looking at her. He wouldn't speak. He would just stand there and look.

'One evening he attacked her in the sitting room. He had her on the floor, and he was shouting and crying, saying he was going to kill her. We had to pull him off.

'He went away for a while, and Lotta returned to Sweden. Graham seemed better when he came back. He was full of remorse. And things settled down again for a while.

'Then when Steve and I broke up, Graham fell in love with *me*. It was the Lotta story all over again. I didn't give Graham any encouragement. I didn't want anything to do with him. But we were back to him mooning about all over the house. The big-eyes treatment. He told everyone in the house how he was prepared to die for me. It was terrible. The only way I could deal with it was to keep out of his way. He burst into my room one morning before light. Literally knocked the door down. "Don't throw it in my face," he said. "Love is precious."

There were a couple more incidents with other women. In the end we asked him to leave.'

'What're you telling me?' asked Sam. 'I mean, it's an interesting story about some nut, but you can't be saying Graham killed your husband.'

'About two months ago Lotta was murdered in Gothenburg. I couldn't find out much about it. I got a letter from her mother. She was stabbed, and there was a note pinned to her body. Written in English.'

'What did it say?' Sam asked. 'What was written on it?'

'I don't know.'

'Why did you think it was Graham?'

'I didn't at first. I haven't seen Graham for years. He lived here for a while, and he had a girlfriend, Frances. She was strange as well, but she loved him. I heard they went back to New Zealand.

But a week or so after Lotta was killed I saw them in town. And I realized they were back. Then I got frightened.'

'This could all add up to nothing,' said Sam.

'Except for Terry,' Jane pointed out. 'And the knife, and the notes.'

'Have you told the police?'

'They weren't interested in a murder in Gothenburg. Inspector Delany was more interested *after* Terry was killed. He said they'd try to find Graham. I gave him a description.'

'What he looked like then?'

'I suppose so,' said Jane.

'What do you want me to do?' asked Sam.

'I'm frightened,' she told him. 'I want a bodyguard. I don't want Graham bursting in on me in the middle of the night. The police still haven't found him. I want him found. I want you to stop him.'

'OK,' said Sam. 'Can you finance it?'

'Forty pounds a day,' she said. 'It's better than dying.'

'Plus expenses,' Sam told her.

Walking back to the car park Sam noticed a homeless boy on the other side of the street; he had one shoe off and was trying to pad it with newspaper. He had a sign in front of him on the pavement: HAMELESS AND HUNGRY. There had been a time when Sam had seen the world from a similar position. It was difficult to find a way up from that far down. Without some kind of help it might even be impossible.

He watched the people passing by, the kid's head moving from side to side like he was at Wimbledon. Sam felt himself getting angry. He knew he was angry at himself, at his own impotence, his inability to provide a solution. But the anger came bubbling up nevertheless. When Sam himself had been on the street things had looked different. Then, everyone who walked past had looked capable of a helping hand. He walked over the road and dropped all his loose change into the kid's lap.

Chapter 13

Funny how things turn out. You take on a matrimonial case and find you're tracking an international serial killer. Only problem is, where do you start?

Sam had the names and addresses of the people who were involved in the communal house. There was a possibility that one or the other had kept in touch with Graham. It was also possible one of them had a photograph of the guy.

Jane Deacon was going to stay on at Terry's brother's house until after the funeral. Then she would move back to the cul-de-sac. Once that happened Sam would have to stay close to her, so now was the time to try to track Graham East down.

Well, not exactly now. Saturday night a man needs to relax a little. And wandaful Wanda had palmed the kids off on her husband again.

Volume Two of *Biograph* was playing loud on the tape deck as Sam shaved. He watched the lathered face in the mirror singing along with it. *Visions of Johanna.*

By the time he'd finished splashing after-shave around, the man had drowned all memory and fate and Sam was punching numbers on the telephone keypad.

'How're you doing?' he asked Wanda when she repeated the number.

'I thought you weren't going to ring.'

'I've been working,' he told her. 'Just got in. What's the landscape like?'

'Clear. What's the music?'

'Dunno, some Jewish guy,' he said. 'I'm on my way.' Sam hung up as his doorbell rang.

★

'Yorkshire TV, Calendar,' the guy said. 'You Sam Turner?'

'Yeah.'

'I understand you found the body the other night. Can we talk to you?' The guy motioned behind him, and Sam took in the van and two other guys unloading camera and sound equipment.

'You gonna pay me?' Sam asked.

The guy smiled. He was short, flabby. Wearing a £500 suit. He had a wide tie, striped, seemed to cover most of his chest. 'We didn't think that would be necessary,' he said.

'Who's we?'

'We're covering a news item.'

'I'm going out,' said Sam.

The guy with the tie smiled again. 'Would payment keep you at home?' he asked.

'Not for long,' Sam said. 'Depends how much you're thinking.'

'Two hundred pounds?'

'How about four?'

'Three. I don't think we'll do better than that.'

'Try three-fifty,' said Sam. 'It might be your lucky day.'

'I think you'll stay home for three,' the guy said.

Cash?'

A nod.

Sam shrugged. 'You know what?' he said. 'You read me like a book.'

They brought the gear into his room. Lights, cameras, moving furniture around. The tie guy told him what questions he was going to ask, listened to Sam's answers. The whole thing took two hours. Wanda rang in the middle of it and Sam told her to hang on, he was making money for Christ's sake. Course he was coming, soon as he could get away.

Towards the end the doorbell rang again. This time a reporter from the local news. Sam told him to wait in his car. 'Count your money,' he said. 'I'm doing TV at the moment.'

The tie guy gave Sam three hundred. 'Thanks,' he said.

'Yeah,' Sam told him. 'Tell me something. How'd you get my address?'

'Police contact. Somebody I know.' He laughed. 'This man works in the police station, calls himself X. Real cloak-and-dagger stuff.'

'What else he tell you? This X guy?'

'Not a lot,' said the tie guy. 'But if anything develops, I'll hear about it.'

'That kind of info would be good to know,' said Sam. 'Can I buy into it?'

The guy scratched his chin. 'You're going to stay on the case?'

'All the way. I'm retained by the widow.'

'So if you come up with anything, *I'd* get to know about it?'

'Sounds like a deal,' said Sam.

The guy from the local news had been joined by a tall lanky Liverpudlian from the *Daily Express*. Sam picked up another hundred from each of them. Answered their questions, posed for photographs. By the time he was through Wanda was on the blower again.

'I'm doing my best,' Sam told her. 'I just have to see these guys out and I'm on my way.'

'I'm lonely,' she said. 'I keep thinking you won't come.'

'Christ, I *wanna* be there,' Sam said. 'Listen to what I'm saying. I'm *earning*.'

'The food's ruined, Sam. I was all ready hours ago. Now I'm sweaty.'

'Fuck. What can I tell you?' he said. 'I'll eat it, whatever it's like. I don't care if you're sweaty. I like a woman who sweats. Christ, Wanda, I'm on my way.'

He hung up. The reporter from the *Daily Express* said: 'You got a heavy night ahead.'

'Nothing I can't handle,' Sam told him. 'If I ever get out of here.'

★

Wanda was stomping mad when he got there. 'I shouldn't even let you in the house,' she said. 'The way you treat me.' Mascara had run a little, but her make-up had turned to war paint like she was ready for a fight. 'Look at this.' She pointed to a casserole of chicken breasts, butter congealed on the top.

'Hell, just warm it up,' he said. 'I didn't eat all day.'

You could at least apologize.'

'I've been apologizing all night,' he said. 'Christ, you run around all day. You end up playing nursemaid at this time, whatever it is.'

'Eleven-fifteen,' she said, clenching her fists.

'We got all night then,' he said, taking his jacket off and sitting on Wanda's plush sofa. He held his arms out. 'Come and tell Sam all about it.'

Wanda waited a few moments in the doorway; Sam could see it was a touch-and-go situation. Then she walked slowly over and sat next to him. 'You're not as nice as I thought,' she said.

Chapter 14

'When you think about it,' Delany said to his sergeant, 'they could have done it between them. The widow and Turner.'

'What about the Swedish bird?' Delany's sergeant was forty-five years old. He wore a suit with pin-stripes, wide turn-ups. He believed in procedure. Statistically, he liked to say, statistically, plodding gets you there in the end, more often than other methods.

'Her as well,' Delany told him. 'Sam Turner could have done her as well. Scam to take us off the scent. Get us chasing this Graham East character.'

The sergeant picked up the fax of the note found on Lotta Jensen's body. 'Whoever chopped Terry Deacon did this one as well,' he said. 'This note is identical. Same size paper, same writing. Look at these Ds.' He pushed the fax in front of Delany. The wording said: LOTTA JENSEN DESERVES TO DIE. The two Ds were distinctive, a large scroll at the top of the letter. 'Exactly the same as the one we took off Deacon.'

'I don't like this Sam Turner character,' Delany said.

'We could bring him in again. Lean on him a little.'

'We'll have to if nothing else turns up,' said Delany. 'What about Graham East's girlfriend? What's she called?'

'Golding. Frances Golding. No, she doesn't know where he is. He disappeared six months ago. She'd say if she knew. She's going to look out a photograph. Destroyed them all when he left, but she's going to look anyway. She hasn't even had a letter from him. Thinks he's back in New Zealand.'

'Oh, yes,' said Delany. 'He just flew over to top Terry Deacon. Have you checked with the New Zealand police?'

'No, sir. You said you would.'

'No, I didn't.'

The sergeant stiffened. 'I'm sorry, sir. But you did say you wanted to do it yourself.'

Delany sighed. 'OK. Get them on the line. Auckland, wasn't it?'

'Wellington, sir,' said the sergeant, picking up the phone. Then, into the mouthpiece: 'Can you put a call through to New Zealand? For Chief Inspector Delany. The Wellington Police Department. Homicide, I think they call it.'

'We're looking for one of your nationals,' Delany told his opposite number in Wellington. 'Name of East, Graham East.' He gave the address that Frances Golding had given his sergeant: Graham's parents' house. 'He's wanted in connection with a murder enquiry. We don't think he's in New Zealand now, but you might be able to come up with an address. Even a photograph would help.'

'Who'd he kill?' asked the New Zealander.

'We're not sure he killed anyone,' said Delany. 'But we do want to talk to him. A woman in Sweden, and a man here. Both knife jobs.'

'We had one here as well,' said the voice in Delany's earpiece. 'A woman called Sarah Dunn, about six months back, with a note pinned to the body.'

'Jesus,' said Delany. 'Sara Dunn Deserves to Die?'

'Something like that,' said the voice. 'How do you know?'

'We're dealing with a global killer,' Delany told him. 'Somebody leaves a corpse in every country he visits.'

'Don't jump the gun, old son,' said the voice. 'I'll get back to you on Graham East. Name doesn't mean anything at the moment.'

Delany hung up the phone and looked at his sergeant.

The sergeant said: 'You're joking?'

'I wish I was,' said Delany. 'Send a fax of our note to Wellington, and get them to send a fax of *theirs* back here.'

Two hours later, Clive Desmond, reporter with Calendar News for Yorkshire Television, received a telephone call.

'X,' said the voice.

'What have you got?'

'Something very strange,' said X. 'The guy, whoever it was killed Terry Deacon, he also killed a woman in Sweden.'

'No,' said Desmond.

'Yes, and that's not all. He killed another woman in New Zealand. Name of Sarah Dunn.'

'This is turning into a very interesting case,' Desmond told him.

'Got to go,' said X. 'I'll keep in touch.'

Clive Desmond put the phone down and took his notebook

out of his pocket. He dialled a number and waited. After a few moments he said: 'Sam? Sam Turner? Have I got news for you!'

Chapter 15

Frances watched the cul-de-sac. The house was unoccupied. She would have to wait until Jane came back. But in the meantime there was plenty to do. A trip to London possibly. Yes, why not? She could buy that hat she'd been promising herself. Kill two birds with one stone.

The policeman was a fool. Frances had wound him round her little finger. That's why there were so many crimes. The police didn't know what they were doing. Underfunded? Yes, of course they were. And they should have much wider powers, of course. Terrorists going around with bombs. Juveniles stealing cars. Some of the kids in this street had been hanging around her car. When she went out of the house they watched her. If she didn't make it absolutely secure, they'd be off with it. No one was safe.

Even when criminals *were* caught they were treated with kid gloves. Videos in their cells. Frances had seen a programme on television. Thugs, muggers, rapists being encouraged to *paint*. Given modelling clay and allowed to cast great ugly statues in bronze. Anything they wanted, they could have it. All at the taxpayers' expense.

Graham had come last night. While she was asleep. He came to her in dreams, when she was dreaming. He could join in her dreams, because he was a poet. Last night was a celebration. He was so happy about Terry Deacon. The world felt much better now.

Frances was worried about her car. She went out every hour

during the evening to check it. She'd told the policeman about it, and he'd agreed that no one was safe.

'Why don't you do something?' she'd asked him.

'If it was up to me, ma'am,' he'd said, 'I'd lock them all up and throw away the key.'

Frances laughed at that. And the policeman, he liked it when she laughed.

He was a fool, but he was a pleasant fool. She loved the way he called her ma'am. A lot of people these days called her Ms. She only had short change for them. Ma'am was a treat. A real treat to hear.

She went to the cupboard and took down the shoe box of photographs. Graham composing a poem at his desk. Frances at the seaside with bare feet and legs. Frances giggling at one of Graham's jokes. Graham looking out to sea. 'Sometimes I think I can see New Zealand in the far distance,' he had said. And then wistfully, 'Or maybe it's Heaven.'

There was a small one of Graham taken in a booth. He looked uncertain in it, as if he wasn't sure when the flash would come. It didn't look like him at all. Frances put it on one side and returned the shoe box to the cupboard.

She took the black Panda and drove to the police station. The street kids watched her every move as she unlocked her car.

'I've found a photograph,' she told the sergeant when he came to the front desk.

'Oh, that's a break,' he said. 'I'd almost given up on you.'

'I'd like it back when you've finished with it,' said Frances. 'It's the only one I've got.'

'You still haven't heard from him, ma'am?'

'No,' said Frances. 'I read about the murder. I'm sure Graham couldn't have done anything like that. He isn't that kind of man.'

'Well, ma'am,' said the sergeant, 'we don't know one way or the other at the moment. We do need to speak to him, though, if only to eliminate him from our enquiries.'

'He wouldn't,' said Frances. 'I just know he wouldn't.'

44

'You'll let us know if he contacts you?'

'Of course,' said Frances.

'And, ma'am. Thanks for the picture. I'll get it copied and let you have it back.'

Frances drove home via Bishophill. She didn't stop the car at the cul-de-sac, but drove slowly past. The house was still in darkness. The Cortina wasn't there either. The *man* in the Cortina, he wasn't there.

Chapter 16

Sam talked to a nice homely old lady called Miss Allison. She had been friendly with the people who lived in the communal house and especially friendly with Graham East. She remembered Graham well. 'He was a sad boy,' she told Sam. 'He couldn't really manage the world.'

'Who can?'

'None of us, really, I suppose. But Graham was a special case. He needed help.'

Sam took a ginger biscuit from the silver cake stand. 'D'you mind if I dunk?' he asked.

Miss Allison laughed. A good laugh, ringing out of her wiry little throat. The best laugh she'd had in a long while. It did her real good, eyes coming alive and shining at Sam now. If she had any spirits in the house, booze of any kind, Sam had a silent bet with himself, she'd be getting them out.

But maybe Quaker ladies didn't drink anyhow. Except in secret. Sam didn't know. They sure made good tea, though, in fine china cups with handles too small to get your finger through. Or if you got it through, you got it stuck there, maybe need an operation to get free again. Be easy enough to snap the handle *off*, but Sam wouldn't do that. Ruin the old biddy's life.

'I'll join you,' she said, taking a ginger biscuit from the cake stand and dunking away. Sam thought it would take a heavy-goods vehicle to get that smile off her face now. Grinning away like a speed freak. One more good joke, she'd be dancing a jig.

'Did you like him?' Sam asked.

'Graham? He was a nice boy,' she said. 'He wanted the world to be different. He would have been happier with a genteel world. He was a conservative, a kind of eighteenth-century aristocrat.' She glanced at Sam. 'I'm not giving you a very good description?'

'I've got a picture of some guy in a wig and tights,' he said. 'Patent-leather shoes with high heels and a buckle.'

That laugh again. Jesus, better slow down here. Don't wanna give her a heart attack. Yeah, there you go, have a sip of tea. Don't get no fuckin' crumbs stuck.

'He was an oddball,' Miss Allison said. 'In a class of children he'd be the one everyone picked on. He'd be a scapegoat; he'd be bullied. He'd say the wrong thing, or he'd say the right thing in the wrong way.'

'Could he have killed someone?'

'No. Not in cold blood. He had a temper. A bad one. He attacked one of the girls in the house once. I think anyone could kill on the spur of the moment. But he couldn't plan it. Do it like that. Not Graham.'

'People change,' Sam said.

'Do you think so?' Miss Allison's eyes sparkled. 'That's not my experience.'

'You brood about something a long time,' Sam said. 'It gets to play on your mind. You need to free your head. Doctor Freud and all that.'

'I've never been too impressed with Doctor Freud,' said Miss Allison. 'According to his theories, women like me should be psychotic. But I feel all right.'

46

Sam looked hard at her. He knew what she was saying. 'It *could* happen,' he said. 'People sometimes go over the edge.'

'It's a theory,' said the old lady. 'Yes, it could happen. But you ask me if I think Graham East, the Graham East who lived in that house, was capable of planning and executing cold-blooded murder.' She looked at the palms of her hands and shook her head. 'I have to say no,' she said. 'I can't believe he was capable of it.'

'You knew everybody who lived in the house?'

'Fairly well,' she said.

'OK. You tell me. Which one done it?'

'I'm not Miss Marple,' she said with a grin. 'They were all nice people. Motivated. Idealistic. I don't think any of them was capable of that kind of crime.'

'It has to be one of them,' said Sam. 'Three murders, and the only link is the communal house.'

'Not quite,' said Miss Allison. 'The link is not the house. It is Graham.'

'You just said it wasn't . . .'

'I said Graham wasn't the murderer, but I didn't say he wasn't the link. This woman in New Zealand, for instance. She had no link with the house, but I'm fairly sure she had a link with Graham.'

'Sure, they both come from the same country.'

'More than that,' said Miss Allison. 'They come from the same town. Listen, I'll tell you something else. When Graham was an adolescent – I think he was fourteen or fifteen – he was seduced by his next-door neighbour. He used to come home from school and she would invite him into her house. I don't know if she was unhappily married. She might have been a paedophile – is that what it's called? When people prefer children? Anyway, it was a messy affair. He never told me her name, but she was much older than him, a married woman. She used him. There was a scandal, and Graham and his parents had to leave the area. I think you'll find that the dead woman is the same woman who seduced him.'

You just convicted the guy,' said Sam. 'If he didn't do it himself, maybe he paid somebody else to do it.'

She shook her head. 'That doesn't sound like Graham, either.' She leaned forward and poured more tea into Sam's cup. Liver spots on her hands. You'd think she was ready for the knacker's yard, but her brain was on a fast track.

'What about his girlfriend?' asked Sam. 'You ever meet her?'

'No. Frances, was it? I never did. That was after my time. I saw her once with Graham in the town, and I heard a little about her from Steven Bright.'

Sam consulted his list of names. Steven Bright had lived in the communal house, but Sam didn't have a current address for him. 'You got his address?'

'Yes, and you should talk to him. Graham and Steven were close at one time. Graham could talk to Steven. Confide in him.' She stood and walked to an antique bureau, coming back to her chair with a purple address book covered in something like velvet. 'He's an architect. Lives in London.' She gave Sam the address and a telephone number.

'There's a couple more people I can't contact,' he told her. 'Jean Granger and Bob Blackburn. Know what happened to them?'

Miss Allison shook her head. 'I have the feeling they were together – you know, lovers. Bob was American. Jean, she was South African Indian, beautiful young woman, all the young men chasing her. I don't know what happened to them.'

Sam stood to leave. 'It's been a real treat,' he said, meaning it.

She smiled at him, eyes dazzling away like little jewels. 'The ginger biscuits, you mean.'

'No. Everything. I don't meet many real ladies. Not many who can think. And laugh. And look like a million dollars.'

'You're a clever man,' she said. 'You know flattery will get you everywhere. You must come back again. You're a sight for sore eyes.'

48

'I'll do that,' he said. 'You invite me and I'll come. We could talk about something else. Sex, maybe.'

That got the laugh pumping away, skinny arms flapping like a penguin. Sam planted a quick kiss on her cheek. 'Oh, my goodness!' she said, clapping her hand to the cheek to keep the kiss in there, not letting it get away. 'Oh, my goodness, Mr Turner, you're irrepressible.'

'Guess so,' he told her. 'And call me Sam, OK?'

'OK,' she said. 'Sam it is.' And she reached up with her thin lips to plant one on his cheek. It landed on his nose, but Sam gave her a point for trying. 'You call me Celia. I'll ring you next week,' she said.

'Don't forget,' said Sam, stepping out the front door. 'I'll wait for the call. Give me an alibi to spend some time with you.'

Chapter 17

Frances walking down the street, consulting her watch. Thinking, still time to get to the West End, buy a hat before catching the train home. Heading for the Angel. A day out in the big city. Sunshine, too. Feeling good.

Remembering the time with Graham when they booked into a bed and breakfast opposite King's Cross station. Graham paid the money before Frances looked at the bedroom, and when she saw where they were going to sleep she cried. The room was no bigger than the bed, and the sheets hadn't been changed. They hadn't been changed in a long time. Graham went straight down to the woman and demanded his money back. The landlady wouldn't give it, though. Graham got their bags and took Frances by the hand, led her out of there and booked into the Great

Northern, *en suite* bathroom, a little bar in the room. A kind of honeymoon.

He could be masterful sometimes. Masterful and creative and sensitive. Frances had given up everything for Graham. Her husband and three children, her respectability. Her status. And she didn't regret it. He was her man. Her destiny.

Turning into the Angel tube, Frances stopped and walked back the way she had come. It was him, coming out of the station, and walking behind her. The *man*. The man in the Cortina. Had he seen her? Was he following her now like he had followed Jane? ˎ

Frances never panicked. She crossed the road and stopped at a shop window. She watched his reflection in the window. He walked on by, never giving her a second glance.

Frances knew where he was going. She felt that big, big smile coming on. Sam Turner, that was his name. She'd seen him on the television. Thought he was a private detective, but he was a public fool.

She watched him take the same route she herself had taken an hour before. When he turned the corner and was out of sight, heading for Arlington Way, Frances entered a phone booth and rang 999. She spoke in a gruff voice and attempted a foreign accent, not very successfully, something between Scottish and Texan. Graham had always laughed when she tried to speak with a New Zealand accent. She came out of the phone booth smiling. That would fix Mr Sam Turner. She had to laugh again at the accent. Graham would have thought it was wonderful.

Frances changed to the Victoria Line and rode through to Piccadilly Circus. There was a little hat shop somewhere around here she had visited once with Graham. Hats changed Frances; she had the kind of face that disappeared under a hat, was transformed by it. Lots of women, when they wore a hat, they looked like they always looked, but with a hat on. Frances, when she changed her hat, she changed her personality.

This was it, yes. Little side-street. Grubby kind of shop from the outside, tiny windows, but when you opened the door – oh, she remembered the bell, two chimes – it was brightly lit, larger than you expected, and hats everywhere.

The woman, as well – an old lady milliner, who spoke absolutely correctly. Called Frances mad*am*, and was forever moving the steps around to get different hats from the shelves. Nothing was too much trouble for her.

Frances loved the unpredictability of hat shops. The whole experience was an adventure for her. You never knew beforehand what you would end up with. You went into a hat shop with some kind of idea, but after an hour or two you came out with something completely different.

She had been fairly sure she was looking for something with a brim today, even a broad brim; but here she was heading for the underground carrying a box with a brimless hat. Black it was, circular, with an imitation veil and a thin strip of synthetic animal hide running all the way round.

'Sophisticated,' is what the old lady had said. 'It makes mad*am* look very sophisticated.'

Frances knew she was right.

Chapter 18

Sam Turner had lived in Islington for two years with his first wife, knew his way around. Felt like old times on the Northern Line. A whole day without the Cortina, which would never have made the trip. Sitting around on trains drinking crap coffee and cracking those little pork pies out of their cellophane. The sun shining like a foreign country, feeling younger. The smell of Islington brought back a stream of memories. Donna and her brothers. Donna walking round the flat in a mini skirt. Donna pregnant. No point in getting morbid, though. Stay in the present. Stay on the job.

The Angel! Jesus. Donna legless, sat on the bottom step. 'Take me home and fuck me, Sam.' And then taking her home, *carrying* her home over his shoulder, putting her to bed. Tucking her in, leaving a bucket by the side of the bed just in case. Sitting downstairs with a bottle, while she sleeps like a baby up in his room.

Donna coming down in the morning in her knickers, white as a ghost. Covered in ribs. Reminding him of everything he ever wanted with her warehouse eyes. 'Did you do it to me?'

'No.'

'D'you wanna do it now?' Desperate to lose her virginity. Get rid of it. Get free.

Donna. Donna. Where are *you* today?

Sam shook his head free of it all, walked out of the Angel and took a left, following the directions Steven Bright had given him over the phone. Bright had been easy to talk to: yes, he remembered Graham East very well. Hadn't seen him for years, though. Gloomy type. Bright thought Graham was the type might kill *himself*. Could imagine *that* more than him killing somebody else. He knew Frances too. She was crazy about Graham, possessive. Big woman, muscular, like a man, except she had a woman's mouth.

'One time,' Bright told him on the phone, 'she came round to my flat looking for Graham. It was while I was living in Leeds. Graham used to call round occasionally, two, three times a year. Just chew the fat. Anyway, Frances turned up on the doorstep. She was worried about Graham, she said. He'd been depressed. She couldn't lift him out of it. I invited her in and we had some coffee. Somehow in the conversation I mentioned Graham had been round a couple of months before. Then she did a double take: "When was he here?" she wanted to know. "He never told me he came here. He's always doing that. He just lies to me."

'She was really agitated. One minute she was calm, then the

next she was a nervous wreck. I couldn't figure her out. "He's not reliable," she said. "I put everything into this relationship, and Graham, he carries on writing his poetry and dreaming his life away. How would you like it, living with someone you can't trust?"

'She was paranoid. They were both paranoid. They'd both been kicked about so much, they didn't know where they were. They had each other, that's all. And that was a kind of mixed blessing.'

Sam turned into Arlington Way and counted the houses down to 102. Fairly quiet street, a pub on one side with the door open, three guys and a woman perched at the bar, one of the men legless already. Number 102 was just another house in the row. Didn't look like an architect's house. Sam knocked on the door.

No sound or movement from inside, but the guy was expecting him. Sam thought he might have slipped out for something, or maybe he was sleeping. He knocked again, then stood back and looked at the upstairs windows. Drapes. Nothing to see.

Hell, he'll be back in a minute.

OK, he knelt down on the pavement and pushed the letter-box open. A car was coming down the street fast. Sam looked into a dark hallway, a little light coming from the opposite end, probably a kitchen window. Nothing else, except . . .

The car screeched to a halt behind him. Sam looked round to see both doors open and two cops getting out, all their eyes on him. Tall one with a moustache and a smaller sidekick. Both of them moving fast, like they wanted to run him through the wall.

'Turn round, face the wall.'

'OK.' Sam did as he was told.

'Hands on the wall.' One of the cops kicked his feet apart and frisked him. Then they turned him round and the one with the moustache said: 'What you doing?'

'Being abused,' Sam told him.

'Smart bastard,' said moustache, and pushed Sam in the chest so his head banged against the brick.

Sam rubbed his head. 'See what I mean?' he said.

'You live here?'

'No.'

'What you doing here?'

'I'm visiting,' said Sam.

'What's your name?'

'Sam Turner.'

'ID?'

'There's a driving licence in my back pocket,' said Sam. 'But if I reach for it you'll crack my head on the wall.'

'Too fuckin' right,' said the cop.

Sam half turned and the cop took his wallet out of his back pocket, flipped it open and looked at the driving licence. 'Who lives here?' he asked, looking at the house.

'Guy called Steven Bright,' said Sam. 'But he's not altogether at home.'

'Don't be smart with us, mister, said moustache. 'You been in there?'

'No, it's locked.'

The other cop pushed the door to check. He nodded to moustache. The door was locked.

'We've proved it, then,' said Sam. 'Can I go now? Got to see my dentist.'

The moustache twitched like the guy behind it was going to laugh, but it was a false alarm. 'We come down the street,' he said, 'you're kneeling at the door. What's that about?'

'I'm a Moslem,' Sam told him. 'Eighteen minutes past eleven every morning I have to open a letter-box and say my prayers.'

Moustache made to shove him again but Sam intercepted the man's arm, gripping him tight by the wrist, leaning forward. Sam hissed through his teeth. 'Don't push me about,' he said, holding eye contact, speaking through tight lips. 'I've taken enough shit from you.'

The cop shook his hand free. When he spoke again there was some kind of begrudging respect to his tone. 'We've had a report of a murder,' he said. 'Or attempted. Caller said somebody called Sam Turner was trying kill a guy named Bright.'

'Bright's dead,' said Sam. 'Or it looks like it. Sam Turner had nothing to do with it.'

The eyes on both the cops widened. The little one, his mouth opened as well, his face in a kind of formation dance.

'Look through the letter-box,' Sam told them. 'That's what I did.'

There was a moment when both cops tried to look through the letter-box at the same time. It didn't last more than a second, just a push and a shove, before the little one gave up and left it to moustache. 'I can't see anything,' he said.

'Other end of the passage,' Sam told him. 'There's a shoe on the floor, left-hand side.'

'Yeah, I got that.'

'It's attached to a leg.'

'Jesus,' said moustache, standing and going for the car. 'Better get on to the station.'

'Don't try anything,' said the little cop to Sam, squaring his shoulders now he was in charge of the prisoner.

'Yeah,' said Sam. 'Or you'll blow me away.'

They waited in the car until reinforcements arrived, then they broke the door down. It was Steven Bright's shoe, foot, leg, and badly mutilated body, complete with note, just like the others.

Two other cops, younger, took Sam to the Met. He drank coffee from paper cups for two hours. Time to think. Wanda had been a mistake. She seemed like a fair bet, but she was too greedy. Ringing him all the time. Time to pull out of that one before it got too complicated. If it wasn't too complicated already.

You never could tell. There was that point at the beginning of a relationship where you had to make a leap of faith, go for it or leave it. And all you had to go on was a hunch. What women called intuition. Sometimes you win, sometimes you lose. Like a black ball game it can go either way.

It was time to unload that lady. Real pity, though, because physically she was there. The red hair, the willingness to play. But she also needed carrying, and Sam couldn't carry. A woman would be nice, but she would have to be independent. Something like Celia Allison, only thirty years younger. Maybe Jane Deacon?

Leave it alone, Sam. You're sitting in the Met, they're gonna lay God knows what on you, and all you can do is think about women.

Islington's a good old town. Everything happens there. You meet a girl and fight her family. You start a family of your own and lose it. You come back years later and find a dead man. Someone's got it in for you.

Sam's head was awash with caffeine when they came for him. They took him to an office where a Chief Inspector Wilkinson was playing *Aida* on a tape deck. 'Thought you worked in Oxford,' Sam told him, taking the only available chair.

Wilkinson hit the stop button, removed the tape and replaced it with another. 'Got any Grateful Dead?' Sam asked. 'More my style.'

The telephone rang and Wilkinson picked it up. He listened for a while, then said, 'Send them up,' and put it down again. He leaned his elbows on the desk and clasped his hands together under his chin, looking at Sam but saying nothing. After a moment Sam leaned *his* elbows on the desk and clasped his hands together under his chin. He looked back.

Wilkinson smiled. Sam smiled and said, 'I'm getting to you, aren't I?'

A few moments later there were footsteps in the corridor, a knock on the door, and Delany and his sergeant were shown into the room. Wilkinson and Delany shook hands and introduced themselves. The sergeant stayed in the background.

'I told you not to leave York,' Delany said to Sam.

'You *asked* me,' Sam told him.

'Murder follows you around, Turner,' said Delany. 'You'll have to come up with some pretty smart talking to squirm out of this one.'

'You think I killed Bright?'

'Who else? You were at the scene.'

'They should make a film of this,' Sam told him. 'Me stabbing a guy to death through a letter-box.'

Delany looked at Wilkinson. 'He was at the scene?'

Wilkinson shook his head. 'He was outside the house. Door was on a Yale, though. He could have been inside.'

'Were you inside?' Delany asked Sam.

Sam shook his head. 'I had an appointment with the guy. Got there too late.'

Wilkinson turned to the tape deck. 'I want you to listen to this,' he said.

'Not the fuckin' opera,' said Sam.

Wilkinson hit the play button.

A strange voice began speaking. Not hurried. Calm, with some kind of impossible accent. A horse, throaty voice.

'Listen,' it said. 'I'm only going to say this once. The address is 102 Arlington Way. Sam Turner is there now, with a knife. He's going to kill Steve Bright. You'll have to hurry.'

There was a click. Wilkinson hit the stop button. 'That call came in just after eleven,' he said. 'My officers apprehended Sam Turner at the scene at fourteen minutes past.'

'When did Bright die?' asked Delany.

'He was still warm,' said Wilkinson. 'He'd been dead less than an hour. Much less.'

'That voice,' said the sergeant. 'Anybody recognize it?'

They all looked at Sam.

'Closest I could get,' he said, 'would be Hercule Poirot. Either him or that guy Sherlock Holmes was always chasing round. What's he called? Morifuckinarty?'

'Funny man,' said Delany. Then to Wilkinson: 'You gonna hold him?'

'No,' Wilkinson said. 'No prints, nothing to connect him except the tape. Might want to see him again, though.'

'*I* might have made the call,' said Sam. 'Put you off the scent.'

'You ain't got the wit,' said Delany. 'That call must have been from Graham East, and I know a way to check it.'

'Frances Golding,' said the sergeant. 'She'll recognize the voice.'

Delany nodded.

'Can I go home?' asked Sam.

'Yes,' said Wilkinson.

'Don't suppose you're going in my direction?' Sam asked Delany.

Delany smiled. 'You know what?' he said. 'We're going the other way.'

'Cheers.'

'And, Turner?' Delany continued. 'Get off the fuckin' case. If we find you at even one more murder scene, or anywhere near it, you'll do time.'

'I'm retained by Jane Deacon,' Sam said. 'I'm going to see it through.'

'Give it up,' Delany warned. 'I don't want to see you again. I especially don't want to see you again on television. Do you read me?'

'I'll consider it,' Sam said, 'if you give me a lift home.'

'Go on the fuckin' train.'

They left Wilkinson's office, and Sam followed Delany and his sergeant out of the building. The two cops turned towards the car park, and Sam began walking towards the underground. 'Hey, Turner,' Delany shouted.

Sam stopped and walked back towards them. This Delany had second thoughts, perhaps. Give him a lift back to York.

'You ever been to New Zealand?'

'What is it with you, Delany?' Sam asked him. 'You spend your life dreaming of far-away places. Maybe you should take a holiday.'

Chapter 19

Terry Deacon's body was released on the Monday, and the funeral was the following Thursday. Sam went along to pay his respects to a past employer, see who was there, and confer with the widow.

There were several groups standing around the church. All the men from the men's group stood close to the church door. Sam nodded at them as he walked over to Celia Allison. 'You heard about Steven Bright?' he said.

'It's a terrible business, Sam. Did you manage to talk to him?'

'I was fifteen minutes too late. Celia, is there anyone here I should talk to?'

'Yes,' said the old lady. 'The woman over there in the strange hat. I'm sure that's Frances, Graham's girlfriend.'

Sam had a quick word with Clive Desmond, the Calendar reporter. 'There were two people who lived in the communal house we haven't been able to trace,' he said.

'Yes,' Desmond said. 'An American called Bob Blackburn and a woman name of Jean Granger.'

'The most likely event is that one or the other of them contacts the police,' said Sam. 'You don't know if that's happened?'

'I know it hasn't,' said Desmond. 'The police are still looking for them.'

'I'd like to talk to them.' said Sam.

'We've got a deal,' Desmond told him. 'Soon as I hear anything you'll know about it.'

Frances Golding was standing with Delany and his sergeant. She had a hat on Sam couldn't believe. Little round job with a strip of leopard skin. He walked towards her, nodding at Delany and the sergeant as he passed. They both ignored him.

Frances's face was a mask Sam couldn't read. 'I'm Sam Turner,' he said, extending his hand. She wore black gloves, and gave a strong handshake.

'Yes. Frances. Frances Golding.'

'I'm working for Jane,' he told her. 'She suggested I talk to you.'

'I saw you on the television,' said Frances.

'Right. I love your hat, by the way.'

Something happened to her face. A kind of colourless blush, perhaps. She looked ridiculous. Delany and his sergeant moved away.

'Did they play you the tape?' he asked.

'Yes. It wasn't Graham.'

'Can you be sure?'

'I know it wasn't him. It didn't sound anything like him. Graham isn't a murderer.'

'Did it sound like anyone you know? Anyone connected with Graham?'

'I don't know who it was,' said Frances. 'I've never heard anything like it.'

Sam changed tack. 'I'd like to come see you,' he said. 'Graham was a poet, right?'

Frances nodded.

'Have you got any of his poems? Anything he wrote? I'd like to know how he thinks.'

'He took everything,' said Frances. 'I found a photograph I gave to the police. But that's all.'

'Yeah,' said Sam. 'I saw it in the paper. But I'd still like to talk. You might find something.'

'If you think it will help,' she said.

The funeral cars arrived in the churchyard. Jane Deacon got out of the first one with Terry's brother and his family and went into the church. Other family members and friends began filing in after them.

'We'd better go inside,' Sam said. He looked hard at Frances again, glancing at the headgear. 'It really suits you,' he said. 'How does it feel to have your head under something like that?'

Jane Deacon had thought about the funeral service. The preacher was kept out of it as much as possible. Terry Deacon's brother gave an address, and then another one was given by a friend, Sam didn't catch the man's name. It was short on sentiment and Sam was moved despite himself. When they followed the coffin out of the church Tom Waits sang *Sailing Away*. The widow looked like a million dollars. Used notes, but who'd turn it down?

They put Terry Deacon in the biggest hole Sam had ever seen in his life. Must've gone down four metres. A cul-de-sac.

Back at home Sam opened a large envelope from Yorkshire Television. There was a note inside from Clive Desmond, the reporter, saying: 'We get more mail for you these days than we get for us'.

The envelope was full of mail addressed to Sam Turner, or Sam Turner Private Detective, or the Turner Detective Agency.

Sam opened them one after the other, read them, and then set them aside. About a third of the way through the pile he stopped and stuck the tape of *World Gone Wrong* into the deck. Listen to the Bluesman.

When he'd read all the letters, he sorted them. Two were anonymous, both death threats. Five were offers of marriage, all from nutters, except one Sam hoped was sane because she turned him on already. The remaining sixty-two were offers of work. The majority of them matrimonial cases, but several others from firms, including two local solicitors who were dissatisfied with their present arrangements.

Sam turned the volume up and did a little dance round the room.

★

The snooker hall was empty apart from the two of them. All the
other tables dark. The bar in a pool of light, abandoned. Gus had
lined the reds up in a straight line down the centre of the table,
the colours on their spots. When Sam arrived he had potted the
reds around the blue and was starting on the pink.

'How're you doing?' Sam asked him.

'Thirty-eight,' said Gus, missing the pink. 'Fuck. Look at that,
talking when I'm down on the ball.'

Sam laughed. 'Real hive of industry, here,' he said.

'Thursday's crap,' Gus told him. 'Sometimes think I'll go mad.
Shall I set them up?'

'Yeah. Only one frame, though. Busy.'

The snooker hall was in a cellar in the centre of the town. In
the evenings, sometimes during the late afternoon, the place was
humming with players of all ages, mainly men, though women
had started coming in greater numbers during the last few years.
Sam sometimes found the bar a problem when he was here,
especially after a game when people would sit around drinking.
Usually he paid for his table and left.

It was run under tight management and though from time to
time a table of drunks would start shouting and whooping, like
they were in a western saloon, usually the place was quiet.
Everyone concentrating on potting that one ball and leaving the
cue ball in a good position to pot the next one. The game was
about self-discipline and intuition, required insight and enlighten-
ment, a meditative atmosphere, the western equivalent of a Zen
temple.

'You found the axe-man yet?' Gus racked the reds and rolled
the brown down to the baulk. Sam collected it and put it on its
spot.

'No,' Sam told him. 'Look, I'm getting more work. Gonna
need some help.'

Gus walked down to Sam's end of the table sanding his cue.
'How much? And what do I have to do?'

'How much they pay you here?'

'Twenty a day.'

'How about thirty?' Sam got down on the table and broke up the reds. The cue ball skimmed the blue on its way back to the baulk, finished up three inches from the cushion. A red hovered over the left-hand corner pocket.

'When do I start?' Gus asked him, feathering the white. He was younger than Sam, maybe thirty years old. Tall and skinny, wearing Levi's with a maroon waistcoat, a day's growth of beard on his face. He potted the red. The cue ball collided with the black and knocked it into the pack. 'Why did that happen?' he said.

'Too much side,' Sam told him. 'Jane Deacon's gonna go back to the house tomorrow. One of us will have to be with her most of the time.'

'Twenty-four hours?' asked Gus, taking on a long blue, missing it by a mile, but fluking the cue ball into a safe position.

'No. She'll be at work during the day. But evenings and all night.' Sam picked out a route for the cue ball through a tangle of reds, left it tight behind the green.

'I saw her photograph,' said Gus. 'Real nice.' He got down on the ball, stood up again and chalked the end of his stick. 'All night? In her house?'

Sam smiled. 'She's newly widowed,' he said. 'She'll be nervous. You'll have to be nice.

Gus played the ball, missed the reds by a whisker and hit the blue. 'Fuck,' he said. 'I *am* nice. I was just thinking.'

Sam nodded, going to the table. Can't blame somebody for thinking. You look at Jane Deacon, you start thinking right off. She's that kind of woman, makes you think when you look at her, and when she's gone you just carry on thinking. 'You've got a woman, anyway,' he told Gus.

'Sure I've got a woman,' Gus said. 'You think somebody's got a woman, they stop thinking? Go brain-dead?'

Sam picked a plant out of the pack and made it, finishing

straight on the black. 'It happens,' he said. He potted the black and went on to a twenty-seven break.

'What else I have to do?' Gus asked.

'Lot of matrimonial cases coming in,' Sam said. 'You follow the husband or wife about. You write down what they do, who they meet. Take photographs. You make a report.'

'Piece of piss,' said Gus. 'I get a company car, or I drive that heap of shit you use?' He fluked a red and pushed the pink over the middle bag. 'Sorry,' he said.

'We do it right,' Sam said, 'the money comes in, we both get company cars. In the meantime we use mine.'

Gus potted the pink, split the reds, and settled into a break. 'It's cool,' he said. 'Great car when it starts.'

'You're talking about a friend of mine,' Sam told him.

When he left the snooker hall Sam almost tripped over a homeless boy sat on the pavement outside the entrance. It was the same kid he'd seen before, hollow-eyed and unkempt and he was still trying to stuff his shoe with newspaper. Sam walked past and then walked back again. He took a tenner out of his wallet and handed it to the boy. The kid looked at it for maybe half a minute. Sam watched his eyes wondering for a moment and then walked off. As he got to the corner the kid shouted after him, 'Hey, mister, *thank you.*' Sam carried on walking, raised his arm in acknowledgement, but kept going to the car. Before driving away he adjusted the mirror, caught his own reflection. 'Conscience money,' he said. He rolled a cigarette and lit it before looking back at his reflection again. 'So what you want me to do? Take the kid home?'

He got to Celia Allison's house early evening. The table was set for two, the smell of beef stew and dumplings oozing from the kitchen. 'My mouth's watering,' he told her.

'It's going to be a few minutes,' said Celia. 'Sit down and read the newspaper. Make yourself at home.' She went back to her kitchen.

64

The local Press had a photograph of Delany looking like a detective who'd lost his way. Chief Inspector Delany, the officer in charge of the investigation, it said, was attending an international conference in London. The conference, to be attended by investigating officers from New Zealand and Sweden, as well as representatives from the Metropolitan Police, had been organized to collate and share information. 'We need to computerize everything we know about the killings so far,' Delany was quoted as saying. 'This man has got to be stopped.'

'With you on his tail,' Sam told the photograph, 'guy must be shitting himself.'

'Let's eat,' Celia said, placing a large pan of stew on the table.

'We should get married,' Sam told her after the first mouthful. 'A woman who cooks like this shouldn't live alone. It's immoral.'

'I thought you'd appreciate it,' she told him. 'When was the last time *you* cooked a meal?'

'I don't cook much,' Sam confessed. 'Rice sometimes, potatoes, I grate cheese over them. I buy those tight lettuces and cut slices off when I need them. Make Brenda's salad dressing and dunk the lettuce in. Survival rations.'

Celia shook her head. 'Don't worry,' she said. 'I'm not going to mother you.'

'I get along OK without a mother,' Sam said. 'What I need right now is a typist. More like a secretary.'

'I know,' said Celia, an ironic twinkle to her eye. 'The story of my life. I offer a man food, home comforts, the traditional things he's supposed to need. He wants me to type a letter. Is it letters?'

'There's a lot of work coming to me,' said Sam. 'Paying work. I don't want to screw up on the admin. You've got a word processor. You probably write good.'

'I taught English for forty years.'

'That's what I mean,' said Sam. 'I write a letter, I'm three-quarters of an hour in the dictionary. When it's finished it doesn't say what was in my head. Lady like you can do the same thing better in ten minutes.'

'All right. Let's give it a try.'

'You can work from home,' Sam told her. 'I want some cards saying 'Sam Turner Detective Agency', with your telephone number as well as mine. People can't reach me, they get through to you. Can you handle that?'

'Let's say we'll give it a try. If it works for both of us, we'll carry on. If one of us feels it's not working, or it's too much, we'll call it a day. I suspect you'll need your own office sooner or later.'

'What I'd like,' said Sam, 'is an office somewhere in the town. Maybe down by the river. Second-floor job with the name on the door. And the same name on the window facing the street. I saw a film once, it's late afternoon or early evening and a client is sitting in the office. The sun is coming in the window, catching the lettering on the window, and masking it on the client's chest: Philip Marlowe.'

'Romantic.'

Sam laughed. 'Tender as a chicken,' he said. 'Hard on the outside, inside I'm all jelly.'

'I don't think so,' said Celia. 'You're not that simple.'

'You flattering me, Celia?'

'Why not?' she laughed. 'You do it to me. Everyone needs a little flattery. It stops us gnawing away for a while.'

Sam finished his stew and pushed the plate away. 'Were you ever married?' he asked.

Celia shook her head. 'Only to the job,' she said. 'The job and my mother. I took care of her until three years ago.'

'She died?'

'Yes. Ninety-seven years old. It was a great relief.'

'No men? No love affairs?'

She shook her head. 'There was a suitor when I was young, but I wanted to teach.' She laughed. 'I let him get away. Then there was a teacher, a widower, a couple of years before I retired. He wanted me, but he didn't want my mother as well. Who could blame him? So there were no men, really. I had a love affair with English, with teaching. A passionate affair with music. Lots of little

66

promiscuous affairs with Italy, Paris, Shakespeare, the cinema, religion. You?'

'A love affair with Donna, my first wife. Brenda supplied more passion than I could cope with. Lots of little promiscuous affairs with Linda, Joyce, Irene, Stella, and the bottle. Some other names don't mean much now.'

'We've got a lot in common, Sam?'

'You know what, Celia? I think you're right. Anybody else told me that, I'd think they were crazy. But it sounds like we've been chasing the same shadows.'

'Not *been*, Sam. *Are* chasing them. When you stop it's time to lay down and die.'

'I'm not there yet,' said Sam. 'Still got some way to travel.'

'I'm going to read Chandler again,' said Celia. 'See if I can get into this detective business.'

'I've got all them books,' Sam told her. 'I'll bring them round.'

'I've got a couple myself,' she told him. 'I'll read those first. Then I'll call you.'

Chapter 20

'You're sure you want to go back to that house?'

Jane looked at her brother-in-law. He was not unlike Terry, three years older, already greying at the temples. His wife, Dorothy, stood behind him as always, had the same concerned look on her face.

'I feel I have to,' Jane told them, thinking at the same time, You really think I could stay here with you?

'If it's too much,' said Dorothy, coming forward now and

touching Jane on the arm, 'you can always come back. We'd be only too pleased.'

Jane tried a tentative smile, first for Dorothy, and then for Donald. 'I know that,' she said. She kissed each of them on their cheeks. 'You've both been absolutely marvellous.'

And it's been a real pain being here, she thought. They were not real family. They were not her dead mother. Since Jane's mother had died when she was six years old, Jane had longed to be held by her. She couldn't remember her mother ever holding her. She was sure she had, but she couldn't remember it. Whenever that came up, when people talked about three wishes, or when they said, If you could have anything, one thing, what would it be? Jane always thought, what I'd like is just for my mother to hold me.

As a child she couldn't wait to grow up, to be an adult, to get rid of all those childish feelings like wanting your dead mother to hold you. She'd been precocious, acting like a mother herself to her younger sister, learning early to manipulate others, to be the leader whatever the cost. If it meant lying or cheating, which of course it did, then that was all right. The main thing was to be in control. Make sure you happened to the world, and the world didn't happen to you. But still it was there, a long time after the child had disappeared; no matter how hard Jane tried, she would never be able to make her mother hold her in her arms.

Dorothy and Donald had been stage one, the simple part of the operation. Stage two was dealing with Sam Turner once she got back to the house in the cul-de-sac. He was more than interesting. Not at all the grubby little man she'd expected him to be. He was being led, though. Being led by Jane, which was the most important thing. All the time he was with her, looking after her, he wouldn't be out in the world where he might find things that Jane wouldn't want him to know.

He'd nearly got to Steven Bright before Frances. Only a few minutes difference and he would have talked to him. Steven could have told him about Jane and Frances. And that would have blown everything. But Steven wouldn't be talking to anyone now, and no one else knew about her and Frances. Things were moving along.

She'd seen Sam Turner talking to Frances at the funeral as well. But Frances had handled it. Frances and Jane – when they had a secret, they wouldn't tell anyone.

Important to remember, though, Jane told herself again, Sam Turner was not at all a grubby little man. He was much sharper than she had imagined. The best policy was to keep him as busy as possible. As busy as possible looking in the wrong places.

Maybe that blue cashmere suit would come in for a little more work with Sam Turner. That would keep his eyes in the right direction, for a few weeks at least, which is all the time Jane needed.

Sam was a lady's man, anyone could see that. And Jane, she was a real lady. He was a gentleman as well, in his way; he would respond to her predicament, her obvious distress. Slowly he would come to do what she wanted him to. He was a man, and men were like that.

Chapter 21

A day for sorting things out. Start to line up jobs for the future. Work towards that office in the sky. Keep on keeping on.

Sam locked the door to his flat and walked to the car. The flat above his was vacant again, the guy had only been there a month. Three different people had stayed there this year. Some of them you don't even meet before they've gone. Start of the year had been a woman running away from her husband. But the guy had found her and come round every night, shouting up at the window. 'Joan. Joanie. I'm sorry, Joanie. It won't happen again.' Knocking on the door, sitting on the doorstep. In the end she'd believed him, or just caved in under the pressure.

After Joan there was a guy Sam never met, used to play a trumpet or cornet, something like that, long blue notes in the middle of the night. The last guy was an Irishman working black sites, never changed out of his working gear. Dermot. Moved to Manchester, where 'the big money is'.

Driving to the wandaful Wanda's house to tell her she's too wonderful. She deserves something better. End the day with a bummer. Tomorrow buy a gun.

Hell, you think it's OK with a woman and it never works. You cross the line, dive in there and thrash about, listen to the life story, imagine it, and you think it's OK, that's all, just OK. You've got a woman in your arms, on your arm, leading you on, and you're *still* looking for a woman. You know it's not going to work. Only thing to do is tell her and then sit back and listen to what kind of shit you are. How you can't commit yourself to anything. How you've got an attitude. How you're a little boy who never grew up and you can't treat people like that for ever.

And you say, sorry, but it's better to be honest, and duck another cup aimed at your head. And you know something's happening, and you know exactly what it is. You're fuckin' out of it, is what. You're fuckin' nowhere.

Celia Allison has all the advantages. It's fairly easy to ditch Florence when you're sick of it, but unloading Wanda is a whole 'nother problem. It should be easy, like telling her you're an alcoholic and you don't want to screw up her life. 'Cept with Wanda, you tell her you're an alcoholic, she just loves you *more*. She's got so much love she can *cure* you. With the Wanda type, you tell them anything negative about yourself, they think you're being altruistic.

The only thing certain about the whole episode is that you come out of it feeling like a shit. But you have to go through it, because if you stay in there, you know you'll come out of it eventually anyway, only then you'll feel like a bigger shit.

This is where she lives. She doesn't know you're coming. You haven't written a speech. You switch the engine off and hope it'll start again if you have to make a quick get-away. You sit behind the wheel and smoke a cigarette. Put it off a few more minutes.

Walk the path to the front door. Dying in every footstep.

'Sam,' she says, surprised. Maybe thinks you're so keen you couldn't stay away. 'Come in.' The lush sitting room. Central heating way too high. 'You should have rung me.'

'You wouldn't have liked it on the phone,' said Sam. 'It's not the kind of thing to say on a phone.' He watches her eyes dilate. She knows what's coming now, only she wants to hear it. She wants to have it spelled out. Otherwise she won't believe it.

'Have you met someone else?'

'No. But I haven't stopped looking.'

'Oh!' She doesn't want that. She wants it straight on the chin. She glances into the mirror, touches her cheek with her forefinger, sits on the edge of a chair. Her hands are all over. She rubs her chin, fiddles with the hem of her dress. 'I'm not prepared for this, Sam. I don't know what you're saying.'

'I'm saying you and me, us being together, it's not working for me. It was . . . it *is* a mistake. I want to finish it.'

She doesn't blink. Her eyes are like laser beams. She looks directly into Sam's brain. 'And is that it?' she asks. 'Just "I want to finish it", and off you go? Don't I even get an explanation?'

'Wanda, what can I say? It doesn't work for me. There's no point in prolonging it.'

'Is it something I've said, something I've done?'

'No. It's not you. It doesn't work for *me*.'

'Something's put you off, Sam. You were keen enough at the beginning. I must have done something?'

'Look,' said Sam. 'I don't want to criticize you. Anything I say, it's not a criticism, it's just that you and me don't jell. I need more freedom in a relationship. I want a relationship which leaves me completely free.'

'Excuse me,' said Wanda. 'Am I interfering with your freedom? I hardly ever see you.'

'You ring me all the time,' said Sam. 'You hassle me.'

Wanda began to cry. Big tears rolling down her face. Sam wanted to go to her, put his arms round her. Whisper. Tell her a joke. He stood on the other side of the room.

'I don't want to lose you, Sam,' she said.

'Wanda,' he said quietly, 'there's nothing to lose. You never had me. It's was just a dream.'

'To you,' she said. 'It was real to me. I thought we had something going.'

'I *hoped* we had,' he said. 'But it's not enough. And it's too much.'

'Sam, I won't ring you again. I'll never ring. We could give it another go. I'll leave you free.' Wanda wiped another gush of tears from her face.

Sam shook his head. 'I don't want to, Wanda. I want to finish it.'

'That's the crux of it, isn't it?' she said. 'You don't even want to try. You just want out.'

'Yeah.'

'And to hell with me. My feelings don't matter. It's all what you want.'

'Yeah. It's just about me.'

'Fuck off, then,' she said, still sitting on the edge of the chair. 'Go on, fuck off. Get out.'

'OK.' Sam made for the door, opened it and walked outside.

'Sam,' she shouted as he was closing the door behind him.

He hesitated. Almost free. 'What?' he said as Wanda walked into the hallway, her face so close to him now he could reach out and touch it.

'You're a complete bastard,' she said, and slammed the door in his face.

He started the car and drove home. During the journey the question began formulating itself in his head. He parked the car by the side of the road and found his key. Inside the flat he looked at the marriage proposals he had received in the post. Read the death threats. He pushed *Desire* into the tape deck and cut a slice of bread to toast.

While the bread was burning the question came, fully formed, into his mind, and he said it out loud: 'Shit, what have I done? She was a really nice woman.'

Chapter 22

The new estate on the ring road had a company called Lotza Bullets, and that was Sam's first stop the following morning. He pushed the door to go inside and found it was locked. There was a sign said: OPEN. RING FOR ADMISSION. Sam rang the bell.

A tall, clean-cut character with rimless glasses came to the door and let him in. 'I'm on the phone. Be with you in a minute.' Sam browsed the gun cabinets while he was waiting. Several of the names out of *Pulp Fiction* hit him in the eye: Magnum, Smith & Wesson, Mauser, Walther – they were all here, laid out before his eyes. They didn't look as good as they sounded, Sam thought. The names were magic, but the reality of the objects themselves was coarse. They had little style. They boasted of a utilitarianism that was crass.

Sam moved on to a cabinet filled with hunting knives. Perhaps the kind of knife Graham East used was among them? They were certainly an evil-looking collection of weapons. There was a huge Special Forces Bowie could have cut a man's head off, and just below it something else called a Black Jackal Hunter with a serrated edge and a nasty little twist to the point. Designed to put you off ever wanting to be a black jackal.

Sam read a notice on the wall advertising the Shooters' Rights Association, which was an organization dedicated to protecting shooters from police and official harassment. Everybody thinks they've got rights these days.

The guy on the phone was talking about muggers. 'What you gotta remember,' he said into the mouthpiece, 'your average thug is always aware of your hands. He's streetwise. When he sizes you up he's looking for two things. First, he needs to see both your hands, second, he doesn't want any kind of eye contact. You've gotta gun or not, you see the thug walking towards you, even if there's two of them, you make eye contact with the biggest one and you put your right hand into your jacket pocket. Ten to one the mugger will back off.'

Sam couldn't hear what the party on the other end of the line was saying. 'Eliot,' the gun shop proprietor said, 'if he doesn't back off, you take your gun out of your pocket. And if he still doesn't back off, you shoot the fucker.' He put the phone down and came out of his office.

'What can I do you for?' he said, smiling like there was lead in his mouth.

'I want a gun,' Sam told him.

'What kinda gun?'

'Some kind of pistol. I need something not too heavy, fit in my pocket. But big enough, or ugly enough, to put people off.'

The proprietor looked at Sam sideways. 'You gotta licence?'

Sam shook his head. 'No.'

'You putting me on or what?'

'No,' Sam told him. 'I need a gun. Show me the way to the licence.'

'You haven't got a licence, you won't get one,' the proprietor said. 'You a member of a gun club?'

'I go to two solo clubs,' Sam told him. 'That do you?'

The man didn't laugh. 'I know your face, don't I?'

'Maybe on the TV,' said Sam. 'Or the local paper.'

'Yeah, you're the one's after the knife-man. I seen you on the news. What you gonna do when you find the guy?'

'I need a gun,' Sam told him. 'Or some fast running shoes, eh?'

He laughed at that. Sam thought he must've never heard it before. The proprietor got a chair from the corner of the room and took it into his office. 'Come and sit down,' he said. 'I'll put the kettle on. Tell you how it is.' The joke had worked wonders on him.

Sam followed him into the office. Bits of gun scattered all over the place. Boxes of ammunition. Stacks of paper targets. A large notice on the wall said: DIGNITY, COURAGE, VIRTUE, CHASTITY, HONOUR. THE AGE OF THE WIMP HAS FORCED THESE WORDS INTO DISREPUTE. On the man's desk was a frame with another quotation: 'Without hunting, man becomes cut off from nature, adrift in the unpleasant sea of the human condition.' José Ortega y Gasset. Sam looked around for a swastika but couldn't find one.

'You want a gun,' the man said, 'you have to be a full member of a gun club. You apply for membership, you attend regularly, after six months they make you a member. Then you can apply for a licence.'

'I don't have six months,' said Sam.

'You apply for a licence,' the proprietor continued, 'the police come and interview you every day. You got any kind of record, they'll turn you down. You have to prove need. You have to show you have a place to use it. Personal protection is not regarded as need.'

'Look,' Sam told him. 'Every day somebody gets blown away. Seems to me like anybody can get a gun.'

'Not legally.'

'Who cares if it's legal or not?'

'I do,' said the proprietor. 'I'm a licensed firearms dealer. I sell you a gun without a licence, they'll close me down.'

'I only want a little one,' said Sam.

The guy nearly smiled. 'I'd like to help,' he said. 'But my hands are tied.'

'What about the black market?'

'Booming,' the proprietor told him. 'The legal trade's in deep recession. The black market's thriving. Villains don't buy legal guns.'

'Look,' said Sam. 'I need a gun. I don't give a shit where it comes from.'

The proprietor pushed a pad and pen across the table. 'I can't help you,' he said. 'Leave your name and telephone number in case I think of something else. I could help you, I would. But I don't do illegal firearms.'

The telephone was ringing when Sam got back to the flat. 'I heard you're in the market,' said a voice he didn't recognize.

'Where?' Sam asked.

The voice directed him to a lorry drivers' café on the A64. 'It'll have to be today,' the voice said. 'I'll be there in half an hour.'

Sam found the place easily. Bigger than he had imagined. There were a couple of trucks parked outside. Inside there was one driver tucking into a plateful of thick-cut bacon and eggs, while another one played a one-arm bandit. A middle-aged waitress stood by a till at the end of the self-service counter. She looked towards Sam when he came through the door, but continued biting her nails.

Sam bought himself a mug of tea which looked like hot orange juice and took it to the end table in the smoking section. He had a sip of the tea, gagged and pushed the mug away. Lit a cigarette and waited. The only sounds were from the one-arm bandit – an incessant bleating – and from the tea urn an almost rhythmical expulsion of steam.

Ten minutes passed before the door opened and a young driver came in. He wore a khaki bib-and-brace overall with a checked shirt and black boots. Long greasy hair tied back with a rubber band. He got a coffee and walked over to Sam's table. He had a

76

plastic bag with the name of a butcher on it. 'You the guy?' he asked.

'Well, I guess.'

The driver sat opposite him. His shirt was open almost to the waist, thick black body hair pushing the folds apart. The shirt sleeves were rolled up, revealing a tattoo which said the guy's best friend was his mother. Sam thought the guy's mother might like him to shave more often. Or maybe she had a tattoo of her own. Mothers these days, they ain't like what they used to be.

'It's a Walther,' the driver said, nodding towards the plastic bag. 'Called a PPK. Fairly old, but in good nick. Enough ammo for a hundred shots.'

'Where's it from?'

'I know nothing,' the driver said. 'Drivers bring them back from Poland, East Germany. Mainly Kalashnikov's — too big for you. Big trade since the Soviets shut up shop. I'm not the guy.'

'I look in your eyes,' Sam said, 'I know you're not the guy.'

'You give me two hundred notes,' the driver said. 'I walk out of here and leave the piece behind. You want to haggle, I pick up the bag and leave.'

'I heard one hundred,' said Sam.

'You heard shit,' said the driver. 'I can't buy at that.'

'But you're not the guy,' said Sam.

'One-fifty's the best I can do.'

'One-twenty's the best I can do,' Sam told him.

'I told you I don't like haggling.'

'Don't haggle,' Sam told him. 'Just sell me the gun.'

'Fuck,' said the driver. 'One-forty.'

'If I say one-thirty,' said Sam, 'will we be able to compromise?'

'Yeah. OK. Gimme the money.'

'How do I know it works?' Sam asked him.

'You don't. You just believe in it.'

'Where do I get more ammo?'

'You don't know anything,' the driver said. 'I think about it, I'll ring you now and then, see if you're in the market.'

Sam pushed the money over the table. The driver palmed it and tucked it away somewhere inside his shirt. 'I'm walking out of here,' the driver said. 'You wait ten minutes before leaving.'

Sam rolled another one, lit it and waited five minutes. Then he picked up the butcher's bag and left.

He drove along the A64 towards town. He stopped at a layby and took the Walther out of its bag. When there was a lull in the traffic Sam wound down the window and took aim at a tree about thirty feet away. He squeezed the trigger and recoiled violently at the explosion. Shit, it worked. The tree didn't fall over or scream out in pain. Just stood there, stoical, like it had a motto, 'Suffer and Grow'.

Sam put the Walther back in the bag and rammed it into the glove compartment. Got out of there quick, singing *Motorpsycho Nightmare* at the top of his voice. *I dig farmers, don't shoot me, please.*

On the way into town a voice in his head, a voice which came occasionally, totally uninvited, said: 'Why pick on a tree?'

Chapter 23

Frances was going to see Graham. Burn a candle for him. Like in his poem, *Eternal Flame of Love*.

But the man had turned up. The Cortina man. Asking questions. Interfering in other people's business. Wanting to know everybody Graham had ever met. Wondering if she'd found any of his poems? Turned up more photographs? Writing it all down. Writing slowly in big letters, printing them, as if he hadn't had a proper education.

'I've got to go out soon,' Frances told him. 'I've got an appointment.'

'I won't keep you much longer,' Sam said. 'What about his clothes? Did he take everything?'

'No, there were some things left. Things he didn't normally wear. I threw them all out when I moved here. I thought, even if he comes back, he won't want that old red shirt, the boots that needed mending.'

'Don't you think it's strange the police haven't found him?'

'No,' said Frances. 'I think he's in New Zealand. He wouldn't go back to Wellington. He could be anywhere there. When he left Wellington the first time he travelled about. He visited all the initial settlements, lived with old-timers, people who could tell him about the early days. I think that's what he's doing now.'

'Some kind of research?'

'You don't understand Graham,' Frances said. 'He's a poet. He's a dreamer. You carry on thinking he's a killer, and you'll never find him. He told me once, if you ever need me and you can't find me, look for a single flower in a large desert.'

'What does that mean?'

'He thinks the world is an alien place. The desert, the flower, these are things he can relate to. Animals, plants, the earth itself, these are worthy. People are the enemy. Nature is undermined by people. By people and by thinking.'

'So he'll be in the countryside someplace?'

'He hated it in Leeds,' Frances said. 'For a long time he never went out of the house.'

'Did you have neighbours there? Someone he might have known? Talked to?'

Frances shook her head. 'We kept ourselves to ourselves.'

'OK,' said Sam. 'Sorry to keep you. I have to cover every angle.' He stood to leave.

Frances collected a keyring with three keys, and a candle from the table, and put them in her bag. 'I'll come out with you,' she said. 'I'm late.'

She saw the man get in his car. When she pulled away from the kerb in her little black Panda he seemed to be having trouble starting his Cortina.

Frances drove to Leeds. The house close to Potternewton Park looked bleak. She had had the windows boarded up. Squatters were a problem in the neighbourhood. These people believed that everything belonged to them. Even the legitimate neighbours were quite capable of breaking in, taking anything they wanted, smashing up everything else. Frances visited at least once a week to make sure everything was all right.

She set the car alarm. Fixed the steering-wheel lock. Took her bag and went to the house door with her keys. A locksmith had fitted three locks to the door for her. Charged her £65 and said she was a wise lady. She let herself in and closed the door behind her.

Most of the rooms were bare. There were a few sticks of furniture here and there. The odd cardboard box filled with rubbish. Nothing that meant anything to Frances. Nothing important.

She lit the candle, opened the trap door to the cellar, and descended the rickety steps. The floor of the cellar sloped away into one corner, and that corner was flooded with a few inches of water. At the higher end of the cellar was a table and a chair. Frances put the candle on the table and sat on the chair facing the brick wall.

She sat in silence for several minutes, then she said: 'Well, Graham, my darling, everything's going to plan.'

But the wonderful thing about being with Graham was that he did all the talking, he did all the thinking. He knew everything. He even knew about the man in the Cortina. Knew about *that*, though it had happened less than an hour ago.

Insight, that's what Graham had. Insight and sensitivity. He was the gentlest man who ever walked the earth. A man who carried terrible burdens, but who carried them with dignity. Frances would always be with Graham. So long as she lived, no one else would mean as much to her as he did.

He was caring and constant. He loved her and she meant everything to him.

Chapter 24

Sam kept a good distance, but followed the Panda all the way to Leeds. He had intended going to see Gus this afternoon, but the sight of Frances Golding putting a candle into her bag to keep an appointment had changed his mind. Why would she need a candle?

Hell, some women preferred candles to men. Some of the guys Sam had met, he could understand why, but this woman was supposed to have an appointment, so why did she need a candle?

The black Panda took the A64 to Leeds. It travelled fast, easily cutting in and out of traffic. Once it hit the city Sam had to close the gap to make sure he didn't lose her in unfamiliar territory. Her destination in Chapeltown was, in the event, not that unfamiliar.

He managed to pull in to a side-street when she stopped. He left his Cortina by the side of the road and walked back to the corner in time to see Frances unlocking the door of a boarded-up house. This must be where she had lived with Graham? Sam had assumed that this place was finished with. He had not imagined it still existed, or if it did exist, he had not imagined that Frances still had access to it. Did the police know about it?

She was inside for an hour. Burning the candle, of course. The house wouldn't be connected to the mains. But what does a woman do in an empty house for an hour? Was Graham East in there? Was Frances sheltering him? But if that was what was happening, why hadn't she taken any food inside?

The questions were coming at him so fast Sam had to start jotting them down. All of a sudden Frances began to be a whole lot more interesting than she had appeared. As far as Sam knew, she didn't have a job. So where did her income come from? If she owned this house, why didn't she let it out or sell it?

The answers to all his questions must be inside. He would have to find a way of getting into the house without arousing Frances Golding's suspicions. But from this distance the place looked like a fortress. When Frances came out Sam counted her locking the door with three separate keys.

She was a wilful woman. She turned from the door and walked straight to the Panda, never glancing to right or left. She unlocked the car, fiddled around with security devices inside and drove off at speed. Sam followed. He would have a look at the house another time. More important now to stay on this lady's tail. See what else she got up to.

Only there wasn't much to see. Frances drove straight back to her house in York, made her car safe, and went inside.

Sam waited for half an hour, but she didn't come out again.

'I read through all the notes,' said Gus. 'You know what strikes me about it?'

Sam potted the pink and tried to move the black off the side cushion, missing it by more than a foot. 'Tell me,' he said.

'That was a really crap shot,' Gus said, shaking his head. 'Christ, there's kids of twelve come in here can play better than that.'

'I can still pot it,' Sam told him. 'No harm done.'

'If you pot it from there,' Gus told him, 'it'll be a fluke. No one would try to pot a ball from that position.'

Sam got down on the ball and eyed a long impossible black. 'Bottom right,' he said.

'I don't believe this,' said Gus.

Before the shot Sam saw the black going into the pocket.

Sometimes life is like that. It's an impossible shot, but that's why he takes it on. The cue ball struck the black thin, sending it down the cushion towards the bottom-right pocket. 'Well, fuck me,' said Gus.

The black wobbled around the pocket, hesitated for a second, and gave up. 'Serves you fuckin' right,' said Gus, going to the table. He potted the black himself, briskly, then glanced over at Sam with his world-weary look.

'It should have dropped,' said Sam.

Four other tables were occupied, dotted around the room in pools of light. A group of men and two women were talking at the bar. There was a glass partition between the bar and the playing area and, although the drinkers looked loud and animated, it was not possible to hear what they were saying. They were distracting, though, and Sam found himself looking over at the group, feeling irritated. Looking at them surrounded by photographic portraits of professional players.

'Another one?' Gus asked.

'Quickie,' said Sam. 'You were telling me about the case.'

'Yeah. This Graham East character. Everybody who ever knew him says he couldn't be the guy. Everything points to him, but nobody believes he's capable of it. What do you make of that?'

'First, I think he's changed,' said Sam. 'We know he's got a temper. We know he's capable of violence. Maybe he's changed. Whatever it is makes people think he's incapable, that part of him dies, and the violent bit develops.'

'It's not likely, though,' said Gus.

'Then I think, what if he's not working alone? Say Frances has got him cooped up in this house in Leeds. Maybe the guy's flipped. Like Jekyll and Hyde. Part of the time he's a wimp, next day he's a knife-man.'

'How do we get into the house?'

'I want to watch Frances, see if she has some kind of pattern. If we can get into her house in York, get the keys for the Leeds house, it'll be easy.'

'Oh, yeah,' said Gus. 'Specially if you meet a slavering maniac inside.'

'It's all right,' Sam said. 'I can make it.'

Gus laughed. 'That's what you said about the last black.'

Chapter 25

The Cortina wouldn't start. Sam and Gus took turns until the battery went flat. 'This is supposed to be one of the perks,' said Gus. 'My first day and the one and only perk evaporates. Jesus, if this is rock and roll, I want my old job back.'

'I'll get it fixed,' Sam told him. 'Jesus, fuckin' machinery. Never trust it.' Sam got his butcher's bag out of the glove compartment, locked the car and left it.

They walked through the town dominated by the old Minster, dodging tourists, late shoppers, retail people leaving work and hurrying home to their normal lives. The weather had turned and a sharp breeze was coming from the north. Sam turned up the collar of his jacket. Cutting through the Coppergate Centre, three doorways in a row housed homeless people, two of them with homeless dogs. 'Didn't used to see that,' said Gus.

'Nobody gives a toss,' said Sam. 'They starve to death, freeze to death, the government won't even notice.'

'You need more employees,' said Gus, you know where to come.'

Sam stopped. 'We do.'

'Hang on,' Gus said. 'It was a joke.'

'Not funny, though,' said Sam. 'The kid in the doorway, it's like he's been haunting me. Every time I go out I bump into him.'

He walked back to the last occupied doorway, Gus following. The guy in the doorway was about eighteen years old going on twelve, had a puppy with him. A scrap of card by his leg said, HAMELESS AND HUNGRY.

When Sam stopped in front of him the guy held his hand out. His face was streaked with dirt and his eyes bulged. 'You wanna job?' Sam asked him.

'Got fifty pence, pal?' the youth said. It was a Geordie accent.

'No. I asked you something else,' Sam said. 'Do you remember me?'

'For a cup of tea?'

Sam crouched in front of him. 'Do you want a job?' he asked.

The youth pulled his legs up and shoved himself backwards against the door. 'I'm hungry,' he said.

'You can earn some money,' Sam tried again. 'I could give you a job.'

The youth looked right through him. 'I couldn't sell Barney,' he said. 'He's my friend.'

'Jesus,' said Sam, standing up.

Gus took his place, touched the youth's arm. 'The man's offering you a job,' he said. 'You could earn some money. Buy some food.'

The youth said: 'I can't defend myself.'

Sam walked off and then came back. He threw a handful of coins into the doorway. 'Come on,' he said to Gus. 'We've got work to do.'

'The guy's a hospital case,' said Gus.

'What did you expect?' Sam asked him. He stopped and kicked the window of the Viking Museum. A middle-aged American couple started running down the road. 'Jesus,' said Sam. 'Nobody can make a profit out of you, they shove you in a fuckin' doorway. If you're really lucky, you get a dog called Barney.'

Gus took his arm and got him walking again. 'You kick all the windows in,' he said, 'it's not going to help him or the dog. You wanna be a social worker, you find better tactics.'

85

Sam spat in the gutter and walked on, grim-faced. As they approached Bishophill he lightened up. 'I'll just introduce you,' he said. 'Then you can go. Come back and relieve me about two.'

He knocked on the door and the blonde let them in. The puffy eyes had gone. She was all smiles. Dressed in a maroon business suit, tight skirt, white blouse, collar like a ruff. 'I thought you'd be earlier,' she said.

'Sorry,' said Sam. 'The car broke down.'

'Oh,' she said. 'You can use Terry's if you like. The police had it, but I got it back today. It's too big for me.'

'The Volvo?' said Sam.

Gus's face broke into a smile. 'Would be very useful,' he said. 'Until we get ours back on the road.'

'This is Gus,' Sam said. 'My associate. He'll be here some of the time. He'll be here when you get up in the morning.'

Jane Deacon gave Gus her hand. 'Pleased to meet you,' she said through her tiny mouth.

'Yeah,' said Gus. 'Pleased.'

'OK,' said Sam to Gus. 'See you later.'

Gus walked to the door, then turned round and came back. 'Have you got the keys?' he asked.

'How're you doing?' Sam asked her when Gus had gone.

'Not too bad,' she said. 'After the funeral it was difficult. I feel better now.'

'What's it like coming back here?'

'Strange.' She smiled, then became thoughtful. 'Not as bad as I expected. I'll manage. I think I can get used to it.'

Sam made eye contact for the first time. 'You wanna talk, I'm here,' he said.

'Thank you. I probably will. I'll try not to get in your way.'

Sam laughed. 'A lady like you gets in my way,' he said, 'that's a good day.'

Did she flush? Sam couldn't tell. No, hell, she'll have guys coming on to her all the time. Brush them off like flies.

'Can I get you anything?' she asked. 'I thought I might make some coffee.'

'Real coffee?'

'Filter coffee. That's all we . . . *I've* . . . got.'

'Yeah,' said Sam. 'I can't drink the instant stuff. Tastes like p— Well, I can't drink it.'

Jane Deacon smiled. 'You can say piss if you like,' she said. 'I'm not going to smack your hand.'

Sam shrugged. 'Piss,' he said. 'And you ever feel the need to smack my hand, you only have to ask.'

'I think we're going to get along fine,' said Jane. 'I'll make the coffee.'

'While you do that,' Sam said, 'I'll have a look round the house. You don't mind, I'll wander round?'

'Fine, go wherever you like.'

He went to the third storey, started at the top and worked his way down. Two rooms on the top, both with single beds. Twin beds with matching covers in separate rooms. Must be guest rooms. Nothing in the wardrobes or chests of drawers.

Second-floor front was her room, had been *their* room not so long ago. Carpet you could lose your feet in. Kidney-shaped dressing table with three mirrors, perfume bottles, mascara, pink tissues, small bottle of three-star cognac. Wardrobe with the door open, blue cashmere jacket poking out, two dozen other dresses inside, and must be fifty pairs of shoes.

Terry Deacon's wardrobe stuffed with suits and jackets, only twenty pairs of shoes, modest man. One of those little racks to keep ties on.

Bedside tables with lamps and books. On his side Paul Scott's *The Raj Quartet*, which he would never finish. On her side John Fowles's *Mantissa*. Sam picked it up and opened it at the marker. 'Still perched on an arm', he read, 'she runs a hand gently down his chest, and makes a little smoothing circle round his navel.' Sam placed the book back on the bedside table. She wants to read rude novels, who cares, it's a free country. Least it used to be. Or so they say.

The central room on the second floor was a study. Large antique desk, personal papers, unanswered letters. Two fountain pens. Company stationery, envelopes. The walls covered with box files, company records all neatly labelled.

The back room was a bathroom and toilet. Huge blue bath. Separate shower. Radiator spanning the length of the room. Piles of towels in primary colours.

'Coffee's ready,' Jane Deacon shouted up the stairs.

'Coming,' said Sam. 'Just inspecting the bathroom.' He went down to join her in the kitchen.

'There's hot water all the time,' she said. 'You can use it if you like.'

'On the way here,' Sam told her, 'we passed a guy living in a shop doorway with a dog.'

'Oh, dear,' she said. 'It shouldn't be allowed.'

Sam took the coffee and added a drop of milk. He couldn't work out if she meant the guy should be moved on, or homelessness should be abolished. He decided to leave it. 'I might try the shower one time,' he said.

She showed him where coffee and tea were kept, the bread bin, the fridge. 'Take anything you need,' she said. 'You might get hungry during the night, fancy nibbling on something.'

Sam smiled but kept it to himself.

'We'll use the front room,' he said, 'if that's all right.' He went to the door of the kitchen, which led out to a garden. It had a good lock and bolts at top and bottom. 'No one's going to come in this way. Can we keep this bolted?'

'I only ever use it to get to the garden,' she said. 'Weekends, during the day. There's no access to the street.'

'I need to talk finance,' Sam said. 'Don't know how long this is going to take, but the expenses are mounting up. Gus costs. I don't have the capital to carry it.'

'It's not a problem,' she said. 'I feel better with you around at the moment. They're talking about a management buy-out of the business. I'll end with half a million, maybe more.'

'Christ,' said Sam.

'And there's the insurance. Terry left me very well provided for.'

'Sounds like it,' Sam told her. 'You ever think of getting married again, I'd like to put in a bid.'

She smiled, fingered the edge of the table for a moment. 'I'd have thought somebody would have claimed you by now?'

'I've had offers,' he said, 'but nobody who could really afford me.'

'You've been married?'

'From time to time. I never learned how to do it. Keep getting it wrong.'

'Is that why you joined the men's group?'

'You want my life story?'

'I'm sorry. I'm being pushy.'

'I didn't think that,' he said. 'I spent a lot of time thinking I was getting it right, then more time knowing I was getting it wrong. I joined the men's group because I wasn't sure how to pronounce Esperanto.'

'You don't find it interesting, people's lives?'

'Yeah, I do. *Other* people's lives. I find it interesting when people change patterns. I didn't manage to do that yet. I'm still trying.'

'I can see you are,' she said.

Sam didn't know what to say to that.

She went upstairs to bathe, change her clothes. Sam continued his inspection of the house. The front room he'd seen before. Last time it had a body in it. Now there was a rug where Deacon had lain. He looked underneath it, make sure the body had gone. There was a stain somebody had scrubbed at, but the trace of it would remain for ever. It was a big room, piano with a photograph of Deacon on it, television, stereo equipment. Three shelves of

CDs. Classical, early music. The man's *Greatest Hits*. Some Beatles. Not a lot to while the night away, unless he wanted to educate himself. OK, he'd done it before, could do it again. Next time he'd bring some of his own tapes. He stashed the Walther PPK behind the stereo system. No point in letting Jane see it. Don't want to freak her out.

The middle room was for sitting in. Bookshelves taking up the whole of one wall, books meticulously arranged in alphabetical order. Some Hemingway. Agatha Christie by the barrowload. Simenon might be worth a try.

Back in the kitchen Sam took a mouthful of coffee from his cup. Stone cold. He spat it back again, threw it in the sink and rinsed the cup. Trouble with looking at CDs, books, who knows which are hers and which were Deacons? Who knows which one played the piano?

Sam couldn't make the blonde out. He looked at her, this woman who'd lost her husband, a few days ago, for Christ's sake, and it's like she's already stopped grieving. When Brenda walked out it had taken Sam months, most of them in an unconscious daze, and she was still walking about inside his head. Donna he would never get over. So what was that? People are so different? Can this woman with the body and the small mouth shrug it off after a few days, bottle it all up somewhere inside and start treading the footlights? The show must go on.

Sam shook his head. She's back at work. She's already counted the cash. Even put a rug over the fuckin' blood stains. Had she been in love with her husband? Must've been one of these back-to-back arrangements, *Cosmopolitan* gutless marriage, each partner deposits their feelings in a stainless-steel bucket right after the ceremony. Either one of them ever goes near the bucket again gives the other one grounds for divorce.

He heard Jane Deacon come out of the bathroom and pad down the hall to her bedroom. Some minutes later she moved to the middle room, do her accounts or something. Make sure she was getting the market price for the business.

Sam realized he was getting a downer on Jane Deacon and told himself to stop. He didn't know shit about her. She might be straight up, just good at hiding it. If that was the case, it'd show. She'd break down sooner or later, let it all spill out.

She came down about ten. Full-length plain dressing gown touching the floor, slippers without heels. Under the dressing gown something looked like green silk. She wore no make-up and looked even better. Slightly dark under the eyes, not sleeping properly. Waking up in the night. Waking up in the past, then remembering it's not the past, it's the ever present. Switching the light on and knowing immediately that it's better in the dark.

'Are you OK?' she asked. 'I didn't realize what time it was.'

'I should apologize,' Sam said. 'I gave you a hard time before. I shouldn't have done that, sometimes my negativity gets out of hand. Sorry.'

She pursed her lips together, frowned, then let it go. 'I didn't take it personally,' she said. 'You've a right to your privacy. Since Terry's death I've been trying to take stock. I'm seeing my whole life from a place I've never been before. It's difficult to recognize myself sometimes. When I asked about you I was really asking about me.'

'I know,' Sam told her. 'I should let you get away with it. Next time I'll be more open.'

She hooked on to his eyes while he was speaking. Sam looked back. There was a movement in the contact between them. It started out with her listening to him, him telling her he would be more open. A moment or two later it was her telling him something, though she didn't speak, and him telling her the same thing back. Sam faltered, looked away for a fraction of a second, and when he came back the moment was dead.

Jane opened her mouth and felt around for something to fill the void. 'I should get to bed,' she said. 'Busy day tomorrow.' Her arms were loose by her sides, and while he watched she clenched her fists and let them go.

'Yeah,' he said. 'Tomorrow.'

She went up the stairs. Sam waited about half an hour, expecting her to come down and tell him something, but it didn't happen. He turned to Simenon.

About midnight he cut six slices of bread and made sandwiches of cheese and ham he found in the fridge. Chutney on the cheese. He found a freezer bag and put the sandwiches into it. Then he read more of the Simenon until Gus arrived at two.

He showed Gus where the Walther PPK was stashed. 'Somebody comes to the door, I shoot them?' said Gus.

'Use some discretion,' Sam told him. 'Might be the milkman.'

'You wanna take the Volvo?' Gus asked, dangling the keys.

'I'll walk,' Sam told him. 'Might need it tomorrow, though. You take it home. I'll collect it if I need it.'

Clear night, OK if you walked, but a bit of a nip in the air if you were in a shop doorway. Sam walked to the Coppergate Centre and found the doorway with the Geordie and his dog. Both of them huddled together. Sam leaned down to place the freezer bag with the sandwiches between them. Four eyes watched him. Neither the dog nor the boy moved, but their eyes never left Sam for a second.

'Something to eat,' said Sam.

There was no recognition of the fact that he was there, that he had said anything, just the eyes. 'OK?' he said. 'Hope you like chutney.'

Chapter 26

Sam woke to the telephone ringing just after eight. He swung his legs out of the bed and answered the telephone in the nude. 'What?'

It was the TV man, Clive Desmond. 'Got some news for you,' he said. 'The missing couple have turned up. Living together in Leeds.'

'Just a minute,' Sam said. 'I'll get a pen.'

He wrote down the address of Jean Granger and Bob Blackburn, who were now called Mr and Mrs Blackburn. 'Have you seen them?' he asked Desmond.

'Yes, but we're not allowed to broadcast anything. The police think they'll be in danger if Graham East gets hold of their address.'

'Police are sometimes right,' said Sam. 'I'll go see them today.'

'You heard they're putting it on *Crimewatch UK*?'

'Yeah,' Sam told him. 'I did a bit of recording for it. Voice-over for that and for the same programme in New Zealand and Sweden. It would be nice to hear what kind of response they get.'

'Don't worry. I hear anything, I'll let you know. Oh, and something else,' said Desmond. 'I've got more mail for you. You're getting a lot of business out of this.'

'Can you drop it off? Or shall I collect?'

'I'll send it round,' said Desmond. 'Might have to hire a delivery van.'

Jean Blackburn answered the door. Tiny olive-coloured woman, hair so black it was almost blue. Sam told her he was working for

93

Jane Deacon and she let him into a cluttered living room. Two huge loudspeakers dominated the room and a charismatic voice was speaking from them, something about the unity of all things, the invisible thread that emanated from all beings in the universe, connecting the whole to the one, the one to the whole. Smell of dope. A roach in the ashtray. Sam didn't do dope at all now. But there had been a time.

Jean Blackburn switched the tape deck off. 'That's our guru,' she said. 'Barry. Magic voice, don't you think?'

'Should I know the name?'

She shook her head. 'You do now,' she said.

'I thought gurus were all Indian,' Sam said. 'Names like Maharishi, Bhagwan. Never heard of anyone called Barry before.'

'He's Australian,' she said. 'Enlightened, though. Do you follow any teaching?'

'I watch parking meters.'

She did a double take and said, 'You're joking?'

'I'm a laugh a minute,' Sam admitted.

'The police have been twice,' she said. 'I don't know what I can tell you we haven't already told them.'

'If you don't mind going over it again,' Sam said. 'There might be something useful.'

She told him to sit. 'We haven't really kept contact with anyone from the communal house,' she said. 'We found a different path when it all broke up. Bob discovered Barry, and he's become our whole life. We try not to think about the past. There *is* only the present. The past is a burden which stands in the way of personal progression.'

'I can go with that,' said Sam. Quick snapshots of Donna and Brenda. Wanda with tears in her eyes. 'This place is only half a mile from where Graham East lived with his girlfriend. D'you ever see them?'

'No. Bob saw Graham once, about a year ago. But Graham didn't recognize him. We went to see Barry in Australia three months ago. We didn't know anything about all this business until we got back.'

'When was that?'

'Three, four days ago. Bob said we should stay out of it, but I rang the police. We're the only ones still alive, apart from Jane, of course.

'You should be more careful,' Sam told her. 'You let me in, you don't know me from Adam.'

Jean Blackburn smiled. 'You get a feeling about people,' she said. She put her hand on her solar plexus. 'You felt all right. Barry was speaking on the tape deck. If something's wrong, I feel it inside, right here.'

Sam sat forward. 'This Barry,' he said. 'He's psychic?'

'He's enlightened,' Mrs Blackburn said. 'He's in touch with himself.'

'Yeah, but he knows everything, right?'

'Oh, he certainly knows,' she said.

'So you could ask him where Graham East is?'

'I don't think Barry would be interested in playing those kind of games.'

'Games?'

'Cops and robbers,' she said. 'Something like that's just a diversion.'

'Exactly,' said Sam. 'That's what we're trying to do. Divert the guy.'

She looked off into the far distance. 'You don't understand.'

Bob Blackburn arrived home looking tired, but he smiled easily when Sam was introduced. He was a tall man with a distinctive American accent that Sam immediately placed in Ohio.

'You're close,' Blackburn told him. 'Kentucky, actually. You must know the country?'

'Not that well,' Sam admitted. 'I was there about eight years. Three in LA, a year travelling round, then I spent the last four years in San Francisco.'

'Frisco! Jesus, I was there a couple a years,' Blackburn said. 'Lived just off Fillmore.'

'I was in a squat in Berkeley the first year,' said Sam. 'Then we moved over to Oakland. Great climate.'

'Yeah,' said Blackburn. 'We used to sit by the window and watch the fog trying to get in.'

Sam laughed. He remembered something Mark Twain was supposed to have said, something along the lines that the worst winter he'd ever spent in his life had been in San Francisco in July. 'I've never seen anything like it,' he said. 'Great banks of fog coming off the Pacific, eating up the city in chunks. When were you there?'

'Late seventies,' said Blackburn. 'Just before I came over here. You?'

'Bit earlier than that,' said Sam. 'The Campus shootings.'

'You saw it?'

Sam shook his head. 'I *heard* it, though,' he said. 'Made me think again about the land of the free.'

'There's no such place.'

Sam looked at Blackburn. 'You ought to be careful,' he said. 'Maybe get some kind of chain on the door. When I arrived Jean just let me in, no questions.'

Blackburn looked over at his wife. 'Yeah,' he said. 'We'll talk about it. I don't believe Graham wants to kill us, though.'

'Neither did Deacon,' said Sam. 'Or Bright. Their convictions didn't do much to keep them alive.'

You don't understand! Shit, Sam had wanted to tell her, you sound like a fuckin' stereotype wife. Three people left alive in this case and two of them are voluntary zombies. Graham East, or whoever is committing these murders, finds out where the Blackburns live, all he has to do is use a deep voice. He sounds convincing enough, they'll kill them*selves*. This is Barry speaking; listen, I want you to stab yourself in the eye. Oh, sure Barry, any particular spot?

One thing Jean Blackburn had said was worth following up.

'When the communal house broke up,' she said, 'we found a different path.' So what path was the communal house into? Terry Deacon had been a Buddhist, and now these two were into some kind of New Age thing. There was a possibility that the killings were cult-related. What if Graham East was a guru spurned? Seeking revenge on his disaffected followers.

Every lead, Sam told himself. Every lead is worth following.

The Volvo handled like a dream. Little touch on the pedal and he sailed past the tourist coach in front. Sixty or seventy bored Germans watching him go by, on their way to a medieval fort. It would be hard going back to the Cortina after driving this beast. Just sitting behind this wheel is what living in the moment is all about.

People live in such impossible dreams. Living in the moment, refusing to face the past, the creed of every guru since day one. Sam lived in the moment when he first saw Donna. Donna stood at the top of the escalator, Donna coming down, walking down as well as being carried down. Donna skinny, Donna pregnant, Donna dead. Sam lived in moments when every moment he ever lived came crowding down into the present moment. Twelve years old, hanging from a tree. Thirty years old, hanging from a bottle. Sam saw a million Sams from all the stages of his life all cramming themselves into the same moment. He could see himself laughing until he thought his sides would split; screaming with pain and incomprehension at the blind totality of destiny; snarling like a cornered animal and striking out with head and fist; weeping with joy at the touch of his daughter's hand, a twist of fate. And it was all in the moment. The fury of the moment.

People like Jean Blackburn, Sam would shake them to pieces. Come on woman, man, fuckin' machine, whatever you are, open your stubborn eyes and *see*. This is not the *way* you dumb shit, this is a cul-de-sac.

Quick call at the garage confirmed the Cortina had made its last journey. Something else to get used to.

Celia Allison was inconsolable because she couldn't offer Sam a biscuit. 'Celia,' he said. 'I don't like biscuits. I liked the ginger biscuits with tea because we dunked them and it reminded me of my childhood. Every time I come here I don't want to be reminded of my childhood. OK Now can we drop it?'

She gave him a stock of cards for his wallet: Sam Turner Detective Agency. And showed him the matching stationery she'd designed.

'I've replied to about half the people who wrote in,' she said. 'And I've set up a couple of interviews for you. One of the solicitors is desperate for a new investigator.'

'You don't hang about, Celia. I knew you'd be good. I heard earlier there's a lot more mail.'

'Bring it round,' she said, 'I'll sort it. The telephone, what I've done is arrange that all calls come through to your number. If you don't answer, they are diverted to me. That way anybody who needs to contact us is sure to get an answer. Four calls today, all from a lady called Wanda, desperate to see you.'

'I don't need to see her.'

'She sounded nice,' Celia told him. 'A little disappointed.'

'I used to know her.'

'She's not finished with you, Sam.'

'She's OK, Celia, but she hassles me. Always ringing up.'

'You know your business better than me,' Celia said. 'But I think I'd give her another chance.'

'Well, maybe.'

The old lady smiled. 'Tell her exactly what you want and what you want to give. She can make up her own mind.'

'After this case,' Sam told her, 'I'm gonna take you out for a good meal, then we go on after that and do a little dancing. How's that grab you?'

'Oh, my goodness, Sam. You are a one.' Her face like a smiling garden. 'I haven't had such excitement for years. The meal sounds lovely, but we could miss the dancing.'

'Tell you what,' he said. 'There's a place in the town you can do both. We eat first, have a little drink, you not me, then after the coffee we take in a waltz or two. You a bit rusty? I'll give you a refresher course.' He put his arm round her waist and waltzed her round the floor.

'Goodness me,' she said, looking up into his eyes. 'I've gone back twenty, maybe thirty years.' She closed her eyes. 'A man named Grey.'

'When you dance with Sam Turner,' said Sam, 'you don't muse on about old boyfriends. OK?'

Celia stopped the waltz and pushed him away. She wagged her finger at him, still with the gleam in her eyes. 'I don't know,' she said, 'but I suspect it's against my religion, dancing in the afternoon.'

'I have to go anyway,' Sam told her. 'But, Celia, next time?'

'Yes, Sam.'

'I'll expect biscuits.'

Sam dropped the Volvo off at Gus's house and walked to the Coppergate Centre.

The young Geordie had already claimed his doorway. He was staring out at the passers by, his dog Barney sat by his side, partly obscuring the Hameless and Hungry sign.

'You wanna job?' Sam asked him.

'Spare a copper, pal?' The response was immediate, uncon- scious. Sam didn't reply and the youth looked up at his face, about to repeat his question. There was a gleam of something, could have been recognition. It hovered for a moment as they stared at each other and then vanished. 'D'you want sex?'

Sam shook his head. The Geordie picked up Barney and held him close to his face. The pup licked him around the eyes and nose. Sam felt in his pants pocket and rattled some change. He dropped a couple of pound pieces into the Geordie's lap. 'I'm gonna keep on asking until I get a sensible answer,' he said.

As he walked away he heard the Geordie say, 'I wouldn't be any use to you.'

Chapter 27

Sam let himself into the house in the cul-de-sac and checked the downstairs windows and the back door. Looked at the Walther, make sure it hadn't been discovered, disappeared, or been tampered with. He was checking the upstairs rooms when Jane got home from work. She came into the house singing something Sam recognized, Billie Holiday number, 'Foolin' Myself'. Imitating the Holiday voice, that slightly squeaky, all the way vulnerable sound.

'Good day?' Sam asked.

'Yes,' she cut into the song to answer him, then went back to finish the line: '*I may pretend, but in the end, I 'm just foolin' myself.*'

'It's a nice song,' Sam said. 'You sing well. Like you mean it.'

'It was on the radio in the car,' she said. 'It took me back.'

'Halcyon days?'

She grinned at him. 'You've been around a lot, haven't you?'

'Here and there. I've been to Leeds today, see an old friend of yours. Jean Blackburn, used to be Jean Granger.'

'Oh, so she married Bob in the end? How did you find her? How was she?'

'I got a tip,' he said. 'She was nutty.'

Jane laughed. 'She always was a bit nutty. People don't change, do they? Both her and Bob were into peace and love like it was a mission, in the same way the astronauts must have thought about a moon landing. Slightly frustrating.'

'They've got a guru, somebody called Barry.'

'Don't know him,' said Jane. 'They had a guru before. In fact they had two gurus. One each, different brands. There was always a question about whether they'd stay together.'

'This house you lived in,' Sam asked, 'was it a religious commune?'

'Not really. Yes and no. We were supposed to be working towards a combination of spiritual and social endeavours. But it never really got going, lasted about eighteen months. We argued all the time.'

'About?'

Religion, sex, people changing partners. We were nearly all professionals, we argued about commitment. We were young. Jean and Bob were faithful to their gurus; Terry was getting more and more interested in Buddhism; Graham was into some kind of esoteric Christianity. Everybody had a different angle.'

'What was yours?'

'A loose kind of theosophy, I suppose. I thought we should try to be a bridge, some kind of structure where different disciplines could cross over and meet each other.'

'Idealistic,' said Sam.

'Yes. We were very young.'

'And what do you believe now?'

'Nothing,' she said. 'Terry did that for both of us. He used to talk about Buddhism sometimes; I can relate to that in a way, but I'm very much of the world. I can't easily withdraw, don't meditate. How about you?'

'Some of the people I've known,' Sam told her, 'some of the dead ones – I'd like to think we'll get together again some time. I can't believe it's over, what we had, what we could have had.'

'Is that your wife?'

Sam nodded. 'Among others,' he said.

'Do you want to talk about it?'

Sam shook his head. 'Not now,' he said. 'Maybe sometime. Need to talk about cars, though. Mine's gone to the graveyard.'

'Oh, just use the Volvo. I don't need it.'

'I'd like to make it more formal than that.'

101

'You want to buy it?'

'I want to, yes. But I don't have the readies.'

'I'll give you the papers,' she said. 'Pay me when you can.'

'Just like that?'

'You had something else in mind?'

'No,' Sam told her. 'I thought it was impossible.'

'Look, Sam, I'm not short of cash. You need the car, just take it. When you've got some money you can pay me.'

She came downstairs about one in the morning, that dressing gown touching the floor with the green silk thing underneath. Sam was playing *Another Side* on her tape deck, volume turned down low.

'Couldn't sleep,' she said. 'Who's this?'

'Jus' a tape,' he said.

'Cocoa?'

'Yeah, if you're making.'

She padded through to the kitchen. Sam laid back in the chair, listened to the tape with the chinking of cups in the background, heard her open and close the fridge door. Cocoa! Jesus, it must be years.

'Is this folk music?' she asked, coming back with a mug in each hand. She handed one to Sam.

'Somethin' like that.'

She sat on the couch opposite him, one side of the dressing gown falling open, exposing her legs encased in the thin green stuff. Shiny green legs. She listened to the whole of *My Back Pages* without moving. When the song was finished she looked up at him. Sam thought she might speak, or maybe she expected him to say something. When the next track started she continued looking at him. Sam looked back. The song disappeared into the background. Sam was happy to see it go, it reminded him of Brenda.

Jane said nothing and said everything. Sam hoped she'd follow through, come over to him or maybe pat the sofa next to her,

102

invite him over there. She just looked. Looking for a lead, maybe? A leader?

Tonight Sam wanted to be led. Neither of them moved and gradually the songs on the album came back into the foreground, a barrier and a bridge between them. A barrier neither tried to overcome, a bridge neither would use.

Go away from my window, leave at your . . . She was nodding, her eyes closing right through the last track. When the tape stopped she was asleep, her head fallen over to the left.

Melted back into the night. The green silk thing was pyjamas, wide trousers like culottes. One of her backless slippers had come off, the left one. She no longer wore a wedding ring. Sam let her sleep while he made sandwiches for the Geordie and his dog. Then he woke her, touched her on the shoulder, shook her a little.

'It's quart to two,' he said. 'Gus'll be here soon.'

She was confused for a few seconds. 'The music,' she said. 'Must have made me nod off.'

'You'll sleep now,' he told her. 'Jus' get into bed.'

She turned at the door for a last look. 'Good night.'

'Sleep well,' said Sam.

Geordie and Barney were flat out but wide awake. Sam put the sandwiches down and looked at their eyes. 'Ham and pickle, cold beef and cucumber, cheese and chutney,' he said, enunciating each word carefully. 'Four chocolate biscuits, two each. OK.'

Geordie nearly smiled.

'You absolutely sure you don't want a job? said Sam. 'Earn some money, make your own fuckin' sandwiches?' He felt in his pocket and found two pound coins. Placed them on top of the packet of sandwiches.

He walked back to the flat and let himself in. The place upstairs was still empty. On his doormat a note from Wanda. 'Please contact me. I won't hassle.'

Sam tucked the note into his pocket, undressed and got into bed. Cold beef and cucumber, for Christ's sake. Is that edible?

He fell asleep dreaming of green silk culottes. Warm ones.

Chapter 28

'Come you, you can't sleep here.' Geordie felt someone kicking his foot.

The same copper as the night before, the night before that. He scrambled to his feet and tucked Barney under his arm. 'Don't leave rubbish behind,' the copper said.

Geordie collected the packet of sandwiches the guy had left and walked along the path. 'Don't let me catch you here again,' the copper said after him.

The next spot was down by the river, through a hole in the fence and into the park. Bit colder than the Coppergate Centre. He opened the sandwiches there and made Barney beg for his share. The little dog sitting up on his hind legs, his tongue hanging out. The dog had followed Geordie one day. Just followed him everywhere he went. A homeless dog. Join the club.

They settled down on the steps of the Film Theatre, but it was beginning to get light, and Geordie couldn't sleep. The guy made good sandwiches, the best for a long time, if not ever. But what did he want? No one had ever offered Geordie a job, no one except the guy in Manchester who wanted beating on the bare arse. Call that a job? Ten quid's worth of red stripes on the guy's arse. Other men had wanted straight sex, and Geordie had done it too, when he was hungry enough. He had said he wouldn't do it, but then felt differently about it after not eating for three days. Not eating for a while made you think about a lot of things differently. Nothing was free. That was absolute. Nothing was free.

So what did the guy want?

Geordie didn't want to trust him. Geordie didn't want to trust anyone. Fuck, your mother runs off with the landlord, leaves you alone in the house. They take you into care, and nobody cares about you. Even your own brother joins the Royal Navy and never comes back, never sends a postcard from foreign. You run away and they bring you back and you go again and don't get far. Then one day you go and they don't find you. You get into a lorry and just keep going and end up in Wales. And still no one gives a fuck. No one ever cares at all, unless you're sleeping in their doorway. Then they care enough to call the cops.

You learn fast. You find out where the handouts are, where the restaurants dump the left-overs. You go into a charity shop when it's snowing, they might give you an overcoat. Even a hat and gloves. That happened once. Wool gloves, nearly like new except for the hole in one of them. Life savers, those gloves. Best gloves in the whole world. Could use them now, even if it wasn't snowing.

So what does he want? The man? The sandwich man? Another fuckin' pervert probably. Likes little fat boys. Feed Georgie up on cold beef and cucumber, chocolate biscuits, make him fat enough to fuck. Only what he doesn't take into account is Geordie's not going to let anyone fuck him if he's not hungry. The guy's going the wrong way about it. Something wrong with his head, like those meths drinkers in Micklegate, shouting at the traffic, pissing themselves. One of them threatened to eat Barney. Sick fuckin' cannibal bastards.

They're everywhere. Every town you ever go, you find them. Even in Sunderland. Geordie went back there one time, look at the house where he used to live with his mother and brother, before it started to go wrong. There was a whole family in that house now. Little kids, one boy and lots of girls, running in and out as though they owned the place. No sign of his mother.

105

Geordie thought there might be a card from his brother in foreign, but he didn't go to the door and ask. They might call the cops. Who wants a card anyway?

The sun came up. Clear sky. Nice to feel the sun warm you through. Barney stood and shook himself, went to a bush to have a pee. Then he came back, looking enquiringly at Geordie. What we doing today? Begging?

'No need,' said Geordie. 'The guy left us two quid. Still got cheese and chutney to eat. We get hungry we can buy some soup.' Geordie picked Barney up and found a sunny spot on the grass. Still wet, but when was it not? 'Go to the drop-out centre later,' he said. 'See if we can get you a bone.'

The derelicts came round the corner and walked over to where Geordie and Barney were sitting. One of them had a bottle sticking out of his pocket. 'Got any drink?' he said.

'No,' Geordie told him. He wasn't the one had threatened to eat Barney, but Geordie had seen him before. A mad man.

'Gis a fackin' drink,' he said. The other one laughed a toothless laugh. 'Gis a fackin' drink will yus?'

'I haven't got anything,' Geordie said.

'Yus fackin' lyin',' the derelict said. He took the bottle out of his pocket and smacked it across Geordie's head. Geordie didn't even see it coming. He fell to the side and cracked his head on one of the ancient stones in the park. He tried to scramble to his feet, but both of the men were on top of him, ripping his pockets. They found the sandwich and tore it out of its wrapping, throwing it to one side.

Geordie put his hand in his trouser pocket to protect the two pound coins, but the derelict kicked him in the neck and then stamped on his back. Geordie went to sleep.

When he woke up the derelicts had gone. Barney was licking his face. Geordie couldn't move much, only enough to see that the money had gone. 'Jesus, Barney,' he said, 'you're supposed to be looking after me.'

Chapter 29

Jane was happy at work today. There wasn't a lot to do any more. Her lawyer had said the management buy-out was now going through smoothly, another month should see it completed. Lovely, then she could be off. See the world. Do all the things she'd never been able to do when Terry was alive.

She'd found Terry's gun at last. Very difficult to look for anything in the house with Sam being about all the time. But there it was, still in the box with cartridges and instructions. Top of his wardrobe, wrapped in that frilly dress shirt he'd only worn once. She hoped she wouldn't ever have to use it, didn't even know if she would be able to. But still, it was good to find it, to know it was there. It might be necessary.

There was a little part of her was getting very attached to Sam, though. She hadn't had to do anything to make him see her. He'd seen her from day one. The man was all eyes. Very slow, but if he followed his eyes he would find her sooner or later.

This wasn't love. She wasn't falling in love with the man. That would be easy to do, but would complicate everything. Jane didn't want a complicated life. She'd had that before. Now she wanted everything to be simple. Lust was fine. A noble emotion.

Sam wouldn't have any problems with that. None at all.

Jane had even toyed with the idea of taking him with her, but she somehow couldn't imagine him on a white beach. He'd probably want to take a tape deck with him and play his silly tapes all the time. Not that she minded his music – if he liked it, that was his affair – but he was too rough and ready for the life Jane had envisioned for herself. Maybe they could just keep in touch, get together whenever she was in England.

In the meantime it was important not to dream too much. Sam was a potential danger. She had to divert him, especially from Frances. It had not been too difficult up to now, and Jane was confident she could keep it up. Even though Frances was a little unpredictable.

Frances had telephoned Jane only a few minutes after she had stabbed Graham to death, and Jane had helped her bury the body. The stupid man had had an affair with some little floozie and then come home and told Frances all about it. Frances had always been somewhat unpredictable, emotionally volatile. Graham was her whole world. When he told her about the affair she destroyed him.

But even before they buried the body Frances had begun reconstructing the event. She had blocked out the bloodiness of the murder, started calling it a mercy killing. Now she was well on the way to deifying Graham. Sometimes it was as if she *was* him, as if the two of them had united together, spiritual avengers. But most of the people Frances saw as the culprits were dead now. Once they were all eliminated Frances would kill herself, join her Graham in the great unknown. Jane's main task was to keep Sam Turner occupied until Frances was finished. And Jane, she knew how to do that.

The thing with a man like Sam was to get him into your bed. Once he was there he would forget everything. Forget his own name.

'And I might forget my own as well,' Jane said to herself.

Chapter 30

Gus sat in the Volvo, two blocks down from Frances Golding's house, checking yesterday's notes. She had come out of the house at nine-fifteen, then driven into town and walked around the shops. She went into Next and Waterstones, bought nothing in either. Then drove home again for ten-thirty-five. Bored lady.

He checked his watch, eight-fifty, and waited. Nine-fifteen passed, but at nine-twenty-five she came out the front door and got into her car. 'Where we going today?' Gus said to himself, turning the key in the ignition.

Similar routine. Frances followed the road into town, parked opposite the Castle Museum and walked to the town centre. She wandered along Parliament Street and went into the Electricty Showrooms, looking at washing machines, opening and closing the hatches, reading the advertising blurbs, passing on after a while to cookers.

After that she walked round to Liberty's and tried on a few coats. Obviously doing nothing. She crossed the river and ended up in the Co-op canteen. Got a small chocolate log and coffee, sat by herself in a corner. Seemed to be talking to herself for a while, but Gus was too far away to hear what the conversation was about.

He followed her back to the car park, watched her get into her car. This time she took a different route, driving through Bishop-hill instead of going straight home. She slowed at the cul-de-sac but didn't stop. Gus saw her looking down there, though, real interested, pumping the brake and changing right down into first gear.

She arrived home at eleven-ten, fixed all the locks and alarms on her car, and went inside. Gus finished writing up his log and waited.

Sam arrived at one-thirty. He opened the passenger door of the Volvo and got in. 'Sorry,' he said. 'You tired?'

'Nodding off,' Gus told him. He passed the notes over to Sam and waited until he'd read them.

'Similar to yesterday,' Sam said. 'Some people go running in the morning, Frances walks round the town.'

'Not for long, though,' said Gus. 'If we're gonna break into her house, it doesn't give us much time.'

'We'll have to be quick,' said Sam. 'But give it a few more days. Make sure we know what she's doing.'

'The drive through Bishophill was interesting,' said Gus.

'Yeah. She slowed right down at the cul-de-sac?'

'Sure, I thought she was gonna stop.'

'Why's she interested in that?' said Sam. 'We're missing something, Gus. Some connection.'

'If she's hiding Graham in the Leeds house, maybe she cases the victims first. When she's sure they'll be at home alone, she picks up Graham from Leeds, lets him do the job, then drives him back again.'

'Yeah, maybe,' said Sam shaking his head.

'You mean I've cracked it?'

'I don't think it's going to be that clean or that simple,' Sam told him. 'But the only way to be sure is to have a look at the Leeds house. We'll watch Frances a few more days, then make our move.'

'Something else,' said Gus. 'Two of us isn't enough to cover everything. We're already stretched. We get more cases coming in, we won't manage.'

'I'm working on that,' said Sam. 'But something else for you. Had a visit from the TV reporter this morning with the forensic report on the notes. Complete copy of it. One set of prints they assume are Graham East's. The notes were all written at the same time, about six years ago, with the same pen.'

110

'Six *years*!'

'Yeah, six. And all the notes have been stuck on a wall with Blue Tack. The guy wrote the notes, decorated his room with them. Lived with them for six years and then started acting on them.'

'We're dealing with a complete looney,' said Gus. 'Why would he do that?'

'The answer, my friend,' said Sam, 'is blowing my mind.'

'But if he had them on a wall in his house,' Gus said, 'Frances must have seen them. She must have known they were there.'

'Unless she wore a very big hat,' said Sam.

'So what does she say about that?'

'I'm going to ask her,' said Sam. 'Now.'

Gus yawned. 'I'll come with you.'

'You better go home get some sleep. I'll fill you in later.'

Frances was scrubbing the inside of the cooker – far too expensive to buy a new one – when the door bell rang. She rinsed her hands and looked through the curtain. The detective, the man who thought he was a detective but couldn't write proper writing, printed everything.

She let him in, still drying her hands on the towel. Gave him a seat in the kitchen, a hard one at the table, sat opposite him, make sure he didn't get too comfortable.

'I wanted to ask you about the notes,' Sam said.

'Notes?' What notes does he mean? Frances wasn't ready for him. The man looks you in the eye and you look back but there's nothing there. He's a blank.

'There was a note left on Terry Deacon,' said Sam. 'Another one on Steven Bright. All the bodies had notes, the same notes. Have you seen them?'

'The inspector showed me one of them, wanted to know if it was Graham's handwriting. I told him it wasn't.'

'Are you sure?'

'Graham used a fountain pen, fine nib. The note I saw was written with felt-tip.'

'So you're not sure?'

'I never saw Graham using a felt-tip.'

'And the note,' Sam said. 'Had you seen it before?'

'Before the inspector showed me it? No. How could I?' The man is devious. He knows more than he's saying. Frances pulled open the table drawer a crack, saw the knife inside.

'The notes are all the same,' Sam told her. 'They've all been hung on a wall somewhere. Got Graham's prints on them. Written years ago.'

'How do you know they're Graham's prints?'

'I don't for sure. But let's assume they are, and that he wrote them. Where would he hang them?'

'Why should I assume that?' she asked. 'I don't believe they are Graham's prints. Everybody wants to blame Graham, but I knew him, I lived with him, and I'm telling you he couldn't have done it.'

'Because if they are his prints, the only place he would have hung them on the wall is the place he lived,' said Sam. 'And if you lived there as well, you must have seen them before.'

'What is this?' said Frances. 'You're not the police. I don't have to talk to you.' Coming in here, telling her how it was. Who does he think he is? How can he know things like this, anyway? The man's not exactly intelligent. Smiling at her now.

'No,' said Sam. 'You don't have to talk to me. I just wondered what you thought about it.'

'I don't think anything about it,' said Frances. 'It's a crackpot idea. If Graham had hung things like that on the wall, I'd have taken them down. He'd have to be mad.'

'Yes, he would, wouldn't he?'

He gave her the long stare. 'And he wasn't,' she said slowly. 'He was as sane as you or me.'

'*That* sane?' said Sam.

Frances wanted to kill him. Stop him insinuating. She could

easily pull the drawer open, get the knife and stick him right in the eye. Just stick him and stick him till he stopped talking, stopped moving. It would be worth the mess in the kitchen just to shut him up. See his face when she pulled the knife out. See what kind of a man he was then. He'd be like all the others, helpless when it came to the point.

'You're deep in thought,' said Sam. 'Did I say something?'

The doorbell rang. Frances stiffened, pushed the drawer closed with her thumb. 'Who's that?' she said.

'Search me,' said Sam.

Frances went to the curtains and saw the inspector at the door. She let him in and showed him through to the kitchen where the stupid detective was still sitting at the table.

'What you doing here?' Delany asked Sam.

'Investigating. How about you?'

'He annoying you?' Delany asked Frances.

'I was just going to ask him to leave,' she said.

'Look,' Delany said. 'The man's got no credentials. You don't have to talk to him. If he's annoying you, you can bring charges. Just give me the word, I'll lock him up.'

Sam stood to leave. 'I'm going anyway,' he said. 'She doesn't know anything about the notes. Never seen them before; least ways that's what she's gonna tell you.'

Sam walked out of the kitchen and down the hall, pulling the door shut behind him. Frances turned to the inspector and motioned to the same chair the stupid detective had vacated. The inspector didn't seem to notice her at first. He was stood in the middle of the kitchen clenching his fists, his mouth in a grim set. Looking like he might explode.

Chapter 31

Sam drove home in the Volvo. He could imagine the two of them back at the house, Frances and Delany. Delany going through all the same questions Sam'd just put to her, wondering how the hell Sam knew about the notes. And Frances, for a moment there, just before the doorbell rang, she'd got herself quite rattled. If Delany hadn't turned up at that moment, she might have let something slip. When she'd gone to let Delany in Sam had been tempted to pocket the three keys in the fruit bowl. Keys to the Leeds house. It would have been so simple, except that she'd have noticed. Instead he removed the lock from the kitchen window, make it easier to break and enter.

Sam dropped the new stack of mail off at Celia Allison's house. It was similar to the last bunch, three death threats this time, only one proposal of marriage. He didn't fancy any of them. About forty possible jobs. Celia wasn't at home, so he left them on the back porch, scribbled a little note saying, 'See you later, Alligator, gone to hire an army of detectives'.

Wanda's house looked deserted as well, but she answered the door as soon as he knocked. She was wearing jeans, something he'd not seen before. She always wore a dress or skirt. She seemed calm.

'Good to see you,' she said. 'Glad you came. Come and meet the girls.' She took him upstairs to the children's room and introduced her two daughters. The eldest was a four-year-old called Samantha, flaming red hair like her mother, seemingly Super-glued to an enormous teddy bear. The younger was a little blonde two-year-old called Kelly, already destined to be a heart-breaker. Samantha didn't speak, though she smiled sweetly from behind the teddy bear. Kelly shook hands and asked Sam if he liked chocolate. When he said he did, sometimes, she asked him if he had any with him.

'I'm going to talk to Sam downstairs,' Wanda told them. 'If you're good, I'll bring some juice and cake upstairs. You can have a picnic.'

'They're great kids,' Sam told her when she'd delivered the picnic. 'You're lucky.'

Wanda smiled. 'More hard work than luck,' she said. 'The picnic won't last long. I wanted to apologize.'

'Hell,' Sam said. 'What you got to apologize for? Anything you said I gave you good grounds.'

'I don't like to lose my temper, Sam. Being abusive. It doesn't help.'

'And sometimes it does,' he said. 'I'm not holding anything against you.'

'You caught me off guard,' Wanda said. 'Coming in the house and laying all that stuff on me. I just reacted. After you'd gone I had time to think about it.'

'There's not a lot to think,' Sam told her. 'I still feel the same. If we go on like before, we'll get into a mess.'

'Sam, I think you like me.'

'I'll go along with that.'

'And I like you.'

'But it's not enough, Wanda.'

'It's all we've got,' she said. 'Two people like each other, they have some things in common, they make mistakes at first but eventually they learn to respect each other's space. There's nothing wrong with that.'

'I respect your space,' he said. 'It was all those fuckin' telephone calls. I can't be crowded when I'm working.'

'I know that,' she said. 'I was wrong about it. I'm sorry. It won't happen again. Or if it does, I'll be sorry about it again. I don't want to crowd you.'

'I don't know . . .'

'Sam, you dump me one day not because of what I've done, but because of your own hang-ups. You think if you're not committed to me in some way, you should let me go. You think I'm looking for commitment. You judge me. I'm not looking for commitment. I only want to get to know you better.'

'I've heard this kind of thing before,' Sam told her. 'Open relationships don't work. Not for me, anyway.'

'It's not an open relationship, Sam. It's just me and you. We see each other sometimes because we want to. The alternative is that we never see each other again because you're frightened.'

'You sound like you're talking sense, Wanda, but there's a part of me doesn't want to listen, feels like I'm being led astray.'

'Think about it,' she said. 'Not now, when you've got the time. But you know I'd like to see you. You want to see me, give me a ring.'

'It won't be for a while,' he said. 'I'm working hard at the moment.'

'Whenever you're ready.'

'See, that's the kind of thing I don't want to hear,' he said. '*Whenever you're ready*. It's like you're just sitting here waiting, being compliant. Every minute I don't ring you, I'm being a shit.'

'No, Sam. That's in your head. I'm not sitting here waiting. I've got two daughters upstairs, downstairs, all over the house. I've got relatives, friends, I go to the solo club. I'm not sitting here waiting at all, I'm living my life. All I'm saying is you can break into it occasionally if you want. Is your life totally fulfilling?'

Sam smiled. 'Only when you tell me off.'

'But you understand what I'm saying?'

'Yeah. You're getting through. We can be friends.'

'We can be anything. Sam, you'll ring me one time, if you ever get round to it, I'll be doing something else. I'll just tell you, sorry

I'm doing something else. I won't be lying. I'll be doing something else. If I'm not doing something else, I'll do it with you.'

Sam realized he'd been smiling for several minutes. 'I needed someone to tell me,' he said. 'I just didn't think it would be you.'

'People surprise you sometimes.'

'Women've been surprising me since the day I was born.'

The two girls came tumbling downstairs and into the sitting room for more cake and juice. Wanda walked to the door with Sam, kissed him on the cheek. 'Celia sounds nice,' she said. 'We had a long chat on the telephone.'

'About me?'

'Yes, we compared notes.'

'And the verdict?'

'You're one of the good guys.'

He walked through the doorway and then turned back to her. 'You look really great in jeans,' he said.

She laughed, closed the door, went back to her daughters.

Chapter 32

One time Graham had been a poet and a lover. Frances used to think of him then as a big intelligent bear. He was quiet, he knew how to listen, and that's what Frances needed then, someone who could listen.

Frances's marriage and the birth of her three children had reduced her to a skivvy. When she met Graham at the Chapeltown Carnival it soon became obvious that they were meant. That's what Graham had said. 'You and me, Frances, we were meant.' Looking back now, Frances couldn't imagine how she had walked away from her family. Simply given up everything and followed him. But that's what she did. During the first year she would sometimes watch the children being collected from school, keeping herself hidden. But since then she had not seen them at all.

Bernard, her husband, had remarried and moved away. She didn't know where. Never tried to find out. Slowly Graham had filled all the spaces in her life. She knew he would, and he did, because they were meant.

He was a big bear, a virgin. Technically he was not a virgin because of the brutish woman who had seduced him when he was a boy, but emotionally he was a virgin. He didn't know women. He knew poetry and he knew how to listen, but he didn't know women.

Graham knew Frances. He said he had known her throughout time. He had known her through innumerable incarnations, since pre-history. He and she had always been together. And Frances knew what he meant. They were not separate beings, Graham and Frances. They were one. If Graham's mood swung, she felt it immediately, and it worked the other way as well; something would upset her and before she had time to think it herself Graham would be at her side. 'Are you all right? Don't worry, I'm always with you.'

The world went past them. Whatever happened, nothing could touch them. They were greater than the world. 'Relationships like ours,' Graham would say, 'are the reason that the world exists.'

But the Devil is wily. The Devil screams with pain when faced with the beauty of a relationship like that. He can't stand it. He summons all at his command to break it up, his pimps and his prostitutes, his fornicators. He gets them all chipping away at it. Trying to break it down, make it turn sour.

You have to be vigilant. You have to be strong.

The beginning was wonderful. Graham had left New Zealand to search for his destiny. He had travelled across the globe. And he had kept going, whatever came in his way, he had not given up. Frances had been born in Leeds, she had never left, knowing that one day someone, something would happen. She didn't know what it would be. She never dreamed it would be Graham. But that is what it was. She fixed to a spot that he was inexorably drawn to. It was like in the fairy stories. But it was real. Graham said all the fairy stories were real, but people now, they were too sophisticated to understand them.

Graham, in his simplicity, had known more than she. Frances had only known *something* would happen. But Graham was actually looking for her. He knew what she was called, what she looked like. He dreamed about her for years before they met.

The first year, the first two years, had been wonder after wonder. Having found each other at last, the two of them blossomed. They grew in each other's company, grew together like a flower that had been separated root from stem and then, miraculously, reunited.

That was the period of the best poems, *The Frances Poems*. During those two years they had spilled out of him. 'They write themselves,' he said, excited. 'They fall off the end of the pen. I hold your image before me and the poems come tumbling down.' Two years of grace. Grace and happiness.

Then the visions started.

The Devil and his henchmen began to break through. Somehow, working away from the inside, they undermined Graham's fragile, poetic sensibility. He was too sensitive, too open, to withstand the constant bombardment. He'd been weakened by the ministrations of the pimps and the prostitutes along the way. Especially the ones in that house in York. The house of sin.

Frances had tried to calm him. She'd kept the visions at bay, or explained them away. She'd done that for years. But as time went by they grew a little stronger, until, eventually, he had been consumed by them.

The first visions were of Sarah Dunn, the next-door neighbour who had seduced him when he was still a boy. She would come to him in dreams, whenever he closed his eyes. Frances would cradle him in her arms until he slept, but then the seductress would return and Graham would wake screaming in the night.

Then the Swedish woman would come, Lotta Jensen, and eventually they would all come until Graham could not rest at all. He paced around the house night and day, his eyes blazing. 'Keep them away, Frances,' he would say. 'For God's sake, keep them away.'

Frances suggested he should write a poem about them, thinking there must be some way to exorcise them. He worked through the night. Frances didn't sleep. There would be periods of pacing, periods of silence. In the morning he came into the bedroom. 'I've done it,' he said. 'I've written a poem about Sarah. Got rid of her.'

He led her through to his work room and there it was on the wall.

> **Sara**
> **Dunn**
> **Deserves**
> **to**
> **Die**

And it seemed to work for a while. Keep her at bay. The others followed quickly until they covered one wall in his room. Frances didn't think they were proper poems, but she didn't mind, anything to give Graham some peace of mind.

But peace of mind was not really on the cards for Graham any longer, nor for Frances herself. The visions continued and Graham's health deteriorated. He never slept for more than an hour at a time, was always tired, towards the end he hardly knew who he was. Sometimes he didn't recognize Frances. She would walk

120

into a room and he would start screaming, 'Keep away, keep away from me.'

Graham didn't leave the house for half a year. He wouldn't even look out of the window. Kept the curtains of his workroom and their bedroom closed at all times. 'In case,' he said. 'In case.'

In the end it had been a mercy killing. Frances had collected thunder-bugs, Spanish fly, dried and ground them and fed them to Graham in his breakfast cereal. They gave him diarrhoea, weakened him physically, but didn't put him to sleep. In the end they would have worked, cumulatively. But they weren't fast enough. They weren't merciful.

Frances waited until he was asleep and slit his throat. She held the pillow over his head until he stopped struggling. But he was terribly weak. He didn't struggle for long. He knew what she was doing, and he wanted it as well.

The very next day he came back and told her so. They would be reunited soon. But first the pimps and prostitutes had to be dealt with. The ones who had separated them. The ones who had worked against them.

Frances took the poems off the wall in Graham's room, handling each one carefully, so that her fingerprints would not give her away before the job was complete. You have to be very careful when fighting the Devil. You have to be vigilant. Leave nothing to chance.

And now the job was nearly done, just a couple more to get rid of. Everything going smoothly and the Devil plays a new card. The stupid detective. Putting his nose in. Knowing too much already, or thinking he knows.

Frances could have killed him today. She was on the point of it when the inspector arrived. She might have to do it. If he kept getting in the way. There was no poem for him, but it was obvious which side he was on.

Chapter 33

Jane Deacon arrived home from work at the same time as Sam. Shoulders hunched, a glum, far-away look about her. She tried a formal smile on him but it fell flat. 'What happened to you?' he asked.

'Oh, nothing. Some legal points holding up the transfer of the business.'

'So it might not go through?'

'No, nothing like that. It's just going to take longer than we thought.'

'You in a hurry?'

She looked at him and the next attempt at a smile fared better. No joy in it, but a fairly good piece of acting. 'Once it's settled I can go away,' she said.

'You're leaving?'

'I'm going away. In the short term I'll keep the house on here, but I want to be somewhere there's some sunshine. Somewhere I can relax, think about the rest of my life.'

'Spend some money?' Sam said.

'Yes, that as well. I'm a virtual prisoner here.'

'You're gonna be a prisoner wherever you are until we find whoever it was killed your husband.'

'Graham, you mean?'

'If it was Graham, yes.'

'You mean there's some doubt about it?'

'It's not been proved yet.'

'Sam, there can't be any doubt about it. It has to be Graham.

There is no one else.' Her voice was rising, not hysterical, but it was certainly going up the register.

Sam had been on the point of telling her about the notes, the forensic evidence, but he sensed she was too highly strung. 'No, there's no one else,' he said. No point in making her nervous. The client wants to think it's straightforward, the client's right.

'I don't see how it could be anyone else but Graham,' she said. 'He's got the motive, everything.'

Sam took a chair and placed it next to her, sat her down. 'Jane, I was being semantic. You're right. It must be Graham.'

She settled a little but was still anxious. Sam couldn't understand why. The lady had been fairly cool up till now. Just a passing remark and she goes to pieces.

Jane got up from the chair and started making coffee. There was something odd about this woman. Some ways, she doesn't seem to be affected by the death of her husband. Sam had noticed this before and thought she must be holding herself together by an effort of will. He'd thought she'd crack. She buries the guy and goes back to work, arranges to sell the business, counts the insurance money, now she's planning a holiday. She's the main, the only, benefactor from Terry Deacon's death. The only reason she isn't the chief suspect is because Sam Turner knew she was nowhere near the house when Deacon bought it.

She was having her portrait painted. Or was she?

She went into the painter's house, left her car in the drive. Sam sat outside the house a couple of hours. She could've gone in the front door and out the back. Gone home, killed Deacon, and come back the same way.

OK, here's a hypothesis. Jane Deacon starts an affair with the painter, what's his name, Watson. They fall in love and decide to kill Deacon, get his money and ride off into the sunset. Jane sets it up with Deacon to hire a detective to follow her, so when she kills her husband she has a cast-iron alibi.

Perfect.

But it doesn't explain Sarah Dunn, Lotta Jensen, and Steven

Bright. Doesn't explain the notes left on each body. Doesn't explain why Graham East has disappeared off the face of the earth. Doesn't explain . . . enough.

'Where've you gone?' Jane said.

'Sorry,' said Sam. 'Train of thought. Look, d'you want to go out somewhere? Get out of the prison for a while?'

'Where?'

'Wherever. What do you like to do? Take in a movie, have a drink, walk in the park? We don't have to sit here all night.'

'I don't think I could concentrate on a film,' she said. 'A walk might be nice, even a drink.'

'Tell me when you're ready,' he said.

Jane went upstairs to have her bath, get changed.

Here's another hypothesis. The painter, what's his name, Watson, is really Graham East in disguise. That's why no one can find Graham East. Jane Deacon's affair with Watson is really an affair with Graham. Sam, you've done too many movies. The blonde lady cracks so you start to put her in the frame. You said she would crack under the strain of everything that happened to her, and then as soon as she does, starts to act normal, you think she's a mass-murderer.

Leave it.

Sam finished up his coffee and did his nightly checks. The Walther, the downstairs windows and back door. Two more chapters of Simenon while waiting for the lady. She came downstairs in a sleeveless mauve dress, short, very short, V-necked, buttoned down the front, slim gold chain at her throat. Tanned legs that seemed to go on for ever, and flat shoes. Some eye make-up, but nothing on her lips. 'Is this over the top?' she asked.

'Yeah,' said Sam. 'Perfect. Where we going?'

'Shall we just walk? See what happens?'

It was a rare, humid summer evening which brought people pouring out on to the streets, into the parks. Girls and women in cotton dresses, men in shirt-sleeves carrying their jackets, the old folk occupying every inch of bench space. Every public house or

124

drinking place had a gaggle of youths and girls outside the entrance, sitting on the pavements drinking and laughing.

In the normal course of things Jane Deacon turned heads. This evening, walking through the park, Sam noticed she drew the eyes of young and old, men and some women – they'd get an eyeful and then turn round for another one. Jane didn't seem to notice. She must have, but she didn't seem to.

'What's happening with the painting?' he asked.

'The portrait? It's not finished. I was supposed to have one more sitting, but I don't know if I'll bother now. It was for Terry. What would I do with a portrait of me?'

'You could give it to me,' Sam told her. 'When you've gone off to your island in the sun it'll remind me of the time I walked through York with the best looker in town.'

'Looks don't mean much,' she said.

'Maybe not, when you've got 'em.'

'It's just fashion,' she said. 'Today's face is good for a laugh tomorrow.'

'I was still thinking about today,' he said, staring back at a guy on the pavement giving Jane the all-over up and down and up again. 'Look at him, the guy's in a trance.' Jane turned to look and the guy suddenly became conscious, pushed his hands into his pockets and hurried off along the pavement. 'Wait,' said Sam, 'he'll turn round in a minute.'

They watched the guy until he came to the corner. There he stopped and looked back quickly before disappearing round the bend. Sam and Jane laughed, carried on walking. 'Gone to change his undies,' said Sam. Her hand brushed against his momentarily, long enough for him to take hold of it if he wanted. He did want, but he didn't do it.

In the Theatre Bar he got her a white wine and a tonic for himself, took them over to a table she had colonized. 'You don't drink? she asked.

'Yeah. More than most,' Sam admitted. 'But only when I'm miserable.'

'You really want the portrait?'

'I've got this huge wall with nothing on it. Needs breaking up.'

'OK, you've got it.' She touched his hand with her index finger across the table. A light touch and then she withdrew. Little electric shock. Sam closed his eyes and opened them again. The tingle still there. He gave no sign, aware that he was playing a game in spite of himself. A touch here, a look there, something he or she said, storing them all up. Leaving them alone, letting them stand until there was no other way out. Playing with dynamite. Like sitting in front of a bottle of whiskey, reading the label, unscrewing the top, smelling it, maybe, not touching a drop. Sitting through the night with the bottle between your legs. See how long you can go.

They walked through the Museum Gardens, passed a couple of winos who shouted abuse at them, something unintelligible, the only clear message being that Sam and the blonde should be shagging each other. Sam didn't need anyone to tell him that.

'How do you get like that?' she asked, watching as one of the winos fell headlong into a border of flowers.

'It's easier than it looks,' he told her.

'But completely out of it. They don't know where they are.'

'You just drink your way to the bottom of the bottle,' he said. 'Then you start on a new one. It doesn't take long.'

'The voice of experience?'

'I know where they're at,' he said.

'But what makes somebody do that, give up like that?'

'Poverty, any kind of deprivation, inadequacy, emptiness, insolvency, want, need. Shall I go on?'

'If you can.'

'Distress, destitution, insolvency, starvation, nothingness, nothing particular, a broken heart, infatuation, yearning, failure, success. Anything you can't or don't want to cope with. There're as many reasons as there're bottles.'

'Are you an alcoholic?'

'Only when I'm drinking.'

They walked back to the cul-de-sac in silence. All the way home nobody looked at her twice.

'Thanks,' she said, going up to bed, 'for taking me out. I needed it. It was nice.'

'I blew it,' Sam said.

She lingered on the bottom step. 'Not necessarily.'

'Yeah. I'll try harder tomorrow.'

Chapter 34

Geordie didn't lie down in his doorway in the Coppergate Centre. He stood there for a while, then sat and waited for the guy. There were bruises all over his body and his neck was stiff, his left arm felt numb, but more than any of these he was hungry. Some drunk had thrown the remains of a bag of fish and chips away outside the Viking Museum and Geordie had shared them with Barney, but not more than a mouthful each.

The guy usually came just after the clock struck two, and that was about ten minutes ago. Geordie counted, telling himself the guy would come round the corner when he got to a hundred. When the guy didn't come he started counting again. He was on his third hundred, number sixty-three, when the guy arrived.

'Christ,' said the guy. 'What happened to you?' He brought up a hand to touch Geordie's black eye, but Geordie moved away in time. 'That's a real shiner.' He held out a packet of sandwiches and Geordie opened them and took a bite, tore a piece off for Barney. Cheese and chutney.

'And hungry,' said the guy. 'So, what's the answer today? D'you wanna job?'

Geordie took another bite out of the sandwich. He didn't think he wanted the kind of job the guy would offer. Before he got the sandwiches he thought he might say yes, but now he'd got the sandwiches, now he was eating one, he wasn't so sure.

The guy felt in his pocket and took out a handful of coins. He offered them and Geordie tucked the packet of sandwiches under his arm so he could take the money. 'No chocolate biscuits today,' the guy said. 'You got all that was left yesterday.'

He walked off. When he'd gone a few steps Geordie followed him. The guy turned round to look, and Geordie stopped. The guy stood and stared for a few seconds then carried on walking. Geordie followed.

If he wants sex, Geordie thought, I won't be able to do it. His body ached all over. I'll be able to do it but it'll really hurt. Something about the guy made Geordie think he wouldn't want sex. Not his build, not the way he carried himself. You couldn't tell by things like that. Some of the guys who wanted sex were like women, some of them like men, big ones, small ones, tough, weak – you could never tell by looking. But there was still *some*thing about this one. Geordie would be surprised if he was after sex. But he'd been surprised before, more than once.

The guy walked faster than Geordie could go with his limp, getting a little farther ahead all the time. But Geordie kept after him. He didn't want to spend another night with the fuckin' derelicts beating the shit out of him. Once they knew you had money they kept coming back. No matter how little you had, they'd never leave you alone. Only thing you could do, move to another town. But you moved wherever, the derelicts would find you in the end.

The guy got about a hundred yards ahead and turned a corner. Geordie tried to go faster, not wanting to lose him now. When he turned the corner the guy had slowed down, only a few paces in front again.

Two more corners and the guy stopped at a door, got some keys out of his pocket and opened it. He stood holding the door until Geordie walked past him into the dark flat. 'Welcome to my humble abode,' he said ominously. Closed the door and put the light on. 'If you don't mind me saying so,' the guy; said, 'you stink something rotten.'

Geordie couldn't smell anything.

'Just stand there,' the guy said. 'Back in a minute.' He went through one of the internal doors and disappeared. Geordie stood on the spot looking around the room. Everything was neat and tidy, clean, bright. Like the place was not lived in much. There was a cooker and a sink. Over in the corner a stereo system and piles of tapes. An old battered sofa and a table with two chairs. Row of hooks with bright red mugs hanging. A telephone. Nothing on the walls. From the room the guy had gone into came the sound of splashing water.

When the guy came out of the room, steam came gushing out after him. 'Your bath's ready,' he said. Geordie walked to the door of the bathroom and looked in. He couldn't see much at first because of the steam, but as his eyes became accustomed he saw that it was a very small room with a bath, small wash-basin and lavatory. If the guy was planning on getting into the bath with him, they wouldn't be able to move. The guy was on his hands and knees now, scrabbling about in a cupboard under the kitchen sink. When he came out of there he had a large black plastic bag, kind they put in dustbins to save the men making two journeys. Geordie had used one to sleep in once. You slept in one of those, it kept the wet out and the cold in.

'OK,' the guy said, handing Geordie the dustbin bag. 'You strip everything off and put it in the bag. Then you get in the bath and have a good soak. When you're finished you leave your clothes in the bag. There's some pyjamas in the bathroom, dressing gown. You put those on.'

Geordie nodded. 'What about Barney?' he said.

'Same with Barney,' said the guy. 'He smells nearly as bad as you.'

Geordie went into the bathroom, Barney following at his heels. He left the door open, but the guy closed it behind him, leaving him alone with the dog. Geordie touched the water in the bath to test the temperature. A little too hot maybe. Maybe not. He undressed with some difficulty. There was a bad cut on his right heel and his sock was stuck to it with dried blood. Eventually it came off and he put one foot in the water. It was OK. He stood in the bath and collected Barney in his arms. 'It's a bath,' he told the dog. 'Nothing to worry about.' Now he knelt in the bath and slowly lowered Barney in beside him. The dog struggled for a few minutes, then seemed to accept it. When Barney was completely settled Geordie lowered himself full length in the water. 'Jeez,' he said. It was so good. 'Jeezus *Christ*.'

Last time he was in water was a couple a months ago when he paddled in the river, just after he arrived in York. Fuckin' freezing it was. Before Barney adopted him.

He lay on his back, his whole body immersed in warm water, just his head sticking out. Barney sat on his stomach, occasionally lapping up some of the water with his tongue, looking confused. Next door the guy was playing music or singing. Hard to tell which.

Geordie woke up to the guy banging on the door. He was shouting, 'What you doing in there?' The water in the bath was almost cold. The door opened a crack and he saw the guy's face peering through. 'Jesus, are you asleep?' He came into the room and Geordie quickly covered his prick with his hands. 'Don't wanna see it,' the guy said. 'Got one of my own. Just wanna make sure you don't die of pneumonia.'

The guy turned the hot tap on, and slowly the water got warm again. 'OK. You can get out now, give yourself a good rub down.' He left the room, taking the dustbin bag with Geordie's clothes, and closed the door behind him. Geordie got himself and Barney out of the bath. Barney did a shake and sprayed cold water all over the room, splashing the mirror and the bathroom cabinets.

When they were both dry he put on the pyjamas and the dressing gown. Had to turn up the trouser bottoms of the pyjamas as they were several inches too long. But the soft cotton felt good against his skin, and the dressing gown was warm. He opened the door and went back into the room where the guy was playing music on the system. Like rock and roll, or whatever it was called – made you feel good, a song he'd heard some of the buskers doing. *No, no, no, it ain't me, babe.* Good song.

'How does it feel?' the guy asked.

Geordie nodded. It felt good. Something had happened to the room while he was in the bath. The guy had put a mattress on the floor, a pillow and a sleeping bag. Narrow mattress, and only one sleeping bag. So the guy didn't want sex. Least ways he didn't want it yet.

'You can go to bed in a minute,' the guy said. 'Just a couple a things. The dog craps anywhere, you clean it up. OK?'

Geordie nodded. What did the guy think? He didn't know how to live?

'Tomorrow I want to get you some clothes, so I need to measure you.' The guy held up a tape measure. 'And those old clothes of yours.' He pointed to the dustbin bag. 'I want to burn them. Any objections?'

Geordie shook his head. He didn't mind burning the old ones if he was getting new ones.

'And still something else,' the guy said. 'I'd like to hear you talk.'

Geordie thought for a moment, then said, 'Thanks, pal.'

'Sam. Call me Sam.' The guy looked at him, then repeated, 'Call me Sam.'

'Thanks, Sam,' said Geordie.

Sam went through another door and closed it, must be his bedroom. Geordie crept into the sleeping bag and laid his head on the pillow. The dog turned round once and snuggled up on the mattress. 'You know, something, Barney,' said Geordie. 'This is the best job we've ever had.'

Chapter 35

In another part of town Gus was reading a textbook on electronic bugging devices, Jane Deacon safely in bed upstairs. He thought it would be simple to put some of these newer devices together. Get the right chips and a little board, his soldering iron and a bright light. Cost a fraction of the price if he made them himself.

Gus was a practical man, could put anything electronic together if he put his mind to it. He'd been messing around with computers for years, built them, fixed them, even had a job at one time mending TVs, going from house to house in a little van, bored out of his skull.

Couple of years ago he'd started a university course, but had to drop out because of the theory. The maths wouldn't stick in his head for some reason. Sam'd said it was because he couldn't think unless he had a soldering iron or a snooker cue in his hand. Might be right, usually was.

If this detective agency thing came together, Gus saw himself with an electronics workshop, building job-specific bugs, miniature cameras and surveillance kit of all kinds. Most of it he'd build himself, prototypes, then farm out the manufacture to other companies, maybe get someone to market devices he'd developed. Security was a big industry already, growing by the day. Get in on the ground floor, make a real killing.

He'd have to farm out the manufacturing, and get someone to help with design as well. Most of the computers he'd built, Gus had housed them in a shoe box, something like that. What the thing looked like didn't matter, he was only interested in what it could do. But people didn't believe in the thing if it was in a shoe box, even people like Sam – he'd say inane things like, 'I've got one of these at home.'

Earlier, after Sam had left, Gus had taken the Walther to bits, cleaned it and put it back together again. Bit crude by today's standards, but he liked the way it was turned. So simple, the whole idea behind a blow-back pistol, giving a hand gun the power of automatic fire. It was one of the larger guns made by Walther, 7.65mm, designed initially for plain-clothes detectives. Then the *Luftwaffe* had adopted it and it became the staple of German staff officers. This one, when it was new, who knows who'd used it? Probably travelled all over Europe during the war.

There was a movement on the stairs. Gus closed the book and went to the hall. The blonde was coming down the stairs looking like shit. Good-class shit, but nevertheless, decidedly ropey. 'Are you OK?' he asked.

She rubbed her eyes with both hands, lifting the long dressing gown a fraction, what appeared to be a blue nightgown underneath. 'Bad dream,' she said. 'I couldn't get back to sleep. What time is it?'

'Four, just after.'

She floated past him into the living room, sat on the sofa and curled her legs under her. 'Sam gone?'

'Yeah, couple of hours ago.'

She was quiet for a moment, still waking up, strangely vulnerable, not quite in her body. Gus eased down into the chair opposite and wondered what it would be like with her, even though he knew he wasn't her type. She was a high-flyer, a guy who wanted her would have to have money or something else she needed. Whatever that was, he knew he didn't have it. She looked up at him and gave him a bright smile, said, 'Have you known him long?'

'We go back quite a way,' said Gus, thinking, *information*, that's what she wants. 'Ten years. Met him at a Dylan concert.'

'He was playing a tape the other night,' she said. 'Nice. Bit old-fashioned, though.'

Gus shrugged. 'You want everything new?'

Jane smiled, shaking her head. 'I take what comes. I find him interesting. Sam, I mean.'

'You fancy him?'

'Yes, I suppose so. He's got something.'

'He has that effect on women. Can't see it, myself. He's a good mate, reliable. He can laugh as well. You find him attractive?'

'It's not a big thing,' she said. 'I'm not going to tell you, you'll go straight to Sam, say, hey, Jane Deacon fancies you.'

Gus laughed. 'Probably will,' he said. 'But he'll know already. Won't need me to tell him.'

'He knows,' she said. 'But he doesn't move on it. Doesn't let on.'

'That's Sam,' said Gus. 'He likes to wait until the apple's ripe. Sometimes he buys a new tape, he won't play it for maybe a week. He reads the titles, all the blurb. He picks it up and looks at it every so often, touches it, you know, feels it. Then a few days later he'll start to play it. I made him a new cue over a year ago. He really likes it, but he hasn't used it yet.'

'Oh, God,' said Jane. 'Come back in a year's time. I'll give you a progress report. What about you? You married?'

'Married? said Gus. 'No. I've got a partner, Marie. We've been together a few years. She's a nurse.'

'Nice,' said Jane. 'She doesn't mind you working nights?'

'It's not permanent,' said Gus. '*She* works nights one week in every three. You get used to it.'

'So what do you suggest? About Sam? Am I doing something wrong?'

'Ask him,' said Gus. 'He'll tell you the truth.'

'He's been married? That right?'

'Couple of times. The last one was a real disaster. Woman called Brenda, real gold-digger. Couldn't ever figure out why she married Sam. He never had any money.'

'And the first one?'

'She was called Donna,' Gus said. 'Sam doesn't talk about her

134

much. I never met her. They had a daughter. She was still a toddler, Donna and the daughter were killed by a hit-and-run driver. The kid was killed outright but Donna was on a life-support machine for some time. Sam asked them to turn it off in the end.'

'That must have been tough,' said Jane.

Gus shook his head. 'Sam,' he said, 'he's got a real downer on bad drivers. Anyone driving over the speed limit, he sees red. And drunk drivers, I think he'd hang them.'

'I'm not surprised. Did they find the man who killed his wife?'

'No,' said Gus. 'The guy's still driving around, probably. I remember one time, we were on the A1, this guy overtook us on the inside lane. Sam took off after him, hitting the horn for about six miles. He forced the guy into a service station. This guy gets out of his car shaking his fist, calling Sam everything under the sun. Sam is livid. I'm trying to hold him back, thinking he's capable of anything, might kill the guy. But he shakes me off and goes over to the guy. "I wanna smell your breath," he says. The guy's still raving. Next thing I know Sam's smacked him one and the guy's on his back in the car park. He gets up and Sam smacks him again. "Every time you try to get into the car," Sam tells him, "I'm gonna smack you. And I'm gonna go on smacking you until you sober up."'

'Is this the Sam I know?' asked Jane.

'Too true,' Gus told her. 'Eventually we get the guy into the cafeteria and pour coffee down him. Sam takes him to the john and washes the blood off his nose. We're with this guy for three hours, until Sam thinks he's sober enough to drive.'

'I suppose he's got a point.' She stretched and yawned. She closed her eyes. Gus didn't say anything, wondered if she was going to sleep or still thinking about Sam. Eventually she stretched again. 'Don't know if it's worth going back to bed,' she said. 'Maybe I'll give it a try.'

'Sweet dreams,' said Gus as she left the room. She looked a

whole lot better going up than she did when she came down. Just as well it was Sam she was into, he thought. Gus wouldn't have been able to resist her, Marie or no Marie. Gus, when he bought a new tape, he ran all the way home with it and played it ten times the first day.

Chapter 36

Sam got up at eight and went straight out the house and into town. The kid was fast asleep. The dog opened its eyes as he went through, but closed them as soon as it recognized him.

Trouble with Jane was simply that she was interested and didn't hide it. Coming on at him, not too much, not too obvious, but still coming on. A couple of weeks ago he'd been working for her husband. The guy's cut down and buried, still warm in his grave, and here she is coming on. Every time Sam looked in her eyes he saw Terry Deacon. If there'd never been a Terry Deacon, or even if Terry Deacon was still alive, he could understand it. Probably he wouldn't even think about it, just go for it. But as it was, it was weird. Why didn't she grieve? Have a good grieve, couple of screaming fits, walk around a while with a long face, hell, Sam'd know what to do. Once she started coming out of it, stopped wearing black, started realizing life had to go on, why then she could come on a little bit and he'd take her on, not bat an eye. She wouldn't even have to come on a little bit, only smile, maybe say hello with a glance.

There was a store in Parliament Street Sam had passed on his way to Betty's, name of Clothes Locker, sold trendy-type clobber for guys about Geordie's age. Sam was the first customer of the day, just after the place opened. He gave the young guy Geordie's measurements, said, 'I want a pair of jeans, boots, shoes, a jacket, two shirts, some kind of sweater.'

'What?'

'What what?

'What kind of jeans?'

'Levi's?' said Sam

'No. I've got Lee's.'

'They're the ones.'

'Boots?' said the assistant. 'Dockers?'

'They'd have to be, wouldn't they?'

'Shoes? Reeboks?'

'I said anything else, you'd think I was square,' Sam told him.

'Square?' said the assistant to himself. He walked away scratching his head. When he came back, put everything into bags, Sam said, 'And three T-shirts, three pairs of shorts, three pairs of socks.'

'Chicago Bulls T-shirts?'

'You got anything better?

'No.'

'Chicago Bulls T-shirts,' said Sam. 'I find out you sold me a turkey, I'm coming back with it.'

The assistant disappeared again. Sam took a cap off a model, Air Jordan written on the front of it and a figure supposed to be playing basketball, number 23 and Nike on the back, little leather tag to adjust the size. He put it on the counter. 'Is that cool?' Sam asked the assistant when he returned.

'Cool?' The guy puckered his lips and nodded his head. 'It's *now*,' he said.

'Wrap it up,' said Sam.

On his way back to the car park he bumped into Brenda. She was already loaded down with bags, if anything more than Sam. There was no avoiding her. Dressed completely in red – shoes, little hat, gloves, suit with a tight skirt, half a centimetre of red silk showing at the back.

'How're you doing? he asked.

'Sam. Shopping? I never saw you shopping before.'

'Needed a few things,' he said. 'Are you all right?'

'I'm shopping. Later I'm meeting somebody for lunch. Staying in town. This evening I'm meeting Derrick, going to the theatre.'

'Derrick? How are you, Brenda?'

'I'm OK. I made the right move this time.'

No eye contact at all. The woman's eyes were fixed on a succession of brightly lit stores, material goods stretching into infinity.

Sam sighed. 'Watch my lips,' he said. 'Brenda, it's Sam, OK? We used to live together. I know you. We were married. I'm asking you how you're doing?'

'For fuck sake,' she said. 'I'm spending the guy's money, aren't I?'

Geordie searched the flat for the dustbin bag with his clothes, but it wasn't there. The guy must have burned them already. Shouldn't have told the guy he could burn them. That was a mistake. Couple of times Geordie had to dress up for perverts, once in girls' clothes, school uniform; and another time in old-fashioned clothes like a Roman or Greek or something.

Geordie went into the guy's room, see if he had any school uniforms or togas. He didn't have nothing. A jacket, spare pair of pants, few shirts, all far too big for Geordie.

Where was the guy anyway? He had a barrow or something, Geordie could empty the whole flat, the telly, the stereo equipment. Must be worth a few quid.

But he didn't have a barrow. Didn't have anything to wear.

The guy was out buying clothes. He'd come back with armfuls of something weird, want Geordie to dress up, maybe take photographs. Then he'd get violent.

The toga guy, Geordie couldn't remember where that was now, somewhere near London. He'd sent his chauffeur, picked up Geordie and another lad, little Tommy, and the chauffeur had driven them out of town to some kind of castle. They were put in showers and given the togas, sent on to a stage. Geordie in an orange one, little Tommy in a very short one, blue. Bright lights in their eyes, and that flash a camera makes. Geordie was supposed to fuck little Tommy but he couldn't do it. He pretended to do it, but the chauffeur came on to the stage and pushed him around. They made little Tommy suck Geordie's prick. Then the guy came on dressed like a devil and fucked both of them. The camera flashing all the time, and the whirr of a movie camera or video. Two other devils came on and both of them fucked little Tommy and he started crying. Geordie tried to run away then, thinking the whole thing wasn't worth twenty quid, but the chauffeur beat him up, kicked him in the head.

Geordie found himself in a ditch next day, took him two days to walk back to London. The last he ever saw of little Tommy was the two devils trying to pull him apart, one with little Tommy's head, the other with a leg, and little Tommy howling something about his mother.

Geordie never got the twenty quid.

The other time, when he had to wear the girls' uniform, was in a council flat somewhere near Tower Hamlets. That guy had taken photographs as well, before getting violent. He'd been tender at first, whispering in Geordie's ear, stroking him, but slowly working himself up. He bit Geordie's lips and started taking bites out of his face. Tied him up and kept him there all night. Next day the guy gave him fifteen quid and let him go, but Geordie had to spend most of the money at the chemist, get some cream to stop the bites going septic.

There were other times as well, in Liverpool, Manchester. Thinking about them, Geordie thought he better get out of this flat before the guy came back. Even if the guy's clothes were too big, it didn't matter. He could take some of the stereo equipment, make a little money.

But the guy came back while he was still thinking about it. The fuck was he called? Sam? Boxes, bags full of clothes. Jesus, here we go again. Whole fuckin' world's full of perverts.

'Got you some clothes,' Sam said. 'You wanna try them on, see if they fit?' He began taking things out of the bags. Jeans, T-shirts, a little hat. 'The hat was an after thought,' Sam said. 'You might think it's shit. Anything you don't like we could take it back.'

These weren't girls' clothes. These were *real* clothes. Geordie moved closer to get a better look. The jeans were real jeans, black jeans. He picked them up. Like the kids in the town. The hat with the name on the front. All the kids wore those, that little strap at the back, fuckin' ace.

What's this? Shorts. Fuck, like underwear. Geordie used to wear underwear in the home and when he lived with his mother. Had to change it every week. His mother used to shout at him, 'Have you brought your dirty underwear down? How'd you expect me to get it clean?' One, two, three pairs!

'You gonna try it on?' Sam asked. 'Or you just gonna pick it up and look at it?'

'I don't want sex,' Geordie said.

'*Sam*,' Sam told him. 'I don't want sex, *Sam*.'

'What I have to do?'

'You have to try on the clothes. You like them, you keep them. Next you have to get shaved, then we go get your hair cut, have something to eat. I tell you about the job. You don't like the idea, you keep the clothes and go back to your doorway. You like the idea, we find somewhere for you to live and you come work for me. Savvy?'

'No sex?' asked Geordie.

'No sex,' said Sam. 'You try to kiss me, I'll punch you in the mouth.'

Geordie thought that might be a joke. Not funny, though. 'I take the clothes in there?' He motioned towards the bathroom.

'No, use the bedroom,' said Sam. 'There's a full-length mirror in there. You can close the door, stuff something in the keyhole if you like. I won't peek.'

Geordie picked up some of the clothes and went into the bedroom. Sam followed him with the rest. 'You want some breakfast?' Sam asked him. 'Egg and bacon?'

'Yeah.'

'How many eggs?'

Geordie had never been asked this question before. He thought of asking for ten, but didn't want to put the guy off by being greedy. 'Six,' he said.

Sam blinked, but didn't seem too put out. 'How many sausages?'

'Six.'

'Let me try guessing the rest,' Sam said. 'Six pieces bacon, six slices toast, six cups of coffee, each with six spoons of sugar? Am I on the right track?'

'I have to eat it all at once?'

'Listen,' said Sam. 'You try the clothes on. I'll make breakfast. I'll make the same for you as I make for me. You're still hungry, I'll make it all again.' He left the bedroom and closed the door behind him. A few minutes later Geordie heard the music and a real good smell coming from the kitchen.

He had the hat on and the Reeboks, still in his pyjamas. He walked around the bed and then back again to the mirror. 'Yo,' he said to the reflection, shaking the index finger of his right hand. 'Yo, man, you look great.'

Sam took him to Betty's. Earlier, at Saks, he'd pointed to the photograph of a model on the wall, and had his hair cut like that. Shaved at the sides, little long bit left at the front, sticking out of his cap now. Big cup of coffee in front of him, he'd have to drink black, 'cause he'd already swigged the cream out of the little jug. Cream cake nearly as big as his head, half eaten and still going down. After two breakfasts. The kid's stomach must be a fuckin' machine.

There'd been a problem with the dog, having to leave it at the flat. Geordie had wanted to bring it along. Barney'd get lonely by himself. In the end he'd settled for taking it walkies, waiting till it did its crap, then feeding it a bacon sandwich.

After eating, Barney settled down for a sleep. 'He always does that,' said Geordie. 'I think something's wrong with him.'

'What you saying? The dog's fine.'

'No,' Geordie insisted, 'if he's going to sleep, he always turns round like that first.'

'Dogs do that,' Sam told him. 'All dogs do that.'

'Why?'

'Some kind of instinct,' said Sam. 'From the wild. They make sure no predators are around. Then they can sleep better.'

It was difficult keeping the kid's attention in Betty's – so many mirrors, little waitresses running around, tourists eating exotic meals. Sam tried to explain what he was doing, what he expected Geordie to do. Told him the whole story about Deacon being killed. The kid nodded, said 'Yeah' between mouthfuls of cream cake and coffee, but didn't know what surveillance meant.

'It's when you're watching somebody else,' Sam told him. 'But they don't know you're watching. You watch them, but you keep out of their way. If they get to know you're watching, you've blown it.'

'Yeah.'

'You understand what I mean?'

'Yeah. I understand it. You hide somewhere and watch them. Or they go for a walk, you follow them, but not right behind. They turn round, you look in a shop window.'

'Right,' said Sam. The kid was bright. 'Also, you have a little book, you write down what time they come out of the house, where they go, when they come back. You write it all down. You can write?'

'Sure. You gotta pen?' Sam gave him a pen and the kid took a paper napkin and wrote on it slowly. When he'd finished he handed it to Sam. It said, in big capital letters, GENTS.

'Right on,' Sam said to himself, then to Geordie, 'You know any other words?'

Geordie smiled, maybe thinking it was a trick question. He took another paper napkin and wrote HAMELESS.

'You're a fuckin' ace speller,' Sam told him.

Chapter 37

Frances lit the candle, went down the rickety steps into the cellar. She placed the candle on the table, sat on the chair and talked to the wall.

Graham thought it was a good idea to get the detective, Sam Turner. But get the others first. The detective thought he knew things, but he was ignorant. It was a lucky guess that Frances had seen the notes. The inspector had wondered about it too, but he hadn't pressed her like Turner. The notes had obviously been stuck up somewhere else, he said. Maybe since Graham had disappeared? But the inspector had also asked to see Frances's passport, obviously wanting to check if she'd been to New Zealand or Sweden. Frances had been to neither place, she told him, she had never been out of the country. She didn't suppose she ever would. Frances didn't think there could possibly be anything to see in another country that she couldn't see here.

Another thing. Graham had been worried that Frances would kill the detective in her own house. She mustn't do that. Everything had to be planned. The detective might come back another time, try to push her too far. If that happened, Frances had to stay calm. She could ring the police. The inspector had already told her she didn't have to talk to Turner. The inspector would lock him up.

Graham was happy that the Blackburns were back. On the way here Frances had driven past the house. Now it was time to plan their deaths. Jean Blackburn would be easy. She took drugs, wouldn't even know what was happening. Graham suggested Frances do it the same as she'd done with Terry Deacon. Knock on the door like it was a social call. Middle of the day. Then wait for Bob Blackburn to come home and kill him too. Get rid of both of them at once.

'When it's all over,' Frances told him, 'we're going to be reunited. I'm fed up of waiting now. I know you're still with me, Graham, but it's not the same. I want to be with you. In the same place as you. I want us to be really together again.'

Graham didn't say anything, but Frances could hear him thinking, in her mind she could see that wispy smile cross his face. 'It won't be long now,' she said. 'As soon as they're all dead I'll be free to come.'

In the place he was, Graham told her, there were no bodies. Everything was like air. There was no pain, no need to sleep or not sleep. He could see the world she was in, see it in all its turmoil and its suffering. And he was beginning to make plans to be born again. When Frances joined him they would decide where to be born together, somewhere quiet, not in a city, not in England at all. Somewhere in nature.

They would bring peace and beauty and poetry into the world. They would be teachers, teaching the old virtues: chivalry, obedience. Tools with which the world could fight evil. It would be a great adventure. And they would be together. Always together.

This last incarnation – the one that had already finished for him, and the one that was almost completed for her – they had been knights. They had fought the dragon and almost lost, but the fight went on and soon it would be won.

Frances took her handkerchief out of her bag, wiped her face. She was sorry, she said, but it did make her cry when Graham talked like this. Tears of joy, though. She was not unhappy. She would never be unhappy again.

Something else Graham had to say after she'd blown her nose, wiped her eyes again. Angels were true. They weren't like in the pictures you saw, or the statues in church. They didn't have feathers. They had long robes, finer than silk, so fine if they touched you you couldn't feel anything. And Graham, and Frances too, they had their own angels, and these angels never left them, ever. They were always there, watching, guiding, making sure that everything that was meant to happen did happen. Frances's angel had told Graham already that they would be reunited soon. There was just one or two little things to clear up. Then it would be time.

Chapter 38

Celia Allison had set the table for three. Sam was bringing someone round to see her. A young man who needed lessons in reading and writing, he'd said, trainee investigator. Celia liked Sam more than any other man she'd met in her life. He was a rough diamond, and Celia knew if she had been younger, she would have been intimidated by him, on the defensive. But she wasn't younger, she was of a certain age. A lovely phrase that, 'of a certain age'. Of an age where certainty did not necessarily have dire consequences when it turned out to be an illusion.

She did not regard Sam's head-on approach as a threat. On the contrary, he was charmingly engaging, like a child with a head full of naïve questions. Celia had met many men in her life, mainly in the teaching profession, who were undoubtedly ingenuous, but very few who could combine it with humour. And that is what Sam brought. Something that had been decidedly lacking in

Celia's experience.

Neither did she doubt that he had a dark side, a part of him that his persona only inadequately veiled. Something she had not met, but which would surface sooner or later should their liaison continue. Celia could not imagine how that dark side would manifest itself, nor how she would cope with it when it did. Could something as fearful as alcoholism, in its worst state, still leave a victim with his nobility intact?

Celia was in mid-cogitation when Sam knocked and came in with the young man and his dog. Polite young man, terribly nervous, took his hat off and shook hands. Celia saw at once that he was either from a broken home or had been badly abused. If she'd had to put money on it, as those American detectives said, she'd bet both. Children of that kind were never easy to teach unless they were really motivated. But this boy was almost a man. Celia had only ever taught children.

She served up crumpets with strawberry jam, obviously a good choice, since they disappeared in the blinking of an eye.

'Geordie wants to join the firm,' Sam said. 'But he has to be able to make written reports.'

'What does Geordie think about it?' asked Celia.

'I can write some words,' he said. 'I can copy words real good. Reckon I could copy a whole book.'

'It does depend on you, Geordie,' said Celia. 'I can easily spend time with you, I can help, but it will only work if you really want it to.'

Geordie looked at Sam. 'This is the job, right?'

Sam nodded. 'Part of it. You wanna try?'

'I can learn things,' he said. 'I know I can. When do we start?'

'We can start now,' said Celia. 'But mornings are best for me. Sam could bring you round in the morning.'

'OK,' said Sam. 'You can have him for a couple of hours now. I'll pick him up around five-thirty'

Celia gave Sam a list of appointments. 'All at Betty's,' she said. 'Ten o'clock in the morning. You can drop Geordie off here about nine, then go on to meet the clients.'

'Life's getting hellish busy, Celia. Don't know if I can keep up the pace.'

'You thrive on it, Sam.'

'What about you? Every time I come round I bring you more work.'

'It's much better than knitting,' she said. 'Before I met you I was supplying half the Third World with socks.'

Sam drove round to his landlord's house and rang the doorbell. Mike Parker was retired now, and the two houses he owned were his pension plan. Lived with his unmarried daughter. Mike was always at home.

'Sam,' he said. 'Come in, long time no see.'

'The flat above mine,' Sam said, going into the house and walking through to the kitchen, 'you got a tenant for it yet?'

'There's a couple of people interested,' Mike said. 'But, no, I haven't let it. You thinking of expanding upstairs?'

'Not for me. But there's a kid working for me could use somewhere to live.'

'If you say the word, it's yours,' said Mike. 'If all my tenants were like you, I could live easy.'

'He doesn't have a lot of cash,' Sam said. 'A small rent to start with, say the first year?'

'Jesus,' Mike said, 'the whole world's trying to screw me.'

'Not another hard-luck story.'

'Fifty a week,' said Mike. 'Take it or leave it.'

'The kid's young,' said Sam. 'Looking for a start.'

Mike went to a cupboard and came back with a key in his hand. 'Thirty-five a week,' he said. 'The kid pays council tax and services. First month free 'cause I'm in a good mood.'

'Mike,' Sam said. 'You changed my life.'

Back in his flat Sam put *Oh Mercy* on the tape deck. Not an album he played that much, but some good songs nevertheless. He'd just played a hunch with the kid, a kind of extended intuition, not knowing where it would go. Now the thing had got its own steam and could go anywhere. There would be no stopping it.

He was tempted to think the worst-case scenario was Geordie ending up back in the doorway, but Sam was not that naïve. There were a lot of people involved now, and as time went on there would be more. If things didn't work out with the kid, all kinds of minor or major disasters were possible. But Sam thought it might work out. It felt good. Geordie had needed all kinds of prodding and pushing, and would continue to need support, but it felt like the guy was at the beginning of a roll.

'We got time for a game?' Gus asked as soon as he arrived. 'I'm sick to death of this detective lark, following people round all the time, staying up half the night talking to sleepy blondes.'

'Got an hour,' Sam told him. 'Time for a couple a frames. That's all.' He told Gus about the developments with Geordie while they got in the car. Then, 'What's this about sleepy blondes?' he asked. 'She been coming on to you?'

'No,' Gus told him. 'She's holding a torch for you, though. Wanted to know how often you fart, how many decibels, even the texture.'

'You jealous?' Sam asked him.

Gus shook his head. 'I'm totally conditioned,' he said. 'I see a blonde like her, my mother and all my aunties start whispering in my ear: "*Trouble*, Gus. Leave it alone. Buy yourself a new jigsaw."'

'I know what you mean,' said Sam. 'I've been holding out, but I think she's getting to me. Disaster's getting closer every time we meet.'

Gus started to hum a tune. Sam pulled into a parking space and they opened the front doors of the Volvo simultaneously and walked fast down the street to the snooker hall.

'Why hold out?' Gus asked when they started playing. 'She looks great, she's rich, and she thinks you're something special.'

'I can't put my finger on it,' said Sam. 'Everything in me says, "Go for it."' He chalked his cue and walked round the table to

148

tackle an impossible snooker. 'Something holds me back. Little voice inside keeps saying, "Wait."'

'Could be *the* romance,' said Gus. 'She take you away to the Costa del Fuckin' Whatever. You wear shorts for the rest of your life, those long baggy ones with flowers on, poppies, sunflowers. Shit, you've got so much money it doesn't matter what you wear.'

'You see me as a gigolo?'

'Yeah. OK, it doesn't fit. But how do you talk yourself out of it?'

'I don't,' said Sam. 'I just wait and see.'

Gus told him about Frances going to the house in Leeds while they set up the balls for the second frame. 'She was in there for about an hour and a half,' he said. 'When she'd left I had a look round. Found a couple of cracks in the boarding I could see through. The place is empty, the ground floor, anyway. Couldn't see upstairs.'

'An hour and a half. What does she do in there? Did she take in any bags, something could have been food?'

'No. A little handbag.'

'You think Graham could be in there?'

'I don't know,' said Gus. 'We gotta get inside, see for ourselves.'

'Yeah. Give it another day. We'll have a go at getting the keys.'

Chapter 39

Geordie watched television with total involvement. Sam had told him earlier that they would watch *Crimewatch UK* with the blonde woman, Jane Deacon, and he had somehow thought they would watch it through a shop window. They didn't, of course, they watched it in the blonde woman's living room, and the people who spoke on the tube had voices you could hear, and even when they weren't speaking you could listen to music coming from somewhere behind the pictures.

Nick Ross, the guy on the programme, said the people they would see were actors, but the voice of Sam Turner was real. Really weird looking at people who were supposed to be Sam Turner and Jane Deacon coming out of the television when Sam Turner was sat on one side of you and Jane Deacon on the other. So close you could smell them, well . . . her. After they were introduced he'd asked her what it was and she'd told him Peach Blossom. 'Hell,' he'd said, 'I'd never have guessed *that*.'

The programme was OK in its way, but it had lots of things wrong. Sam, for instance – the guy who was the actor who was supposed to be Sam – he was driving round in a beat-up old red car, when everybody knew Sam drove a fuckin' big new-looking foreign car. Also the woman who was supposed to be Jane Deacon had the blonde hair but she didn't have the special looks. She was a pretty-looking blonde woman on the television, bit dumpy, whereas the real Jane Deacon, smelling strongly of Peach Blossom, was *beautiful*, more like a film star.

The programme on the television seemed like a million miles away. What it showed had actually happened in this house, in this room. Sam had shown Geordie the blood-stains on the carpet, right behind him now, under that little rug. You just watched the pictures on the television, you had no idea what it felt like to *be* here. To sit in this room and imagine the knife-man coming back in. He came once and killed the blonde's husband, why couldn't he come again and stab the three of them sat on this couch, Barney as well?

Except Sam was here. So it'd probably be OK.

Geordie had spent the afternoon with Celia working on words. She had a way of making them seem easier than they were, and Geordie realized he'd done quite a lot of work on words in the past. In the home and at school, and although the work he'd done then hadn't resulted in much, it had given him a basis for what was now a requirement of the job. Celia said that concentration was the hardest thing to master, but Geordie didn't find a problem with that. 'When you're on the street and you're hungry,' he said, 'you just concentrate on food until you get something to eat.'

'Yes, I suppose you do,' Celia had said.

Apart from watching *Crimewatch UK* Geordie had been concentrating on words nearly all day, and when the programme was over he was going back to the room upstairs to concentrate some more.

First, though, he had something to say, and when Jane Deacon switched the television off he said it: 'Graham East, he left home half a year ago?'

'Something like that,' said Sam.

'When you leave home,' Geordie said, 'the first week or so is OK because you're glad to get away from everything, and because you've been eating regular meals, you're fairly strong. But after that you get thin and your face changes. You start to grow a beard.'

'Good Lord,' said Jane. 'You mean he might be on the street? Like a tramp?'

'Where would he go?' asked Geordie, getting into it. 'Something else as well. When you've been on the street for a while, you get frightened. And when you're frightened you start to look different.'

'Not that different,' said Sam.

'You do,' Geordie insisted. 'It changes you. I've seen people come on the street fresh from home, then you don't see them a couple of weeks and when you meet again you don't know who it is.'

'What're you saying, Geordie?' said Sam.

'That photograph they showed on the programme. I bet he doesn't look anything like that now.'

'You know,' said Jane, 'I didn't think of Graham as a drop-out. But he could be. That was part of his personality. He was a romantic. He had a notion about what he called the "gentlemen of the road" – tramps.'

'Yeah,' said Sam. 'Frances told me when he left home in New Zealand he was a kind of tramp. He lived with old men in different cities, she said.'

'I haven't finished yet,' said Geordie. 'I haven't seen him in York. At least I don't think I have – at hostels or soup kitchens. But he might be in Leeds, or someplace close. If we looked in the drop-out centres, we might find him.'

'He's right, Sam,' said Jane. 'That's why no one's seen him. If he's on the street, he's virtually invisible.'

'Yeah,' said Sam. 'It's worth a try. Good man, Geordie. You're thinking.'

'We could go tomorrow,' Geordie said. 'Get started.'

'Maybe in a day or two,' Sam said. 'There's some other things I want to follow up first.'

'OK, boss.' Geordie picked up his books and left the room. He went upstairs to Jane Deacon's office, concentrate on some more words, figure out how to spell Graham.

'He seems like a bright kid,' said Jane, when Geordie had gone.

Sam nodded. 'He needs to go slowly for the time being. There's nothing wrong with his brain.'

'Look,' said Jane. 'This is just an idea. If you're too busy at the moment, I could go with him. I could drive him to Leeds, wherever, and we could try to find Graham in the places where the drop-outs go.'

'No.'

'I wouldn't mind, Sam. It must be worth a try.'

'No. I don't like it. If Graham's there, he would probably spot you before you saw him. If we do it, we do it without you. But we don't do it yet.'

'Why would he see me? I could wear a wig. Sam, you give me half an hour with some make-up, you wouldn't recognize me.'

'OK, I know all that. I still don't want you involved. More

152

importantly, I don't want Geordie involved yet. I want him to work more with Celia. I want to get him settled, start to live a regular kind of life. I've got some jobs lined up for him, but I don't want him working independently on something that might not lead anywhere. He has to feel that what he does is useful.'

'What if I go by myself?'

'Jane, no.'

'You can't stop me.'

'I can't stop you, no,' said Sam, raising his voice. 'I'm telling you, though, we do this my way, or not at all. There are more important things to do at the moment. If you're wandering round Leeds, I can't concentrate on anything.'

She got up from her chair and left the room.

Sam closed his eyes. Geordie thinking independently was a good thing. He needed encouragement, and Sam would give him that when they were alone. What he didn't need, what none of them needed, was Jane Deacon putting herself on the line. *If* it was Graham East at the bottom of all this, then the best strategy was to wait for him to show himself. The only place he could get to Jane Deacon was in this house, and when and if that happened, Sam would be waiting for him.

Talk to Gus in the morning, get the keys to the Leeds house. There would be something there. Frances Golding knew more than she was telling. Maybe talk to Bob Blackburn again, he might be more forthcoming than last time.

But it was annoying Jane trying to get herself involved. That was the last thing he needed.

She came back into the room and placed a mug of coffee in front of him. She sat in the chair opposite with her own mug, hitched her skirt up a little too high for comfort.

'Why don't you grieve?' Sam asked her after a long silence.

'What do you mean?'

'I don't understand,' he said. 'I was you, I know I'd be tearing my hair out, screaming, I'd be banging my head against the wall.'

'We grieve in different ways,' she said.

153

'I don't see you doing it,' Sam continued. 'You're standing at a crossroads you can't comprehend. But you just don't show it. You've got to cry, Jane. You'll get sick.'

'I know,' she said. She took a sip of the coffee. Looked at him over the rim of the cup. 'I'm trying. But I've got to be strong as well. There's no one to turn to.'

'Forget strong,' he said. 'The world's full of reactions. If you cry, someone'll hold your hand.'

'I wish I could.'

'You want me to, I can be really nasty. Have you blubbering in about two minutes.'

She took a tissue out of her sleeve.

'See what I mean,' Sam said.

On the way home Sam and Geordie walked through the Coppergate Centre. When they got to the shop doorway Geordie stopped. There were two young boys in there, huddled together to keep warm.

Sam walked on and Geordie hurried to catch up with him. 'That's my doorway,' Geordie said.

'You want it back?'

'No,' he said. 'I just wanted to look at it.'

Chapter 40

Jane was frustrated. What did you have to do to get Sam Turner into your bed? She'd made it patently obvious that she wouldn't object. She'd all but given him a year-old Volvo. He said he wanted her portrait and she'd given him that. He didn't have a wife. No regular girlfriend. She'd talked to Gus about it, thinking he might be gay, but he wasn't.

He'd been pushing Frances as well, and that wasn't good. Frances was fine if you left her alone. But if she was pushed, she might start getting angry, and if she got angry . . . Well, Jane didn't want to take any chances.

Everyone else was safe. Gus and Geordie were no threat whatsoever. Jean and Bob Blackburn didn't know anything, and anyway Frances would be taking care of them. The only one who was capable of pushing it to the limit was Sam, and Jane knew she could divert him if he would only give her half a chance.

Jane had never been turned down by a man, and there had been quite a few of them. Often a glance would be enough. Even when she was married to Terry she'd had the odd affair. It had never been a problem to start a relationship. The problems were all connected with endings. Getting rid of a man could be a real problem. But starting, that was easy.

Except with Sam. But why, for God's sake? Was he shy? No, Jane couldn't believe that. Perhaps she should take an interest in his music? That's what she'd had to do with Terry, at least pretend to take an interest in his music. Suggest they go out together again? He'd enjoyed himself walking through the town with her that night. Everybody looking at her. Getting to his vanity. Well, she'd do everything possible.

At first it had seemed important to have Sam close so she could see what he was up to, keep him off the scent. Then having him close had seemed like a good idea in itself. He was the kind of man most women would find attractive in some way. But now having him close seemed like a kind of competition. Could she get him? Would she fail? No, Jane thought, you won't fail. All you have to do is find the key.

But a lifetime of experience had taught Jane Deacon that you don't have to find the key to a man. The man *gives* you the key. You simply have to be observant, make sure you don't overlook what is staring you in the eye.

There is a gesture Sam is making right now which is tantamount to dangling a key right in front her. Jane knows this is happening, and a smile crosses her face, because she begins to see what it might be.

She had wondered before if the key might be Gus. Set one of them against the other, a healthy competition with Jane as the prize. But she had turned this idea down because it wouldn't work with Sam. He'd see through it and walk away. A younger man would fall for it, fight tooth and nail, but this old trooper was a different proposition.

No, the key to Sam was something else altogether. And the man was not only holding it out in front of her eyes, he was rattling and shaking it so it was impossible to miss. The key was Geordie.

Geordie was the son Sam had never had. Geordie was also Sam himself when he was younger, or some subconscious aspects of the present Sam. Geordie was a terribly complex character in Sam's imagination, a tangle of archetypes. He was the prodigal son, the story of the good Samaritan, the outsider rejected and unloved by society. He was all these things and more, for he was also a kind of spiritual prince, the frog who would be transformed by the kiss of warmth and compassion.

Underneath his rough exterior, his apparent indifference and his infuriating patience, Sam Turner was a bleeding-heart liberal. And Jane knew how to deal with *them*, wind them round her little finger. She had lived with one for years, in fact just got rid of him.

So there it was, simple as ABC, and staring her in the face all the time. She went to Terry's wardrobe and took out his leather jacket. Yes, it would fit Geordie a treat. He'd look great in it. Jane looked at the rest of the clothes in the wardrobe. Not all suitable, but all about the right size, and if anything needed altering, well, she had a sewing machine, hadn't she?

Geordie needed a mother, and that was something Sam would never be. Jane could do a little mothering, but with no self-interest, of course. No, it would all be for his own sake, a helping hand so he could find his feet in the world. Whatever he needed, Jane would be there to help Sam's little frog.

Chapter 41

Frances came out of the house at nine-twenty-five and drove off in her little black Panda. In the Volvo a hundred and fifty yards up the street Sam, Gus and Geordie watched her go. When she'd rounded the corner Sam said, 'OK, let's do it.'

He and Geordie left the car with Gus at the wheel and approached Frances's house from the rear. This meant taking a back passageway, just wide enough for a car, lined on both sides by high fences and gates. When they got to Frances's gate Sam clasped his hands to make a step for Geordie, and the kid put a Reebok into it and scrambled over the wall. A moment later Sam heard the bolts on the gate being pulled back, then the gate opened and Geordie's grinning face peered around it.

They were in an enclosed yard, maybe twenty-foot square, on the right a couple of outhouses and on the left a party-wall with the house next door. Stretched from the house to the outer wall of the yard was a washing line with some of Frances's smalls hanging to dry, a pillow slip and a sheet. Sam went to the kitchen window and checked that the lock had not been replaced. 'Pass the sheet,' he said to Geordie.

Geordie looked vacant.

'The fuckin' sheet,' Sam whispered, pointing to the washing. Geordie unpegged it from the line and brought it over to the window. Sam covered the window with several folds of the sheet and asked Geordie to hold it there. He took out of his coat pocket a hammer which he had prepared earlier by covering the head with six socks, and smashed the bottom pane of the window. He pulled the sheet away to look at the damage, and then put his finger to his lips. They waited for about half a minute in silence. But there was no response to the sound of the smashing glass.

Sam reached inside for the catch and opened the window. He clambered inside, telling Geordie to wait in the yard. The keys were in the fruit bowl. He took them and passed them back through the window to Geordie.

'OK, give them to Gus,' he said. 'And don't run. Walk fast.'

Gus waited for Geordie to get in the car and pulled away from the side. Geordie passed the keys over to him while they drove. 'Any problems?' he asked.

'No,' Geordie told him. 'We used the washing.'

Gus let it go. He drove about a mile up the road to the hardware store and took the keys inside. 'Can you do me duplicates of these?' he asked.

The storeman took the keys and went behind the counter. He took some blanks from a rack and started up his lathe. 'You lost the duplicates?' he asked.

'No,' Gus told him. 'The wife's mother's come to live with us. They're for her.'

'You give her these,' the storeman said, 'she'll be able to get out.'

Gus smiled to keep him sweet and walked around the store looking at buckets and brooms, DIY double glazing kits, really fascinating.

When the keys were ready he paid the man and drove back to Frances's house. Geordie took the original keys and didn't run, walked fast round to her yard.

After Geordie took the keys Sam went through to Frances's living room to have a look around. He found what he thought must be Graham's poems, since they were nearly all addressed to Frances. Terrible poems. Sam had written them, he'd have thrown them away in case anybody found them. Maybe Frances was just a liar, said he didn't leave the poems behind because she didn't want to share them with anyone, or maybe she was just embarrassed by them.

He skimmed the poems, not having time to read them all, thank you God, but there was little of interest in them. Except the guy was poor in every way. A pauper. All he had in the whole world was Frances. So why did he leave her?

Some photographs as well. Photographs of Graham, many of them much better than the one Frances had given to the police. It looked very much as though Frances didn't want Graham to be found. The rest were family photographs, pictures of what must be Frances and her sister as little girls, pigtails and long socks. Some of the two sisters with their father, none with a mother.

Sam went upstairs and explored the three rooms there. The bathroom was all female. No man had ever been in there. No kind of contraceptive or contraceptive aid. Tights hung over the bath.

A spare room full of boxes Frances had not bothered to unpack since moving in. Sam opened one or two of them and had a look. Mainly books, some ornaments.

Frances's bedroom had a bed and a desk. The bed made. The desk empty. It was like the house was hardly lived in. There was no television or radio, no sound system. She must sit here in complete silence all the time. What the hell does she think about? Then she drives to Leeds and sits in that house over there, completely empty, not even any furniture.

There was a sound downstairs and Sam froze to the spot for a second. Then he heard Geordie's voice calling his name.

He went down the stairs and took the keys off Geordie through the kitchen window, put them back in the fruit bowl. He climbed back out of the window, then closed it after him and put the lock back on. 'Give her something to think about,' he said.

He and Geordie walked back round to Gus in the Volvo and got in. Gus drove, dropping Geordie off at Celia's house. Sam took over the wheel when Geordie went inside.

159

'We could do it now,' Gus said. 'Take us less than an hour to get to Leeds.'

'No,' said Sam. 'Let's be sure. Wait until Frances goes to Leeds again, then we'll do it the next day, make absolutely sure we don't get disturbed.'

'We might get a game in, then?' said Gus.

'What? In the middle of the day when we're supposed to be working?'

'No,' said Gus. 'I know we've gotta keep at it.'

'Shit,' Sam said. 'You don't take the job seriously. We've just got to stay with it, Gus.'

'OK, OK. It was just a thought. I'm sorry. I shouldn't have mentioned it.'

'Christ,' Sam said, taking a left towards the town centre. 'I have to take all the responsibility, keep the fuckin' thing going.'

'I said I'm sorry,' Gus told him. 'For Christ sake leave it alone.'

Sam made a couple of left turns, pulled up outside the snooker hall and got out of the car. 'Three frames, OK? Loser pays for the sandwiches.'

Chapter 42

Frances felt like she needed a bath. Someone had violated her house. Even before she got inside, while she was still turning the key in the lock, she knew something was wrong. She walked inside quietly and closed the door behind her. She stood and listened. Nothing, but a feeling like the unwanted touch of a man, his hands all over your body. She stood for a while longer to make sure there was no one in the house. Sense of a breeze coming from the kitchen.

160

When she was absolutely certain she walked down the passage and saw the broken window. Something very strange here, the window lock was still in place, only one of the lower panes broken. Whoever it was wanted it to appear that he hadn't been inside. She checked all the rooms, and he had been everywhere. Nothing was out of place, nothing appeared to have been touched, yet everything was tainted.

Frances rang the police and waited until Inspector Delany's sergeant arrived. A few minutes later two other officers arrived to look for fingerprints. The sergeant took a statement. What time she went out, what time she came back. How nothing was missing. 'Oh, well, that's something, ma'am.'

'I don't care about that,' she said. 'Everything's been *touched*.'

'It looks as though you came back just in time,' he said. 'Disturbed them before they actually got into the house.'

'No,' said Frances. 'Someone's been in. I can smell it.'

The sergeant humoured her. 'Still, nothing's missing. You're absolutely sure of that? You've checked everything?'

'Yes,' she told him, wishing he would go. Useless. Really useless. 'Nothing's safe,' she said.

'There are no useful prints,' said one of the other policemen. 'A neighbour saw a youth in a baseball cap.'

'You get a description?' asked the sergeant.

'Yes, sir,' said the policeman. 'A youth in a baseball cap.'

Frances sighed and stood. 'I'm going to scrub the house out,' she said.

'I'm sorry,' said the sergeant. 'This kind of opportunist crime is very difficult.' He stood to leave, then had another thought. 'We're getting a tremendous response to the *Crimewatch* programme,' he told her.

'Oh,' said Frances. 'About Graham?'

'Yes. We've had reported sightings all over the country. Well, all over the world, actually. Tremendous job to check them all out.'

'It's going to take some time, then?'

'Some time,' he said. 'We'll get through them.'

When they'd left Frances took the sheet from the back yard and put it in the dustbin. She rang a glazier and arranged for him to come round and replace the window. Then she rang a company called FeelGood Security, talked to a very nice man called Mr Mitchell, who made an appointment to call round the following day. 'We work with the National Approval Council for Security Systems,' he told her. 'We've been established since 1981, and we are the North's leading installers of intruder alarm systems. Whatever you decide, you can rest assured in the knowledge that all FeelGood installations are carried out in accordance with British standards.'

Very reassuring.

She put her apron on, filled the bucket and began swabbing the kitchen floor. After that she took one room at a time until everything in the house was cleansed. Later, in the early evening, she went to the bathroom and soaked herself. Tomorrow she would wash all her clothes. Everything in the drawers. Rid them of the intruder's smell.

Chapter 43

Sam stood in the kitchen with his soap and shaving kit wrapped up in a towel as if he were going to the swimming baths. 'I'd like to take you up on the offer of the shower,' he told Jane Deacon.

'Oh, of course,' she said. 'Use it now if you like.'

Sam went upstairs, leaving Geordie in the kitchen with Jane Deacon. He got in the shower and turned the heat up until it was almost unbearable. Let the water play all over him for a while before reaching for the soap. When he was rich Sam was going to have a shower of his own. There was something about a bath that disgusted him, soaking in your own muck, that faint scum floating on top of the water. You take a shower, it flushes the whole lot away.

He heard what sounded like Jane and Geordie coming upstairs and going into her bedroom. Geordie was coming along fine. Celia said there was no problem with the language. He was keen to learn and progressing fast. Earlier he'd asked Sam to give him a spelling test. He took the poem Celia had given him and said, 'Ask me any of those words.'

Sam asked him to write JUST, AN, ORDINARY, MAN, OF, THE, BALD, WELSH, HILLS, and Geordie wrote them all down correctly, with the exception of hills, which he wrote with only one l. When Sam asked him what the poem was about Geordie said, 'A guy who gobs in the fire, kind of derelict.'

But Geordie's reaction to the flat was interesting. He'd stood in the middle of the main room for a while, sat down at the table then moved over to a fireside chair. He looked in the bathroom and the bedroom, sat on the bed, then came back to the main room. 'All mine?' he asked again.

'Yeah.'

He did another tour, coming back again to almost the same spot on the worn carpet. 'Fuck, Sam, what am I gonna do with all this?'

'After a while it won't seem so much. You only use the bathroom a couple a times a day, the bedroom only at night.'

'What about Barney?'

'He can sleep in here,' Sam said. 'We get him a basket or something. You prefer it, he can sleep in the bedroom.'

'I cook here?' he asked standing by the cooker, picking up a frying pan, twisting his head to look up at the grill element.

'Sure.'

'I don't know how to.'

'Hell, Geordie,' said Sam. 'You take one thing at a time. I'll teach you to cook. Celia and Jane, Wanda, they'll all teach you to

163

cook. Anything you wanna know how to do it, you just ask. Everybody'll help.'

'I ain't got nothing to cook, Sam. I'll have to buy eggs.'

'Yeah. We can go to the shops. Get everything you need.'

He stood there shaking his head. After a moment he said, 'You don't want me to live with you?'

Sam hesitated. 'You'll be living above me,' he said.

'But you don't want me to live with you downstairs?'

'People need their own space, Geordie. You want me, you're so close you can shout.'

'Space?'

'Yeah, space. Downstairs, that's my space. This'll be yours.'

'From now?'

'From whenever you like. It feels strange now, you've only just seen it. After a while you'll think it's great.'

Sam went downstairs leaving Geordie up there to get used to the idea. Ten minutes later Geordie came down. 'It feels great,' he said. 'Only there's no music, no eggs. Barney, he likes it better down here.'

'You want something to eat?'

'Yeah,' said Geordie. 'I'm starving.'

'Tomorrow we can do some shopping,' Sam told him. 'Get some eggs. Maybe find a second-hand radio.'

OK, Sam told himself, the kid's never had any space before. He doesn't know what to do with it, maybe finds it frightening. Everything's different for him. Celia, Jane, learning to read and write. He's a fuckin' Martian just crash-landed his space ship. The only thing he understands is eggs.

Sam left the shower and padded over to the wash-basin, cleared a patch of steam from the mirror and got out his shaving kit. Under-floor heating! Jesus, you didn't know, you'd think the house was on fire. He got a good lather on his face, pulled the blade down the left side of his cheek. From Jane's bedroom Geordie was shouting, 'Yo, man, that's great. Fuck, Barney, come take a look at *me*.'

He was like a child. Had that openness, the same kind of open-eyed joy and vulnerability you see in little kids on the street. Sam wondered what he would be like when the world chased that away. Wondered why the world hadn't chased it away already, the things the kid must have seen, must have lived through. When Sam was on the street he was already an adult, had been married with a family and was a widower. He was following a self-destructive impulse, a death-wish, casting the world aside because it didn't seem to hold any comfort for him. Searching out hard times in the city. But Geordie had never known a warm or caring world, no one had ever told him he was loved or worthy. His whole life experience had been rejection, double-dealing, a road full of twists and turns, each one meaner than the last. Every cell in his body turned around before it went to sleep, make sure it was safe.

Sam dressed and left the bathroom. Geordie and Jane were still in her bedroom so he shouted, 'What you two up to?' and walked along the hall to the door. It was open and inside he saw Jane with Terry Deacon. Only it wasn't Terry Deacon, it was Geordie dressed in one of Deacon's suits, the whole shooting range: pin-stripe trousers, jacket, waistcoat, white shirt with tie, black shoes.

Geordie turned when Sam appeared in the doorway. 'Hey, Sam,' he said, 'look at this.' He took the suit jacket off and grabbed a leather one from the bed, slipped it on. It was soft brown leather, finger-tip length, just about a perfect fit. 'Whada you think?' Geordie had the collar turned up, hands thrust deep into the pockets, walking with a little swagger up and down the bedroom, his head and shoulders going from side to side rhyth-mically like a soul singer between verses. Little Anthony, maybe, or the twelve-year-old Michael Jackson.

'Could've been made for you,' said Sam, glancing at Jane. She was sparkling. There were clothes and shoes all over the bedroom, like a men's outfitters at sale time. 'You having a clear out?' he asked.

165

'What should I do with all this stuff?' she said. 'Geordie needs clothes. I don't need any of this.'

'What, all of it?' said Geordie. 'Fuck, Sam, I've got more clothes than you now. You wanna borrow anything, I don't mind.'

Jane laughed and went to the door. 'Shall we leave him to it?' she asked Sam. 'Get some coffee?'

'Yeah.' He followed her downstairs, leaving Geordie sat on the carpet trying on a pair of brown brogues.

'It's a nice gesture,' he said. 'Really made Geordie's day.'

Jane gave him a long impish stare. 'Strange, isn't it?' she said. 'Just watching him putting different clothes on – clothes make you feel different, make you look different because you feel different.'

'I met Brenda the other day,' Sam told her. 'My ex-wife. Dressed completely in red, looked like a fuckin' gladiator.'

Jane smiled. 'Red's difficult,' she said. Then as an afterthought, 'Do you miss her?'

'She just kinda wasted my time. All the years I was fighting Brenda I could have been living, *doing* something.'

'Why did it take so long? I mean, you could have just walked out.'

'I didn't know that then,' Sam said. 'I thought I had to stay, see it through, whatever *it* was. I'd married her, felt some kind of responsibility.'

'To make it work?'

'Yeah, I suppose.'

'It can't always have been like that,' Jane said. 'Must have been good in the beginning?'

Geordie came tumbling down the stairs sounding like something heavy and square had been thrown from the top step. He burst into the living room wearing a white sports coat over a bright yellow shirt. No trousers, only his shorts. 'Does this go?' he asked Jane.

'Yes,' she said. 'You could wear it with jeans, sandals.'

166

'And a pair of shades,' he said. 'There's some shades up there.'

'Take them,' she said. 'They're yours.'

He was gone again, bounding up the stairs, sounded like four at a time.

'You were saying?' she said to Sam. 'About the beginning.'

'I don't know if it was good even then,' he said. 'We told ourselves it was. The sex seemed good, but I don't think either of us was thinking about each other.'

'Sex can be misleading.'

'Sometimes I think I married her as a kind of revenge,' Sam said. 'And she did the same to me.'

'Revenge?' Jane didn't understand.

'Something like that,' Sam said. 'Revenge for being so stupid as to like me. Revenge for thinking I could make her happy, for telling me I had the potential, making me try.'

Jane shook her head. 'You wanted to punish her because she got you wrong? Made a wrong judgement?'

'I'm not proud,' Sam said. 'I'm just telling you how it was, how it worked out between us. I met her in town the other day, I look at this woman – can't offer me anything, never could – and I think, I put all my hopes on her. I must've been blind. Brenda's completely incapable of delivering whatever it was I wanted. Most of the time she doesn't even understand what I'm talking about.'

'But you understand her.'

Sam laughed. 'No, it's just the same with me. I don't know who she is. When I think about it, I never did. I laid a kind of template over her, ignored who she was, just saw what I wanted to see.'

Jane didn't say anything, sat there shaking her head.

'We used each other as punch-bags,' Sam said. 'Both of us must've needed one at the time.'

'And now,' Jane said, 'you don't think about her at all?'

'Sometimes,' he said, looking at the floor. When he looked up he said, 'If you see her, say hello – she might be in Tadcaster.'

They were quiet for a moment, listening to Geordie moving

167

about in the upper room. Then Sam said, 'What about you, your life?'

'Not a lot to tell,' she said. 'You met Terry. I suppose he was the main thing.'

'What about before that?' he asked. 'Your sister. What about her?'

Jane had a surprised look on her face. It was only there for a moment before she said, 'Oh, she died. Killed herself.'

'I thought you still saw her.'

'What do you mean? How could I? We never spoke about my sister, Sam.'

She was agitated now. Suddenly unsure of herself. One minute she's calm, the next she starts going to pieces. 'Right at the beginning,' Sam said, 'when you and Terry were setting me up, you supposed to be having an affair but having your portrait done, Terry said to me you were supposed to be at your sister's, but he knew you weren't.'

'You've got it wrong,' she said. 'Or maybe Terry just said that. My sister killed herself some years ago.'

The brick came down the stairs again, only bounced once. Geordie came into the room naked apart from a pair of Bermuda shorts decorated with what looked like spiders, shades on the end of his nose, and a Panama hat. 'Seaside clobber,' he said. 'Celia said she'd take me to the seaside. Now I've got the suit, she'll have to.'

'When did Celia say that?' asked Sam.

'This morning. We're getting fish and chips and eating them on the prom. Candy-floss. That's what you do there. Make sandcastles. She showed me postcards.'

'Maybe I could come as well,' said Jane. 'It sounds lovely.'

'Hang on,' said Sam. 'Don't leave me out. I'm the keenest paddler on the east coast. I'll dig out my braces and plastic mac.'

Chapter 44

After Geordie's lesson the next day Sam left him in the Volvo outside Frances's house. Geordie and Barney both. Surveillance experts. Watch the suspect. Make a report. Sam said probably nothing would happen, but as soon as he'd gone things started.

First a guy in a van arrived, *Wales Glaziers* written on the side. Geordie didn't know what it meant but he copied it down on the pad, together with a picture of what the car clock said when the guy arrived. While the guy was still in the house another guy arrived in a blue car and this other guy went in the house as well. Geordie couldn't see what kind of car it was from inside the Volvo, so had to get out and go for a walk along the street. It was a Vauxhall. He remembered the order of the letters and wrote that down on the pad as well, together with the registration numbers of the two vehicles. Another picture of a clock.

He wrote down what the two guys were wearing as well, anxious not to miss anything out. The first guy had an overall on, but the second guy was wearing a suit and carrying a little briefcase. Geordie didn't know how to spell suit and it took him a while to find it in the dictionary which Celia had given him. When he eventually found it, it said that soot was a black substance, and that didn't seem right as the guy's soot was brown, if Geordie remembered correctly. Geordie thought that dictionaries were probably not always right. So many words in them, some of them would have to be wrong.

By the time he'd got that lot down the second guy was coming out of the house and getting back in his car. Yeah, a brown suit, and a hat. He added the hat to the report.

Then a quiet spell, time to think, get your breath back. Should have brought something to eat. Geordie played one of Sam's tapes in the car stereo, *John Wesley Harding was a friend to the poor* – bit like Sam maybe, 'cept Sam didn't *travel with a gun in every hand*.

Sam was OK. Geordie told himself Sam was OK maybe twenty times a day. Other times in between telling himself Sam was OK Geordie could think anything. He could think the guy was stupid, setting himself up to be robbed. Like now, for instance, Geordie could just take the tapes and split. He could sell the tapes at a second-hand shop, make plenty. Other things in the car as well – a fuckin' camera – he could take everything. Take the car, if he knew how to drive it. When he didn't think Sam was stupid he could think the guy was just biding his time, waiting to introduce some perverted sex thing. Snuff movie or something like that.

But Sam was OK.

Other times he could think Sam was just setting him up. Sam having a good time being a good guy, but one day he'd just get bored and tell Geordie to leave. 'Get outa my house, back to your doorway.' When Geordie thought that, he'd think best to split *now*, make sure you get something out of it. He knew where Sam kept a roll of notes in his bedroom, a wad thick as your hand. Take that lot, you could live for ever. Book into a hotel. With waiters. Have breakfast in bed. Then when Sam comes in in the morning saying, 'Get outa my house,' he's like talking to himself 'cause Geordie's already booked out. And so has the roll of notes. Just a space there where they used to be.

Serve the fucker right.

But Sam was OK.

Last night was good. Sam and Jane getting on like a house on fire. All those clothes. How much was that leather jacket worth? Two hundred quid? Maybe more. Sam and Jane getting close together on the sofa, laughing at each other's jokes, laughing with Geordie, talking about the seaside. It was like a family. Sam and Jane like his father and mother, and Geordie like the son who lived there with them, belonged to them. Making them laugh so

170

much they almost touched each other. And Celia, she'd be like the grandmother, go to the seaside with them, and Gus would be like Geordie's brother, only staying close by, not going off to foreign in a ship and never coming back.

They'd be happy, like normal families, not fuckin' about and ruining everything. 'Cept when they were catching murderers, doing surveillance, all that.

Yeah, Sam was OK. Even Barney liked him.

Next thing the guy in the overall comes out and gets in his *Wales Glaziers* van and drives off. Geordie drew another picture of the clock. He was still drawing it when Sam came back.

'Anything happen?' Sam asked.

'Christ,' said Geordie. 'You aren't gonna read the report?'

Back in the flat upstairs Geordie put groceries in the cupboard. Eggs, bacon, bag of carrots, rice, cans of soup, dog food. Opened one of those and gave it to Barney on a saucer. Barney thought it was Christmas, wolfed it down in two minutes flat. Licked the saucer clean and looked to see if there was any more.

Now what? Music coming from downstairs, but you can't go down there yet, invading another person's space.. Sit on the sofa, put your feet up and relax. Yeah, this is the life, nothing to do. Keep your mouth open and see if you can catch flies. Wait for an hour, then go downstairs, see if there's any *space* left or if the man's used it all up.

Fuck, Geordie thought, I had some tapes and something to play them on, it wouldn't matter. Could listen to the music like other people do. Play them all day, not let anybody else in the place, say, fuck you, man, this is *my* space.

What do you do with a space, man?

Park in it, man.

Could do some words for Celia. He got his pad out and looked at the sheet of exercises he had to finish for tomorrow. Wrote down a couple of words and even checked them in the dictionary. Shit, it would be so much easier to do them in Sam's room, listen to the music at the same time, wait for the telephone to ring and listen to Sam talking in it. Sam, he'd be just sat down there with his feet up listening to the music, looking at a magazine, maybe, or looking at that big picture of Jane Deacon he'd got on his wall. Nothing on Geordie's walls. Just fuckin' big walls with shit paper on, bit starting to curl off in the top corner.

You were really bored out of your skull, nothing to do, you could take hold of that paper up there and pull it. The whole wall might come down, even the house. Sam down there sitting with his eyes closed listening to the guitar picking, Jesus, he opens his eyes and he's sat in a pile of bricks, nothing left but the tape deck, breathing the air around Tom Paine's, people in the street staring at him, saying, 'Evening, Sam. How you doing?' Sam looking round, standing up, saying, 'Fuck, where's my space, man?'

Then he'd want to come up here, live with Geordie, banging on the door saying, 'Hey, let me in, man. I've got nowhere to go.' And Geordie with the key in his hand on the other side of the door not saying anything, pretending he was out, thinking, 'Fuck, what's going on here? Who is that? Guy from downstairs trying to invade my space?'

But, Geordie, he'd let him in. Set himself up to be robbed. Next time he comes home, Sam's split. He's running down the road with Geordie's eggs and his leather jacket, his Air Jordan cap. Dumb fucker, doesn't know when he's winning.

Geordie got up from the sofa and went down to Sam's flat. Sam was sitting in his chair with his feet up listening to the music, *Baby please stop crying*. He motioned Geordie to a chair. 'You eat yet?'

'No,' Geordie told him. 'I bin having 'lucinations.'

'You should try to sleep in the place,' said Sam. 'Lie on the bed and sleep, when you wake up it'll begin to feel like home.'

'That what you did? When you first came here?'

Sam nodded.

'It's Barney, really,' Geordie said. 'He doesn't wanna sleep there till he gets a basket.'

Sam sat up in the chair and leaned forward, coming so close he almost got inside Geordie's head. 'You don't want to, you don't have to sleep there. Upstairs, down stairs, it's all yours, you got a key to both. Tomorrow we'll get Barney a basket. OK?'

Geordie was quiet for a minute or two. 'Barney starts to have 'lucinations,' he said, 'what am I supposed to do? He doesn't understand things. He's only a dog.'

There was that gap in the tape, comes between songs, leaves you with nothing 'cause you don't know if it's the end or not. Then there was the drums and a long trumpet intro, and the guy started to sing with a terrible hollow voice like he'd been 'lucinating for a thousand years, *DO you love me . . . or are you just extending goodwill?* And he's got you. It's like magic. Barney looks up at you from that spot on the carpet, and it's like he's listening too. You watch Sam close his eyes and ease himself down in the chair, and you close your own eyes and feel the tension drain away from your face. A moment or two previous you wanted to talk or eat or something, anything. Now you just want to close your eyes and listen, go with the music.

Chapter 45

What next? Celia was fairly well organized as a rule, but worrying about Sam had got her behind with the various jobs in hand. He managed most of the morning interviews at Betty's, and when he couldn't make it he always told her to cancel. But he was doing far too much, not enough hours in the day for him.

It was typical of a man, for instance, to cover all the practical things, and put the essential things to one side. Wanda, for example, was essential. Through their telephone conversations Celia had come to know quite a lot about Wanda. Become fond of her. She was not one of these young women who was out to get a husband. She had a full life of her own, two delightful daughters, or at least they seemed delightful on the phone. Celia had spoken to both Samantha and Kelly, and whoever picked up the phone in that house it was always interesting and usually a treat.

Celia was invited to tea there this afternoon, and as soon as she ... Oh, goodness, yes, that was what she had meant to do – confirm the retainer details with the solicitor, Mr Forester. Then she would be on her way.

His secretary put the call through and Celia introduced herself. 'I met Sam yesterday,' Mr Forester confirmed. 'Good meeting, I think. We seemed to be able to talk to each other.'

'Good,' said Celia.

'I understand you don't want to be involved in credit references?'

'That's what Sam said.'

'It'll mean a bit of reorganization here, but nothing we can't cope with. We can handle that side ourselves, but everything else we'll pass over to you.'

'The question is how we do it,' said Celia. 'Personal meetings are a bit time-consuming. If we have to meet over every job, we'll get nowhere.'

'Most jobs are routine,' said Mr Forester. 'I could *send* you the details. The odd one is more complicated.'

'We lose a bit of time with the post, though,' said Celia.

'Do you have a fax?'

'No, but maybe we should have. I'll mention it to Sam.'

'That would be best. I could send everything to you on a daily basis. Anything out of the ordinary, we'd have to meet.'

'Lovely,' said Celia. 'Very nice to talk to you.'

'And you, Ms Allison.'

She put the phone down. Goodness, a fax machine. Something else to learn. Celia had conquered her computer now, but when she first got it there were endless problems. The dealer hadn't wanted to know anything about it once he'd got his money. She'd spent weeks trying to make it print before finding out there was a hardware fault, and then several more weeks trying to get a new printer out of the dealer. And she'd got one in the end. Now she was learning an accounting program.

'You look absolutely lovely, my dear,' she told Wanda as soon as they sat at the table.

Wanda smiled. 'Thank you,' she said. 'And so do you.'

'There were times, when I was younger,' said Celia. 'But I never had hair like yours. If I was a man, I'd snap you up in a minute.'

'I don't know if that's what I want, Celia. In fact it sounds quite painful.'

Celia laughed. And then, 'Oh, I didn't mean . . . Well, I didn't mean you wanted snapping up. I know I never did. Well, once or twice I thought it might have been nice. Depends who's doing the snapping, I suppose.'

'How's Sam?'

'That's what I wanted to talk to you about,' said Celia. 'I feel he's under a lot of pressure. Have you seen him?'

'He's been around a couple of times. Never stays long. He's always on his way to somewhere else.'

'Yes,' said Celia. 'That's what I'm worried about. I'm not a worrier generally, Wanda. And I'm sure Sam is quite capable of taking care of himself. Well, look, I'll come straight to the point. I've had a dream about him. Two dreams, actually, two nights running. First let me say this: I don't dream much, and when I do I don't always think it's significant. But I had these two dreams, and in both of them Sam is caught in something, some kind of trap. The first one was a real nightmare, he got caught in an animal trap, by his leg, couldn't move at all. And then last night he'd fallen into this enormous pit, something like a grave. There was no way he could get out.'

'You think it's some kind of premonition?'

'No. More like a warning.' She threw up her hands. 'Is this too fanciful? I don't want to get carried away over nothing.'

'I don't know, Celia. Have you spoken to Sam about it?'

'Goodness, no. He'd just dismiss it as the ramblings of an old lady. That's why I wanted to talk to you. I thought you'd be more sympathetic.'

Wanda smiled. 'I am,' she said. 'I just don't know what I can do.'

'He's under some pressure, you see,' Celia said. 'There's work coming from all directions, and he just takes on more and more. There's Geordie as well. I mean, he's a lovely boy, but he's got lots of problems. Sam thinks the world of him. Have you met him?'

'Sam brought him round last time. He was very quiet.'

'Then there's this Jane Deacon, you know, the widow. You must have seen her photo in the paper. Gus tells me she's after Sam. Can you believe it? Her husband has only just been murdered and she's after Sam?'

'She's very beautiful,' said Wanda.

Celia snorted. 'Not my type at all, my dear.'

'Do you want me to do something, Celia?'

Celia shook her head. 'I wanted to share it,' she said. 'At the moment he's fine, he just takes everything that comes. I worry that something else will happen. You know, the straw that breaks the camel's back?'

'I hope not. Sam seems to have his head screwed on, his feet firmly planted on the ground.'

'To pick up on your metaphor,' said Celia, 'I believe he wilfully strays on to less firm ground from time to time. Might even be tempted by quicksand.'

'You mean Jane Deacon?'

'The blonde lady, yes.'

'What can I do?' said Wanda. 'If he fancies her?'

'I'm not saying he does,' said Celia. 'Gus wasn't convinced. I think he'd be much better off with you.'

Wanda shrugged. 'It's up to him. He knows where I live.'

'I don't want to interfere,' said Celia. 'I wouldn't have said anything if it wasn't for the dreams.'

'If there's anything I can do,' said Wanda, 'I don't mind. If I can help, I will. But I don't think Sam will ask me. It will be up to you.'

Chapter 46

Sam got out of bed and walked through to the bathroom stepping over Geordie and Barney. Only Geordie and Barney weren't there. Just an empty sleeping bag. Sam smiled. Must have gone upstairs during the night.

He washed and shaved, came back to the kitchen and started cooking breakfast. Put some sounds on the tape deck, that'd bring the kid down.

This morning Sam was meeting a guy whose sixteen-year-old daughter had gone missing, eloped with her boyfriend after a family row. They'd checked with relatives and schoolfriends and drawn the big zero. Could Sam find her, make sure she was all right? Hell, who knows? Did she want to be found?

Sam turned the eggs. No sounds from upstairs. Have to wake Geordie. He went up the stairs, knocked on the door and walked in. The kid didn't even bother to lock his door. The bed hadn't been slept in. Where was he? Walking the dog. If he didn't get back soon, the breakfast would go cold.

Sam made himself a bacon sandwich, leaving two eggs, bacon, sausage and toast on the warm plate. The Bluesman was bemoaning the fact all the friends he ever had were gone. Sam poured a second cup of coffee and took it out on the street, see if Geordie was on his way back. Nothing. The street went on for ever. Rain clouds gathering at the far end and coming this way. Nearly time to leave now.

He put on his coat, turned the tape deck off, and sat in the chair a few more minutes. Geordie still didn't come. At the last minute Sam rang Celia.

'Geordie's not here,' he said. 'I was going to drop him off at your place.'

'Shouldn't you be on your way to Betty's, Sam?'

'Yeah, I'm on my way now. I'll leave a note for Geordie, tell him to walk round to your place. But he's gonna be late.'

'Well, never mind,' she said. 'It's the first time.'

He scribbled a note and left it by the frying pan. The first place Geordie would look when he got back. Bloody kid. Where was he?

Nice old guy at Betty's. Not so old really. Maybe not even forty. Really worried about his daughter. It was all his fault. 'We wanted her to concentrate on her school work. That's all. But she wanted to spend all her time with her boy friend.' Well, of course, where've you been? She's discovered sex. What, you want her to pretend it doesn't exist?

Sam said he'd look for her, got the addresses of her best friends, the boyfriend's parents. Didn't promise the world. Forty pounds a day plus. Two hundred on account. New notes. Give it a week, then review the situation.

'My wife's worried sick,' the guy said.

'Yeah,' Sam told him. 'I bet.'

The note was still by the frying pan, the eggs, bacon, sausage and toast untouched. Sam checked the flat upstairs again, looked through Geordie's clothes. Only thing missing was the leather jacket. For a moment Sam entertained the thought that Geordie had split, then, no, he'd have gone straight round to Celia's. Didn't want to be late, didn't even have time to eat.

178

'No,' Celia said on the phone. 'He hasn't turned up.'

'Where is he?' said Sam. 'I thought he'd taken the dog for a walk.'

'Maybe that's what he did,' said Celia. 'Sometimes, boys of that age, they just forget the time. Did he have any money?'

'Little bit. A few quid.'

'Maybe he went to a café. I'm sure he'll turn up soon.'

'I hope so,' said Sam. 'I can't think where he'd go.'

'I'll ring you if he turns up here.'

Sam put the phone down. The guy's voice came back in his head: *My wife's worried sick.* So am I, thought Sam. The old stomach starting to churn. Christ, anything could have happened to him. An accident, some fuckin' drunk driver. Give it another hour then ring the hospital. Maybe the kid was arrested, caught shoplifting, something like that. The possibilities were horrendous.

After an hour he decided to look in the bedroom, see if the cash was still there. That would give him a direction. The cash was still there, he would know there had been an accident. The cash was gone, he'd know the kid had robbed him and split. He didn't look. He sat in the chair and tried to think of something else. A car had come round the corner once before and took his whole life away. He'd hoped it had only taken half his life, his daughter, and that Donna would wake up and start living again. He'd hoped that for ten days before telling them to turn the machine off. Donna would never have woken up, and if she had, she wouldn't have known who she was. He'd held her hand for hours, looked at all those tubes going into and coming out of her. Watched the waveband beating peacefully on the monitor. It felt like wood, her hand. Like a piece of wood. Something you picked up and held, an object with no feelings.

She was out of it. He'd bent over the bed to say goodbye, kissed her on the cheek, on the lips, 'Goodbye, my love.' Nothing. Not even the flicker of an eyelid. She'd already gone. The machine was a lie. The breathing an illusion. Donna was way, way off, in a whole 'nother place. Somewhere beyond pain, beyond any reality Sam could imagine.

Gus came in after another half hour. Sam didn't get out the chair. Gus filled the kettle with water and put it on to boil. He sat in the chair opposite Sam. 'What's new?' he asked.

Sam looked at him, said nothing.

'Something wrong?'

'Geordie's disappeared,' he said.

'Disappeared? When?'

'I don't know,' Sam said. 'Could've been in the night. Could've been this morning. He wasn't here when I got up.'

'Thought he was gonna be a fixture,' said Gus. 'No note, nothing?'

Sam shook his head.

'Anything missing?'

'His leather coat. He took that.'

'Money?'

Sam said nothing. After a moment he put his lips together and shook his head.

'You think he's gone back on the street? What?'

'I don't know,' said Sam. 'Could've had an accident.'

'You checked the hospital?'

'No.'

'You want me to, I can do that.'

Sam nodded.

'You talk to the guy this morning, the missing girl?'

'Yeah. I didn't get round to writing it up. It's in my notebook.' He pointed to the table.

Gus picked up the notebook, took out a photograph of the girl. 'She's young,' he said. He transferred Sam's notes to his own book. 'I'll get on this as well,' he said. 'You going to Jane's tonight?'

Sam nodded. 'Business as usual,' he said, trying a smile, felt like a grin. Felt terrible. 'There's something weird about her, Jane Deacon.' He told Gus about the business with the sister.

180

'Yeah,' said Gus. 'You think she could be implicated in some way?'

'I know she is,' said Sam. 'Checked her marriage record. Wanna guess what her maiden name was?'

'Surprise me,' said Gus.

'Golding,' said Sam. 'She was christened Jane Debra Golding.'

'Jesus. They're sisters? Her and Frances?'

Sam nodded. 'Yeah,' he said. 'But the really interesting thing is why Jane Debra doesn't want anyone to know.'

'If Frances was your sister,' said Gus, 'would you tell anybody?'

'The Goddess of Gloom,' Sam said. The grin came back fleetingly.

'She'll have you howling at the moon.' Gus walked to the door. 'OK,' he said. 'I'll let you know what the hospital says.'

Sam sat in the chair, listening to the Volvo start up, drive away. The hospital is not likely, not thinkable. It's much more likely the kid has split, something Sam said, maybe. He went over the conversations of the last evening, the last day, the last week. Geordie had been reluctant to move into the flat. Could that be it? Sam coming on too heavy about needing his own space. When he didn't need any space at all, just a chair to sit in. The kid could have all the rest of the space to himself. What did it matter? Space? Geordie, just come home, forget about the flat, we could divide this one up between us. Sam could live in the bedroom. Geordie, if you just come home now, I'll live on a fuckin' shelf.

Everything seemed to be working out. That's the tragedy. Everything coming together. So, the kid's under pressure, trying to adapt, learn to read and write, learn to live decent. The pressure's not that bad. It must be better than living on the street. Even somebody's dumb as Geordie can see that.

You got it wrong, Sam. You gave the guy a handout and let him see you doing it. You tried to disguise it, even told yourself it would all come out of his wages, but he saw right through you. Couldn't take a handout, just like you. Somebody offers you a hand, what do you do?

Take a fuckin' big healthy bite.

So, why complain? You'd have done the same. If it isn't something you've worked for, something you've deserved, you don't want it. Geordie, he's just like you. Rather be on his own in a doorway than living off somebody else's charity.

If he comes back, it'll be OK. It'll mean he can make it. Mean he's strong enough to live. If he doesn't come back? Well, fuck him.

Celia arrived, knocked and came in, followed by Wanda. At the same time the telephone rang. Sam thought he should do something but sat in the chair. Celia answered the phone. 'Gus,' she said, and listened for a moment. Then, 'OK, I'll tell him.'

While she was on the phone Wanda came over and knelt beside Sam. 'How you doing?' she asked.

'I'm fuckin' sick,' he said. Then looked towards Celia as she put the phone down.

'Gus checked the hospitals,' she said. 'No one like Geordie has been admitted.' She came over and knelt beside Wanda, placed her hand on Sam's knee. 'You haven't heard anything?'

He shook his head.

'We're going out to look for him,' said Wanda. 'At least he's not in the hospital, Sam. That must be a good thing.'

'We'll be off, then,' said Celia. 'Be in touch soon. If he's in town, we'll find him.'

Wanda planted a kiss on his cheek, then followed Celia out to the street. Sam sat in the chair. He sat for half an hour then put his coat on and walked through the darkening streets to Jane's house.

'That's terrible, Sam,' said Jane. 'He wouldn't just disappear like that. Something must have happened to him.'

Sam didn't answer, vision of Geordie washing about in the bottom of the river. Barney too, a suicide pact.

At one point during the evening she came over to the sofa and

182

sat beside him, placed her hand on his leg. She sat for a while with
her head on his shoulder then kissed him on the cheek and looked
for his lips with hers. She was nervous of his reaction and Sam let
a dry kiss happen to him. He said, 'Look, some other time this
might be OK.'

'I'm sorry,' she said.

They sat close together for a while in silence. After about
twenty minutes she went up to bed. 'It's raining,' she said. 'I don't
mind you waking me. If you need me.'

When Gus arrived Sam walked back home through the Coppergate Centre. It was a cold night, raining hard, and three of the
doorways were occupied. Geordie wasn't in any of them. When
he got back to the flat Sam checked upstairs first. No change
there. His own flat was dominated by the portrait of the blonde.
The kid hadn't been back. Sam got into bed and slept.

At nine Celia arrived and woke him. Her coat was dripping
wet. 'No luck yesterday,' she said. 'I'll try again today. Wanda's
going to Leeds.'

'From a woman's point of view,' he said, 'tell me about Jane
Deacon. What's she up to?'

'I don't think I can be objective about her,' said Celia. 'She
gives me a bad feeling.'

'Me too,' said Sam. 'But I can't work out what it is. Geordie
said she didn't like him, he had a real downer on her, then she
gives him her dead husband's wardrobe.'

Celia smiled. 'That was for your benefit, Sam, not Geordie's.
It's you she wants. She thought she could get to you through
him.'

'But why, Celia? She's only just buried her husband. Why is
she so keen?'

Celia turned her nose up. 'Perhaps she's got no heart,' she said.

Sam had known people, lots of people, whose marriages had
broken up. All his friends, none of their relationships had lasted.
They would come to him and say, 'It would have been better if

183

he/she had died. It wouldn't have been such a betrayal.' They didn't know what they were talking about. A year later they'd come back and say, 'It was all for the best really.'

Dying like that, without giving him the chance to say goodbye, meant that she never died. She didn't live, and she didn't die. She was always there, somewhere near the edge of his consciousness; if he gave her the chance, she would come at him in a kaleidoscope of snapshots, send his mind reeling into a scream.

You learn some things. He could drink Geordie and Donna into a tiny recess in the back of his mind. Too fuckin' right, he could. Just slip down to the shops, buy a couple a bottles. Easy.

But he wouldn't do it.

About five in the evening the rain stopped. A little after that Wanda pushed the door open and stood in the frame. 'I've brought someone to see you,' she said. She stood to one side and Barney walked in. He came across the room and nuzzled against Sam's leg.

Geordie appeared in the doorway looking very small. He had the leather jacket on and that stupid little hat. Sam pushed himself out of the chair and took a step towards him. The kid walked forward too and they came face to face in the middle of the room.

'The wad,' said Geordie with a quiet voice. 'The money, I've still got it.' He moved his hand towards the inside pocket of the leather jacket, but Sam intercepted it. He held Geordie by the wrist for a moment, then put his arms around him, crushing him to his chest.

'Don't say anything about it,' he said.

Geordie put his arms around Sam's back and they stood together for a while, Sam's head buried in Geordie's neck and Geordie's face on Sam's shoulder. When they came apart Sam held him at arm's length, looked at his funny little white face.

Geordie moved towards his pocket again. 'I've got the money, Sam,' he said.

Sam took his wrist. 'I don't know anything about that,' he said. 'I'm going for a walk now. When I come back I'm gonna check

184

my money in the bedroom. See if it's still there.' He looked towards the door. 'What happened to Wanda?'

'Dunno,' said Geordie. 'Must've gone home. You won't be long?'

'Five minutes. Put the kettle on, make yourself a drink. It'll warm you up.'

Chapter 47

It was raining in Leeds as well, not as heavily, but coming down all the same. Jean Granger finished listening to the voice of her guru and began sorting through a heap of dusty tapes, most of which had not been played for years. Some still had the outer cases, but most of those were broken, and many didn't have outer cases or labels. Impossible to tell what they were. One day she'd sort them all, put labels on them, get new cases and put them in alphabetical order in the cupboard. Not today, though.

What was in her head for some reason was Leonard Cohen's *Suzanne*, but she couldn't find it and made do with *Famous Blue Raincoat* instead. *Suzanne* would be there somewhere, probably one of the ones without a label. Still, she thought, when the sound came from the loudspeakers, it wasn't necessarily *Suzanne* she wanted, it was the sound of his voice. She hadn't heard it for years.

Bob told her that someone at work had said that Leonard Cohen was still alive and had made a new album. Jean hadn't thought about Leonard Cohen for years, but when she was very young she had thought that he was the ideal man. Listening to him now, she wondered if anybody could ever be that young.

She rolled a little joint, well packed, and settled down on a cushion on the floor. Later she would do something about the house, meditate a little, then cook something in time for Bob getting home from work. Now she needed to relax.

Someone in the communal house used to play this kind of music. Jean couldn't remember who it was, one of the men, either Terry Deacon or Steve Bright. It was hard to think that they were both dead. Murdered. It was Steve, he used to play Leonard Cohen and Neil Young records. Terry played all classical stuff, and some things that were very old, claviers and lutes. During their brief affair Terry had played lute music when they made love, he used to make a joke about it, plucking and fuckin'. Jean smiled. He'd be doing neither any more. She wondered if he'd used the same joke with Jane, plucking and fuckin'. Probably used it with all the girls.

Jean had been a virgin when she went to the communal house but had ended up sleeping with everyone. She wore green stockings, and when Steve played that Leonard Cohen song, she couldn't remember what it was called now, when it got to that line everyone would look at Jean and laugh. It was an easy time, full of laughter and tears. Feelings, everyone had feelings, lots of them. Feelings splashing about everywhere. Every time you turned around there was another one.

Graham she hadn't slept with, of course, and thank God for that if he was a mass-murderer. But she had made a play for him one time when she'd had the best part of a bottle of wine. Did she pass out? She couldn't remember what had happened. She would have slept with him if he'd wanted, it seemed important at the time that she slept with everyone in the house, all the men. It was a community. It was her contribution.

Since then she hadn't slept with anyone but Bob. The thought of sleeping with someone else had never occurred to her. Strange, though, to move from 100 per cent emotional promiscuity to total monogamy overnight. Or maybe not so strange at all. You did what you could do. None of it was about sex really, the promiscuity or the monogamy. It was about living in the moment,

186

identifying yourself within the swirling spaces of the cosmos and being that, whatever *that* happened to be at the given moment. Graham East, her life with Bob, green stockings, plucking and fuckin', it was all the same thing.

Jean rolled another one. Maybe she'd get the house together tomorrow. Just one more little spliff before meditation. Good old Leonard still croaking away there, maybe he'd been a frog in his last incarnation. *Jane, came by with a lock of your hair* . . . He wasn't a frog now, but he was just as misunderstood, maybe even more so.

Jean didn't know Frances Golding, had never met her, so she didn't know who it was at the door, the woman with the strange hat. She got it right, though, she realized after she let Frances in, she was Graham's ex-girlfriend. 'Oh,' she said. 'It's uncanny, I mean I was just thinking about Graham and there's this knock on the door and it's you.'

'That's right,' said Frances.

'When that happens,' said Jean, 'you just know how everything's connected.' She looked at Frances and she knew it was the strange hat that gave her the good feeling. Anybody who wore a hat like that just had to be all right. I mean, what a hat, perched on her head like that. Good Christ, *please*, give me a camera.

'I'm a bit zonked,' she told Frances. 'You know how it is?'

Frances said she knew. 'But you said you were thinking about Graham,' she said. 'What were you thinking?'

'I was reminiscing, really. But thinking as well how everything is connected. It was to do with this tape – you know this song?'

Frances shook her head, funny little hat going from side to side. Jean almost asked if she could try it, see if it fitted, what it looked like on her. But then she forgot to ask.

'The tape?' Frances prompted her.

'Oh, yeah, we used to play this, well, not this exactly, but another one of his, and it brought everything back, Graham, the others, the way we were then. I was thinking about all that and then there's a knock on the door. You see what I mean? I was connected with Graham, and you were connected with Graham, but we didn't know each other, and then there's this knock on the door. It's like everything's working together. Sometimes it seems like it isn't, but it really is, only we can't see it. Do you want a cup of tea?'

Frances smiled.

'I know what you're smiling at,' said Jean. 'I know I'm a bit disjointed. But do you get the gist of it?'

'Completely.'

'I knew you would. As soon as you came in the door, even before that, when I *opened* the door, I could feel you would understand. It's like when Barry says about positive vibrations, you can actually feel them coming from some people. It's like, almost, well, don't get me wrong, but like I conjured you up. Like we conjured each other up. You're necessary to my development and I'm necessary to yours. It's sometimes impossible to separate things.'

'You're crazy,' Frances told her.

'That's what Bob says,' said Jean. 'The whole universe is crazy, it's like crazy paving – you look at it, all these odd bits of stone, and you can't think how it would all fit together, but it does, in the end it all fits together. It's wonderful.'

Frances began opening her bag. 'Oh, a handbag,' said Jean. 'It's lovely. I used to have a bag like that, years ago. I sometimes think now, whatever happened to that bag? It was so useful, you know, you can get everything in a bag like that, any time you need something you know it's in your bag. And it goes with your hat as well. Oh, that's what I was going to say before, can I try it on?'

'Try it?' said Frances, still fumbling about in the bag.

'Your hat? Only if you don't mind. It's years since I had a hat.'

Frances took the hat off and passed it over to Jean. 'It's new,' she said. 'I haven't had it long.'

'I'll be ever so careful.' Jean looked at it for a while, little strip of animal skin going all the way round. Not real skin, of course, some ridiculous kind of synthetic. She felt Frances push herself

188

out of the chair on the other side of the room and come over to her. It was when she put the hat on her head that she felt a pain in her face. Her first thought was that it was a hat pin she hadn't noticed, could have been that because there was blood dripping from her face on to her hands. Then she thought something had fallen on her. It was a terrible pain and the blood, not just dripping, gushing. While she was still confused about what had happened, beginning to think maybe she needed help with this, there was another pain in her neck and she looked up and saw Frances with the big knife in her hand. Frances smiling like it was all right really.

It must have been the knife fell on her, but from where? Jean had never seen the knife before, it must be Frances's knife. And she watched as Frances brought the knife down again, below her neck this time, into her chest, between the throat and her breasts. And again, and again, and Jean watched her. Frances was saying something which didn't make sense, something about a hat, and all the time she was saying it the knife kept coming down into Jean, cutting her, opening her up, and there was blood on the cushion and the carpet, and the more Frances spoke the more Jean couldn't understand what was happening or even sit up anymore. She fell forward, off the cushion, her face on the carpet in the blood, and now Frances was stabbing her in the back, and Jean knew she couldn't do anything about it. She suddenly heard Leonard Cohen again, but didn't recognize the song.

There was no fight in her. She relaxed and listened to the way her lungs were trying to cope, the breathing tortuous, like nothing she had ever experienced before. The pain in her back ebbed away and she closed her eyes, not knowing why, but knowing with absolute certainty that the moment had come.

Frances was sat astride the body. She looked around for her hat and picked it up off the floor. A few specks of blood on it. She rubbed the hat on the dead woman's skirt and looked at it again. Good as new. She put it on her head.

189

She got off the body and walked over to the chair, sat down. Her knife was still sticking out of the woman's back. Frances smiled, thinking it was a silly place to leave it, pushed herself out of the chair and got the knife. She wiped that on Jean Blackburn's skirt as well, and put it back in her handbag.

Now all she had to do was wait for the husband to come back, kill two birds with one stone, as Graham had said.

She eased herself back in the chair, closed her eyes, it would be some time until he returned from work, maybe five, six o clock. Frances would be ready.

The tape came to an end and switched itself off. Frances was glad to hear it, she wouldn't have known how to switch it off herself, and wouldn't have touched it anyway, she wouldn't touch anything in the house. She didn't know who it was on the tape, she only knew he couldn't sing. Either that or he had a throat infection.

Chapter 48

Sam dropped Geordie at Celia's house and went round to see Wanda. In jeans again, the girls playing upstairs, but coming tumbling down when they heard Sam arrive. Kelly said 'Oh, goody, picnic,' when she saw who it was.

Samantha, older and wiser, told her, 'We don't *always* have a picnic when he comes.' But then looked at Wanda to see if she was right.

Wanda shrugged her shoulders. 'Why not?' she said. 'Sam might like a picnic. But we'll have it on the kitchen table.'

Kelly turned her nose up at Samantha.

'I came to say thanks,' Sam said.

'I didn't hang around,' Wanda said, taking biscuits from a cupboard, juice from the fridge. 'Thought you'd rather be on your own.'

'Yeah. You're worked out. But I owe you a lot. I'm grateful.'

'You don't owe me anything.' She took plates from the draining board and set them on the table.

'I'll get the cups,' Samantha said.

'OK.' Wanda clapped her hands. 'All ready.' Then to Sam, 'You do drink juice?'

'I tried it once before,' he said, sitting down at the table.

Wanda poured juice from a large glass jug and the girls dug into the biscuits. 'You just help yourself,' Samantha explained. 'You like picnics?'

'Especially when they're unexpected,' said Sam.

'How is he?' Wanda asked. She wore a white shirt with a blue cotton jacket to match her jeans.

'He seems fine,' said Sam. 'We talked long into the night. I think he'll make it.'

'He was on Leeds station,' said Wanda. 'Sat on a bench looking lost, staring into space.'

Sam smiled. 'He told me. Thinking of running to London.'

'Yes,' said Wanda. 'I don't know what he'd have done if I hadn't found him. He couldn't make up his mind whether to stay or go. Every time I asked him a question he asked Barney what *he* thought.'

'Did you look for long?'

'Nearly all day. It was a new experience for me. Asking all the homeless people if they'd seen him, talking to groups of teenagers. The station was my last resort. If he hadn't been there, I'd have come home. God, he was pathetic, Sam. Sat on this bench with Barney on his knee. I thought he'd run when he saw me, but he just sat there, and when I got to him he looked up and said, "Hello, Wanda," as if nothing had happened. Then he took the money out of his pocket and said, "Can you give this back to Sam?" I said that you didn't care about the money, that you wanted him back, and then I spent maybe half an hour trying to convince him.'

'And you did.'

'Yeah. He was terrified on the way back. Once or twice I slowed down, thought he was going to jump out of the car. But he managed it.'

'Thank God,' said Sam. 'I really appreciate it. You taking the time.'

She smiled, stroked Kelly's hair. 'He wanted to put the money back, you know. What happened was he took the money, then changed his mind and put it back. Then later on he thought you'd notice that the money had been touched and give him a row, so he took it again and walked out.'

'I shouldn't have kept it there,' said Sam. 'Too much of a temptation.'

'It was partly your fault,' Wanda said. 'What're you going to do with the money now?'

'I've already given it to Celia.'

'He's confused about finances altogether, though,' Wanda said. 'He feels like a charity case.'

Sam nodded. 'What can I do about that? He's not a charity case. He can earn his keep.'

'You're doing something wrong,' said Wanda. 'He sees you giving him money, then you buy him clothes, groceries. He can't see how he's contributing to it.'

'It's really not like that,' said Sam. 'OK I've loaned him some money up front to get started, but it's all coming out of his wages.'

'Maybe it would be better if Celia paid him his wages, then he paid you something off what he owes you?'

'I could try it,' said Sam. 'Don't know what Celia will think.'

'It was her idea.'

'Jesus, you two been talking again?'

'Just comparing notes.'

'You must think I'm a hopeless case.'

Wanda shook her head. 'We thought you look like a man

who's trying hard. Nobody gets it right all the time. But seeing you yesterday, I mean, you were a bit low.'

'The old Achilles' heel,' Sam told her. 'Always plays up when it rains.'

Wanda shook her head. 'More juice?' she asked.

Kelly stood on her chair. 'I'll get it,' she said, reaching for the juice, missing the handle and pushing the jug over towards Sam.

He saw it coming, knew he was too far away to stop the jug falling over. He saw about two pints of red juice hit the table on its way to him. He tried to push the chair back hut it tipped on its back legs. The chair began to go over backwards fast, taking Sam with it. But it didn't go as fast as the juice which jumped from the table and hit him in the groin. The two girls both screamed, Wanda said something like, 'Oh, my God,' and Sam didn't have time to say anything before the chair took him over and landed him on his back on the floor.

After that it was very quiet. Sam lifted his head and felt the top of his trousers. They were very wet. He put his head back down. Wet was the wrong word. His trousers were sodden. Wanda, Samantha, and Kelly were all stood above him, staring down. It was Kelly who laughed first, then Samantha.

Wanda knelt and put her hand on his chest. She was also laughing now. 'Are you all right?' she said.

Sam nodded and smiled up at her. 'But you know what?' he said. 'I just lost all my picnic spirit.'

Wanda insisted on washing his trousers and pants. She could spin them dry, but it was going to take an hour longer than he expected. He rang Celia and told her he wouldn't be able to collect Geordie. Geordie said he'd walk home and meet up with Sam at the flat.

He got in Wanda's bath and soaked for a while. She came in and scrubbed his back, which made it all seem worthwhile, but was called away too soon to a toddler crisis in another part of the house. Sam couldn't remember a time, ever, when someone had

193

scrubbed his back. He'd shared a bath sometimes with Donna in Islington, but it was a bathroom used by the whole house, three other flats, and after you'd been in there you always came out feeling like you needed a bath. Brenda locked the door when she was in the bath. God knows why. She was never shy about taking her clothes off.

Sam, with a towel around his waist, did a wooden jigsaw puzzle of Mrs Tiggy-Winkle with Kelly and Samantha. Twenty-eight pieces. Was a real sweat, but they managed it.

Chapter 49

When he got back home, parked the Volvo, Gus came round the corner. Sam waited for him outside the house. 'You look almost human,' Gus said.

'Just had my pants pressed.'

'I heard he came back,' said Gus.

'He's inside, I hope,' said Sam. 'How'd you get on yesterday?'

'I found the girl,' Gus told him. 'Haven't seen her yet, but I know where she is.'

'The schoolgirl?'

'Talked to all her friends. If they knew anything, they weren't talking. But her boyfriend's mate, he knew exactly. Didn't even have to pay him.'

Sam opened the door and they went inside. Geordie was sitting in Sam's chair with Barney on his lap. In the other chair was somebody Sam didn't recognize at first, couldn't think who he was. Tall guy, skinny, looking like he'd just failed to survive a road accident. The guy got to his feet when Sam walked in, said something in an American accent Sam couldn't understand. Geordie said, 'This is Bob Blackburn, his wife just got killed.'

'I didn't know what to do,' Blackburn said. He was crying, kept brushing tears from his cheeks. 'I went back home, got your card. I can't stay there.'

Sam heard Gus filling the kettle behind him, putting it on to boil. Sam told Blackburn to sit down. 'It would be better if you start at the beginning,' he said.

Blackburn had his head in his hands. 'I'm sorry,' he said through his fingers. 'Been up all night with the police. God, it was horrible.'

'Gus's making some coffee,' Sam told him. 'Just sit tight. When you're ready you can tell it from the beginning.'

The guy was never going to be ready. When he got the coffee he started. 'I always get home about five-thirty,' he said. 'Just yesterday this guy at work was getting married. We went out for a meal, had some drinks, so I didn't get home till midnight.' He took a sip of the coffee. 'That's good,' he said. 'I was drunk, almost legless. I don't drink normally, you see? I had to hold on to the wall coming down the street. Singing old songs. Jean knew I would be late, and I thought she would be waiting. She'd be stoned, you know, but waiting.

'First thing I noticed was there was no light on. So I thought she'd gone to bed and I started shushing myself, trying to be quiet, not wake her up. I'm feeling about for my key for ages, then when I find it it won't turn in the lock, 'cause the door's not locked. I wonder what's going on now, because Jean wouldn't go to bed without locking the door. I mean, where we live you don't do that. There's young guys walking up and down the street all night, just trying all the doors, see if they get lucky.

'Anyway, I sus the door's not locked and go inside. I'm tiptoeing across the room when my foot gets caught in something, and the next thing is I'm sprawled all over the floor. On the way down I'm grabbing at anything in the dark, and what I grab is the

195

stereo system, which comes down with me, bringing the shelf and tapes and albums with it. Also, I'm not alone on the floor. I think I must have tripped on Jean's skirt, and I'm flat out on top of her.

'I didn't know it was her at that point. I know it's a body of some kind, and I realize it's cold. So I sober up. Just like that. Suddenly I'm no longer drunk, not in my head anyway. I still can't control my body, but in my head I'm as clear as a bell. I shove all the stereo equipment off me and get to the light switch.

'Jesus. I've never seen anything like it.'

Sam thought Blackburn was going to cry again, his bottom lip quivering, but he took in some air and kept going. 'I still hadn't put it all together in my head, you know, that she was dead. I don't know what I thought. I thought something like she'd smoked too many joints and passed out, got cold on the floor. I didn't see the blood at first because of the tapes and records all over the floor. It was only when I got down on my knees, started clearing all the rubbish off her, around her, that I picked up the note. Saw the blood on it, read what it said.'

Gus said, 'Jean Blackburn deserves to die.'

The guy nodded, said, 'Granger. It said Jean *Granger*, her maiden name.' Blackburn broke down now, started weeping again. Sam and the others waited for him to gain some control.

When he looked up again Sam told him, 'You're doing fine. Take it slowly. What happened next?'

'I'm not sure,' said Blackburn. 'I got out of there. I just walked out the door, ran down the street. I was looking for a cop, but you never find them when you want one. At some point I stopped a squad car and they took me back to the house, then all hell broke loose. There were so many police cars you couldn't get down the street. Neighbours coming out, radios going, police surgeon, the whole lot. They took me back to the station and I spent most of the time talking to somebody called Delany, three other guys.

'They thought I'd done it. I was covered in blood, so it must have seemed obvious to them. It was only after they realized she'd been dead about eight hours, which placed me at work with about two dozen witnesses, that they started to lighten up. Christ, they were heavy at first. Trying to pin all the murders on me. I told them, fuck, what're you saying? I've been in Australia. How could I've done them?'

'The police got any leads?' Sam asked.

'Not really. There was a black car parked down the road yesterday afternoon, from about three until six. Parked outside a house, the woman lives there noticed it and wondered whose it was.'

'You don't know what kind of car?' Sam asked.

'She didn't know. Just a black car.'

Sam and Gus exchanged glances.

'When did they let you go?' Sam asked.

'About lunch time. I went to the house, threw some things in the car and came here. I can't stay there.'

'He can use my flat,' said Geordie. 'I'll sleep down here.'

'I'll pay you,' Blackburn said. 'I've got money. I'm not looking for a handout.'

'There's only you and Jane left alive now,' Gus said. 'We're covering her already. If you stay here, you'll be covered as well. Just don't answer the door.'

'D'you wanna look at the flat?' said Geordie.

When Geordie and Blackburn went upstairs Sam said, 'God must have been on his side, Gus.'

'Sounds like it.'

He asked Gus if Frances had been out yesterday.

'I didn't watch her,' Gus said. 'I made some enquiries about the schoolgirl, then I spent the night at the cul-de-sac.'

'So she could have been in Leeds,' Sam said. 'There's no way of knowing.'

'I think we should take a look at that house of hers,' said Gus. 'We've got the keys, let's just do it.'

'It's a bit late in the day,' Sam said, glancing at his watch. 'We won't be back in time to cover Jane.'

'Sam, Geordie can be there on his own for a couple of hours. If we leave now, we'll be back around eight. Tell them to barricade themselves in. It'll be OK.'

Chapter 50

Sam drove out of town past Frances Golding's house to check her car was there. They didn't want to walk in on her in the Leeds house.

When Sam came off the ring road and drove alongside Potter-newton Park, Gus said, 'Are we going the right way?'

'You know a better way?'

'When I followed Frances,' Gus said, 'she didn't come this way.'

'She did when I followed her,' said Sam. 'Wait a minute.' He pulled into a side-street and drove back the way they came. He turned into the street where the Blackburns house was and Gus said, 'Yeah, this is it. This is the way she came. How'd you know that?'

'Just a hunch,' said Sam. 'You see that house there. That's where Jean Blackburn was murdered.'

'So Frances was sussing it out?'

'Maybe,' said Sam. 'I can't think of any other reason she'd drive down here.'

They came around again and parked a couple of blocks from the boarded-up house. One of the keys was stiff but worked and they found themselves in a deserted hallway, dark, and smelling of damp. Sam got his torch out and they made a tour of the ground-floor rooms. There was no furniture, a couple of cardboard boxes in one of the rooms, which Gus opened. They only contained rubbish. They were at the foot of the stairs when Gus said, 'Wait. I thought I heard something.'

Both of them stood still and silent and listened. 'There's nobody here,' Sam said. 'You can smell the place is empty.' Still, they trod the stairs warily. The upper rooms were completely empty. 'No attic, I suppose?' said Sam. There was a hatch, but it only led to a roof space with a water tank.

Back downstairs Sam walked along the walls slowly, shining his torch on the floor. 'What you doing now?' Gus asked.

'Frances brought candles with her,' he said. 'Why would she do that? I thought I might find some wax. Unless there's a cellar.'

Gus found the trapdoor in the middle of the kitchen floor. They got it open and Sam went down the old wooden staircase first, shining his torch before him. 'Careful,' Gus said. 'The place is probably crawling with monsters.'

'Ho, ho, ho,' said Sam.

The cellar was empty apart from a table and chair. 'That's interesting,' said Sam.

Gus shivered. 'There's water on the floor over here,' he said. 'Must be a broken gutter or something.'

'And a stub of candle on the table,' said Sam. 'So this is where she comes. But why?'

'Maybe we're too late,' said Gus. 'He was here but now he's moved out. Gone somewhere else.'

Sam moved the chair back and sat at the table. Shone the torch in front of him on to a brick wall. 'Wait a minute,' he said. He got up from the chair and moved over to the wall. 'This has been knocked down and rebuilt.'

Gus joined him and felt the wall. 'Not too long ago, either. New bricks and cement.'

'You think someone's buried in there?'

'Only one way to find out,' said Gus.

Sam said, 'A drill? At least a hammer and cold chisel.'

'Yeah, come back with some tools.'

'Not tonight, though,' said Sam. 'I don't want to leave Geordie all night. We'll try tomorrow.'

Gus shivered again, then sneezed. 'Can we get out of here?' he said. 'It's so bloody cold.'

On the way back to York Gus said, 'I'll drop you at the cul-de-sac, then I'm gonna call on this schoolgirl. What do I do if she won't go home?'

'You can't force her,' Sam said. 'Get her to ring her mother, see if we can arrange a meeting with her parents. That's as far as we can take it.'

Geordie and Jane were in her loft. Sam let himself into the house with his key and couldn't find anyone. He shouted and couldn't make anyone hear, wondered if he should panic for a while. Then he heard them scrabbling about up there. Geordie came down with an old amplifier and Jane followed with a speaker. 'Look at this!' said Geordie. 'There's a tape deck and a record player and another speaker, stacks of records.'

'We used to use it before Terry bought the new system,' said Jane. 'I thought Geordie might as well have it. It's only stuck up there doing nothing.'

'Hell, Geordie,' said Sam. 'You're getting everything you need.'

Jane climbed back into the loft and passed the rest of the equipment down. Then they carried it down to the first floor and stacked it in the hall.

'We watched the news,' Geordie told him. 'There's a big reward for whoever finds the killer. Five thousand pounds.'

'More than that,' said Jane. 'Terry's brother, Donald, has put up five thousand, but relatives of the other victims are offering more. I think Donald's organized it. About twelve thousand altogether.'

She had lilac leggings on, some kind of short smock with part of a cobweb from the loft on the shoulder, her hair was ruffled from climbing in and out of the loft, and there was a smudge of something on her cheek. It was a change, Sam thought: you

200

looked at her most times, she seemed like nothing had ever touched her.

'Will we get it, Sam?' said Geordie. 'The reward, I mean.'

'Maybe,' said Sam. 'We had a bit of a breakthrough tonight. I think we know where Graham is.'

Jane looked at him. 'But you aren't going to say where.'

'Not yet,' he said. 'Still a couple a things to check out.'

They had coffee in the kitchen, Sam found himself watching her as she moved around. Couldn't work out exactly what was different about her apart from the smudge on her cheek. She kept looking back as well, smiling with that little mouth of hers. She was skinnier than he thought, hardly any breasts, long legs. She'd been so self-contained before, but the last few days she'd come out of herself unloading all the clothes on Geordie, now the stereo system. Maybe that was it, needing to get rid of Deacon's possessions. There she was again, looking at him over her cup. Maybe he should tell her about the smudge. Maybe not, she looked better with it. Not so untouchable.

The situation reminded Sam of a story he'd read by Hemingway, he couldn't remember which one it was, where this couple are each savouring the fact that something is going to happen, but neither of them taking the initiative, waiting for a third character, the happening itself. He glanced at Geordie, who was reading an album cover, wondering if the kid picked up anything at all of what was going on. He didn't appear to, seemed to be completely oblivious of the comic lust going on around him.

She moved differently, too. Slower, trying not to confuse him with any swift movements, languidly, so that he could take in every turn, dwell on it, see how her body could glide, stir, hover, even deviate, with a harmony that, whatever else it did, kept you watching.

But two Sams were watching, there was the old cynical Sam as well, who knew that lust was capricious, and though you had to go with it today, tomorrow it could easily seem like a mistake.

She caught him looking and there was that smile again. The

201

smile that said, 'I know what you're thinking.' And she glanced at Geordie as well, with her eyes, not moving her head at all, so the kid didn't even know he'd been scrutinized, a glance that took only a fraction of a second before her eyes were back on Sam. But the glance away at Geordie said a whole lot more than the constant eye contact. It said, 'Oh, Geordie, we love you, but if you weren't here, we could have a real good time.' And it also said, 'So what? We'll wait a little longer. Let it build up so when it eventually happens we'll be sure to be ready.'

'You've got a smudge on your face,' he said.

She brought her hands up to her face, maybe thinking she could feel it. 'Where? It's so filthy in that loft.'

'Usually is,' he said, going over to her. She let her hands fall to her side and stood with her head up, waiting for him to do it. 'Just there,' he said touching her cheek, high up, just under her left eye. Little electric shock in his finger, and on her face as well, the way she tensed, flickered her eyelashes. 'Stand still.' He rubbed at it with his index finger and thumb, showed her the dirt that transferred itself to him. Jane laughing, embarrassed, glancing at Geordie again, wanting them to be alone. 'There,' he said. 'It's only dust.'

They were very close together now. He could feel the heat from her body, her face flushed a little, not so you'd notice unless you were this close. The tip of her tongue showed through her lips for a second, then withdrew and she swallowed, looking for air. Sam's mouth was dry.

'What's a sonorous finale?' Geordie asked, looking up from the album cover.

Jane smiled, closed her eyes for some reason.

Sam said, 'It's when all hell breaks loose.'

But whatever he'd said would have broken the moment. Jane stepped back, said, 'I think I'll have a bath.' Still stood there a moment, though, not speaking, but saying, 'Wish you could come with me.'

Sam had a quick glimpse of Wanda scrubbing his back. Why baths all of a sudden? A new development in his life?

Jane walked towards the stairs and he followed her with his eyes. She turned around to take a last look as she got to the kitchen door, held on to the door frame with one hand and made something like a wave with the other. Sam smiled and nodded, let her go.

'Jesus, Sam,' said Geordie. 'I got a hard-on jus' watching that.'

'You and me both,' said Sam. 'I thought you was reading?'

'Fuck, I had to do something.'

He leaned over Geordie to see what he was reading. Some kind of classical compilation. 'You like classical music?' he asked.

'I don't know,' Geordie said. 'I like that stuff you play, some of it. The one with the guy wearing a scarf and real fuzzy hair.'

'*Blonde on Blonde*?'

'Yeah. I told Celia I'd write down all the words from it.'

'Jesus,' said Sam. 'You learn all those, you won't need any more.'

'You reckon?'

'Well, maybe a few,' he said.

Chapter 51

She took her top off and stood looking in the bathroom mirror. Still a little smudge on her face, and her hair a mess. She moved back so she could see the rest of her body reflected in the mirror. Kicked her shoes off and pushed down the leggings, her pants inside them.

She turned to the side, see what that looked like. She knew she had a good body, had never had any reason to doubt it. Still, a girl has to be vigilant, check things aren't getting out of proportion. Pity Sam couldn't have come up with her, get a man's opinion. Only he wouldn't have had time to look. They'd both of them be straight at it. She brushed her nipples with the palm of her hand, still hard from the contact downstairs. Felt her body tense again.

She turned completely around to take a look at the back view, did the pinch test on her bottom. It was OK, holding up to the strains of life. Maybe too much fat on the backs of her thighs, high up, creasing a little.

He might come up. He had a bit of a bulge in his trousers down there. She knew he wouldn't come up, with Geordie being there, but it was OK to imagine it, fantasize a little. The trick with Geordie had worked out. If Sam had come in this evening and found her and Geordie in separate rooms, he wouldn't have been half so keen, would have spent the time with Geordie, in fact. But because he thought she was interested in helping Geordie, he had to look at her twice. God, what a simple man, it was almost enough to put you off.

Except for the chemistry, whatever it was called these days, the attraction. That was real enough, simple enough. And just in time as well. The sale of the business would be completed in a few days, maybe a week, and then there would be nothing to keep her in England. She'd be off to the sun. If Sam turned out to be really cute, she might take him with her, at least for a while, as long as he could make her body feel like this.

She ran the bath and while it was filling checked her diaphragm in the wall cabinet, pessaries and contraceptive jelly. Use the whole lot, don't take any chances. Hope he remembers to bring some condoms, if not there's some, where? In her bedside cupboard. She'd taken them from Terry's bedside cupboard some weeks ago, so when he got the urge they wouldn't be able to.

Jane tried the bath water with her toe and got in, letting the water flow over her, warm and easy, lapping away like her thoughts. So, Frances had been at it again. Jean Granger was dead as well. She wondered how Bob was coping with that. He'd been a sensitive kind of soul in the old days. Something like that happening could drive him to a breakdown. Except with Frances still on the loose he might not have time.

Jean had been beautiful in the old days. Good fun, even though she was a complete tart. Christ, the men she'd had. Whoever it was you ended up with, you would always know that Jean had had him first. Strange thing was that it didn't matter, even then. Because Jean didn't have them in a real sense, she just kind of branded them and let them go. Oh, and those ridiculous green stockings, like she was living up to an image in a song.

Still, it had made life interesting, Jean being like that. Shown the men that they were not the only ones who could be promiscuous. And it had made sex altogether an easier option for everyone. Made it less of a burden, less of a necessity, something you could do when you felt like it and then forget it. With Jean around, however many men you slept with, you would never catch up.

If she was still in England, Jane would go to Jean's funeral. Pay her last respects to a woman who had been a formative influence.

And what's this Sam said about knowing where Graham was? Still, if he *thought* he knew, that was something to occupy him. He could follow as many leads about the whereabouts of Graham East as he liked. He'd never find him. And when he'd exhausted himself following up the leads, when he was frustrated beyond measure by it all, why, Jane had a soft spot where he could lay his weary head.

She wrapped herself in a bath robe and walked through to her bedroom. She intended to get dressed and go downstairs, but got into bed instead. Must be Geordie playing music downstairs, sounded like Chopin. something in a minor key, dragged your heart out. Jane wasn't that kind of woman, but *if* she were, knowing Sam wouldn't come up and music like that playing in the distance could be enough to make her weep.

Chapter 52

Geordie told Sam that the music reminded him of his mother and his brother and of people that he hadn't met yet but missed already, and Sam said, yes, he could remember feeling like that when he was much younger, but hadn't had the feeling for a long time.

'It's not what my mother and brother are like really,' Geordie said. 'Really they don't care about me; and they've gone anyway. It's more like they *should* have been.'

Sam listened again to the music. It was wistful, that's all. 'What it does,' he said, 'is make you realize you've got a big hole inside you, an emptiness that'll never be filled.'

'Yeah,' said Geordie. 'And it makes you crawl inside that hole. Turns you inside out.'

'Tears you apart.'

'Crucifies you.'

'It's fuckin' terrible,' Sam said.

'Shall I turn it off?'

'No, I love it.'

Gus arrived just before two, sneezing and shivering. 'What you doing?' Sam said. 'Go back home to bed, we'll stay on here.'

'No,' Gus told him. 'I'm here now. I'll be fine on the couch. Must've got some kind of bug.'

'Did you talk to the schoolgirl?'

'Yeah,' said Gus. 'Real nice kid. And her boyfriend too. She doesn't wanna know about her father. He's been abusing her, knocking her about.'

'Sexually?'

Gus nodded. 'Since she was twelve. The girl reckons he's scared the mother'll find out. There's no way she'll go back home.'

How's she gonna live?'

'The boyfriend's got a job. They don't have much, but I get the feeling they'll make it.'

'Her father gave me two hundred quid,' said Sam. 'I'll give him it back and tell him to go fuck him*self*.'

'Why not give it to the girl?' said Gus. 'I'm sure she could use it.'

'Yeah, good idea. I'll tell him his daughter's holding it for him.'

'He might sue you.'

Sam smiled. 'I don't think he will.'

They left Gus in the house, coughing, spitting, eyes watering, looking smaller than usual, and walked through the night. 'You feel terrible when you look like Gus,' Geordie said. 'I was like that in Liverpool. It was raining and I was wet through all the time. Sleepin' in the rain. Thought I would die.'

'Yeah,' said Sam. 'He should be in bed, really.'

Sam had a series of dreams about Jane, finally woke up in the early morning after a really steamy one, little disappointed to find it wasn't real. In the dream she'd been covered in tattoos, birds and cats chasing each other. Birds chasing cats as well as cats chasing birds. Running all over her body, hiding in the places that were available for hiding.

Maybe you should go into analysis, Sam told himself, get yourself sorted out. Donna had been in analysis with a Jungian therapist when Sam first met her. She kept dreaming she was in a glass coffin. Turned out she was in a family which wanted her to be like them; once she left them she no longer had the dream.

If life was only that simple, Sam said to himself as he got out of bed.

Strange thing was, though, if Jane Deacon were covered in tattoos in reality, he would never have fancied her. Brenda had a

207

tattoo on her hip, which was easy enough to forget. It certainly didn't do anything for her. So, one tattoo he could cope with, two? Even three? But not covered in them, Jesus, that would be a nightmare.

Geordie was already up and playing *Another Side* on the tape deck. He'd put his sleeping bag away and was trying to get Barney to sit in his new basket. The dog didn't want anything to do with it. 'He slept with me all night,' Geordie said. Then, 'Shall we ask Bob Blackburn to come for breakfast?'

'Yeah, good idea,' said Sam. 'He's probably going crazy up there.'

Geordie got eggs and bacon in the pan and went upstairs to tell Bob about the invite. The Folk Singer was somewhere around *midnight's broken toe* when Gus arrived with the kid's stereo equipment. Sam went out with him to help carry, telling Gus he looked wonderful.

'I'll be OK,' Gus said. 'After a sleep.'

'We were gonna take that wall down tonight.'

'I'll be OK,' Gus said, blowing his nose.

Geordie and Blackburn came down the stairs and Geordie started taking pieces of the equipment up to his flat.

'Leave it for now, Geordie,' said Sam. 'The breakfast is turning black.' He asked Gus if he wanted to stay for breakfast, but Gus said sleep was all he wanted and left.

Blackburn sat down with them at the table, said how he was starving but didn't usually eat eggs or bacon and did they have any muesli?

Sam got it for him and sat down to his own breakfast. 'What you gonna do when this is all over?' he asked.

'I won't stay here,' Blackburn said, tucking into the muesli like it was real food. 'I'm going back to Kentucky.'

'Where's that?' said Geordie.

'Kentucky? That's where I come from,' said Blackburn. 'You heard of Missouri, Tennessee? Kentucky's thereabouts. Mississippi river?'

'Long since you've been back?' Sam asked.

'About ten years, but I've got kin there. Make a new start.'

'D'you get Indians there?' asked Geordie.

Blackburn interrupted the voyage of spoon and muesli to his mouth. 'Some,' he said. Some half-breeds. My grand-daddy and great-grand-daddy fought the Cherokees. Iroquois as well, from time to time. But they've mostly gone now.'

Geordie forgot all about eating his breakfast. 'Fuck,' he said. 'Cowboys and *Indians*.'

'OK,' said Sam, taking his empty plate to the sink. 'I'm gonna drop Geordie off at Celia's. You gonna be OK here?'

'I'll be fine,' said Blackburn. 'Maybe I can put this stereo equipment together?'

'No, I want to do it myself,' said Geordie. 'You can help me if you like, this afternoon.'

Sam took him to his English lesson, mentioned on the way that he and Gus would be husy tonight and that Geordie would be by himself with Jane.

'That's OK,' Geordie said. 'Me and her get along fine now.'

When Sam got back to the flat the phone was ringing. 'I'm not gonna make it,' Gus said.

'Don't worry,' Sam told him. 'I can manage by myself.'

'You could also put it off,' said Gus. 'I'll be OK tomorrow. We can do it then. It'll be easier with two of us.'

'See how I feel,' said Sam. 'I'm dying to know what's behind that wall.'

'Dying? You wouldn't be the first.'

Sam laughed.

'Oh, Sam,' said Gus. 'Leave it, man. I want to *be* there.'

'I wouldn't dream of doing it without you,' Sam told him.

Chapter 53

Frances knew something was wrong as soon as she entered the Leeds house. It was the same feeling she had when they broke into her house in York. A sense of violation. But this time much more serious. This was her and *Graham*'s house. This was where they spent their life together. More a shrine than a house.

She knew who it was as well. Sam Turner or one of his henchmen. He would have to be stopped. He would have to be stopped very soon. Impossible to tell how he got in, there were no broken windows this time, all the boarding was intact. But he *had* been here, she was certain of it.

The feeling grew stronger as she opened the trapdoor and descended into the cellar. He'd been down here as well. Frances lit the candle and looked around the cellar. A small room, perhaps five paces square. It didn't look as though anything had been touched. Maybe she was wrong? Her feelings were usually right, but perhaps the sense of violation she had felt in the upper rooms had spread down here.

When she sat on the chair, however, all doubt vanished. The chair had been moved. He had actually sat here. In this spot. The chair had been moved back a couple of inches, but enough so that Frances had to lean forward to sit comfortably at the table. Sam Turner, with his longer legs, would manage OK at this distance. But Frances could not. She moved the chair forward.

Graham said she was right. He had been here. He hadn't found anything, of course, there was nothing to find. But he had been here, and there was the possibility that he would return. He might have noticed something about the new wall, Graham wasn't sure about that. But they couldn't take any chances. If he had noticed something about the wall, and came back, tried to knock it down, then all would be lost.

It was up to Frances to stop him. Graham would have liked to deal with Sam Turner himself, but he was sorry to say Frances would have to do it. 'Don't wait too long,' Graham said. 'Be careful. Watch the man, make good plans. But do it soon. Within the next few days.'

'I will,' Frances said. Like a marriage vow, that . . . 'I will.'

She felt Graham smile. But he was serious as well. Very serious. 'Everything else must stop,' he said. She wasn't to worry about Bob Blackburn or anyone else. Concentrate solely on stopping this stupid detective. Stop him with the knife.

Graham had chosen the knife for the other killings as well. It is a pure tool, he had said. 'An extension of the claw and the tooth. The angels smile on the use of a knife when it is for defensive purposes.'

Turner was like the others. He was interfering in destiny, and that was forbidden by natural law. 'He has to be stopped, Frances. Whatever else happens, this man has to be stopped.'

Graham was not often this insistent, but when he was, you had to listen. He thought for both of them, after all. Graham was not only his own master, he was the master of their joint destiny.

Frances would do it anyway, Even if Graham had not brought it up at all, she would still have done it. She didn't like Sam Turner. He was not a nice man, he had no manners. He had been in the way right from the first time she saw him. It had been a mistake to talk to him at all. She should have shunned him from the beginning. Who did he think he was, coming into her house, asking her questions? He wasn't the police. He had no authority whatsoever. She didn't have to humour him.

What she had to do was watch. When the time was right, as soon as the time was right, she would strike. It would be a pleasure.

Rid the world of a piece of scum. For who would miss him?

No one. Even the police inspector would be happy to see him go. That was another thing. Interfering in legitimate police work. The man's conceit was enormous. Setting himself up in opposition to the police, interfering in their already difficult task. No wonder the police couldn't do their work properly. People like this Turner person getting under their feet all the time. Ordinary decent people being mugged in the street, having their houses broken into, their cars stolen. Irish and Arab terrorists running around the country planting bombs in department stores, blowing up planes over Scotland.

All these things the police had to deal with. And they could deal with them, very ably, thank you very much, if the kind of scum represented by Sam Turner would only give them a chance.

'Well,' said Frances. 'It doesn't seem as though any one else is going to deal with it. And it certainly needs dealing with.' Frances would do it herself. Strike a blow for ordinary human decency. Get Sam Turner.

On the way home in the car Graham was still speaking to Frances. She mustn't get herself too worked up, he said. She mustn't forget their primary plan. They hadn't yet disposed of everybody from the community house. Remember, Frances, they all have to die now or we shall have to face them in the next incarnation.

That is the most important thing. Don't forget the most important thing.

Frances agreed with him. She told him so. But what Graham didn't realize was that Sam Turner could stop them finishing that task. It was better to concentrate on him, then go back to the original plan. She didn't tell Graham this, it was no use arguing with him when his mind was made up. He could be very stubborn, could Graham. Very stubborn indeed.

When Sam Turner was dead, then Graham would see that she had been right. He would forgive her. She'd give him one of her big, big smiles, and he wouldn't be able to resist.

212

Chapter 54

Sam told Geordie that Gus was too ill to do the job this evening.

'That means you'll be coming to Jane's house with me?'

'Yes,' said Sam. 'But you'll have to go there yourself tomorrow.'

'OK, boss. Can I have the afternoon off to fix up the stereo?'

'Yeah,' said Sam. 'That's fine. I'm gonna keep an eye on Frances's house. See what she's up to.'

Geordie went upstairs and Sam cut himself a slice of bread. He'd have a cup of coffee and then go to work.

The telephone rang and when he picked it up Jane said, 'How you doing?'

'That's my line,' said Sam. 'People always picking up on what I say. How're you doing?'

'I want to see you,' she said.

'I'm coming tonight,' he said. 'I'll see you then.'

'Well, what I thought was, maybe you could come alone?'

Sam smiled into the mouthpiece. 'Without Geordie?'

'Yes.'

'Or Barney?'

She laughed down the line. 'You're getting the idea.'

'Why would I want to do that?' he said.

'You're playing with me, Sam.'

'No,' he said. 'I just want to get it straight. Need to know if I should wear something special. People have different tastes.'

'Casual dress,' she said. 'Not too much.'

'You're playing with me, Jane.'

'Hoping to,' she said. 'Depends on you.'

'Will you be wearing a casual dress?'

'Oh, very,' she said. 'Something soft and flowing.'

'Anything else?'

'What? Underneath you mean?' Then she made a sound like catching her breath.

'I didn't hear.'

'I said I won't be wearing anything underneath.'

'Think I'll leave Geordie at home,' Sam told her. 'Could be dangerous at your place.'

'What about you?' she asked. 'Underneath?'

'When in Rome,' Sam said.

She laughed. 'There were times I thought we'd never get round to it.'

'Yeah,' said Sam. 'When it's time it's time. But tell me something. Do you have any tattoos?'

'No,' she said. 'I can't provide you with that.'

'Good,' he said. 'I had a kind of nightmare about it.'

'Did you dream about me?'

'I don't want to make you conceited.'

'But you *do* want to make me?'

'Christ,' he said. 'She talks dirty as well.'

Geordie came back into the flat, started opening a can of dog food.

'I don't mind playing a part,' she said.

'I've got to go,' Sam said. 'We can discuss the casting later.' He replaced the handset.

'Who was that?' said Geordie.

'Look,' Sam said. 'Something's come up. About tonight. You wanna have the night off?'

'Could do,' said Geordie. 'Who was on the phone?'

'Only I thought, you know, if you're working alone tomorrow night, maybe you could take tonight off, relax a little. Play with your new stereo.'

'It was the blonde,' Geordie said. 'You hear that, Barney?'

'On the phone?' said Sam. 'Yeah, it was Jane Deacon. Nothing important.'

'You gonna have sex with her?' Geordie asked.

'Hell, Geordie, yes. I'm going to have sex with her. Is that all right? OK by you? You don't have any objections?'

'Fine by me,' said Geordie, looking up at him. 'D'you mind if I watch?'

'Christ,' Sam said. 'The kid's being lewd.'

'Lood?' said Geordie, going out the door, back to the upstairs flat. 'How do you spell it?'

Chapter 55

'There's no instructions with it?' Bob Blackburn asked.

'Structions?'

'Yeah, tell you how to put it together, what fits where?'

'No. This is what we've got. She didn't say anything about structions.'

'OK, we can try,' Blackburn said. They laid out the pieces of equipment on the floor of Geordie's flat. Speakers connected OK, but there seemed to be a lead missing between the tape deck and amplifier.

'Does that mean it won't work?' said Geordie.

'You need a DIN plug to connect them together,' Blackburn told him. 'You can probably get one in the town.'

'OK,' said Geordie, 'I'll go get one.' He took Barney with him, walked into the town and bought what he needed. When he got back Blackburn had set all the equipment up apart from the missing lead. He fixed that and Geordie put Sam's copy of *Blonde on Blonde* in the tape deck. It worked fine and Geordie turned it up good and loud.

'There's part of it I wanna write down for Sam,' Geordie said.

'Called *Jus' Like a Woman*, part of that. Kinda like a present for him.'

Blackburn showed him how to fast-forward and rewind the tape, and he sat with a pencil and paper and played the end of the song over and over again, from time to time scratching his head as he worked out the spelling of a word. When he'd finished he signed it 'Geordie' and took it downstairs, put it on Sam's pillow.

'You know about sex?' he asked Blackburn.

'How do you mean?'

'For instance,' Geordie said. 'if two blokes both love the same woman, only one of them can have her, right?'

'Yeah. Usually,' Blackburn said. 'That's how we do it in the West. Some cultures handle it differently.'

'What? Like sharing?'

'Yeah. There are polygamous tribes, cultures.'

'I don't understand polywords,' Geordie told him. 'Like, if it was me and you, and there was this woman we was both in love with, but she liked me, what would you think?'

'Are we friends, I mean in this hypothetical situation?'

'Hypo*what*?'

'Hypothetical. Me and you and this woman, that situation doesn't exist, you're just making it up. That's not real, it's hypothetical.'

'Yeah,' said Geordie, unsure. 'We're friends.'

'Then I'd talk to you about it,' Blackburn said. 'Say what I thought, see if I could get you to stand down. Usually a friendship can't stand that kind of situation. We'd probably end up fighting.'

'And the one wins gets the woman?'

'Not necessarily. Maybe neither of them ends up with the woman. It'd be up to her.'

'Jesus,' said Geordie. 'So we fight, we're not friends any more, and the woman goes off with someone else?'

Blackburn laughed. 'Maybe,' he said. 'It wouldn't be the first time.'

216

'OK,' Geordie said, 'I've got another one for you. Same two guys and the same woman, but the woman definitely likes only one of them and they have sex. They're really into each other. The other guy, when he sees them together, he wishes it was him. You with me?'

Blackburn nodded.

'Well, the guy who doesn't have the woman, he doesn't want to fight, 'cause he wants to stay friends with the first guy. So what should he do?'

'Is this a real situation?'

'No,' Geordie said. 'It's hypo-whatsit. Jus' something I've been thinking about.'

'Can I come at it from a different angle?' Blackburn said. 'Because when you're attracted to someone, it's usually lust, or it could be love. But whatever it is, it's a kind of energy. Makes you feel randy, or it might make you cry, whatever, because it sets up some kind of energy, it makes you feel different. You think about that woman all the time, want to be with her. Am I on the right track?'

'Yeah,' said Geordie. 'But she's into the other guy.'

'I'm coming to that. What you can do is turn the lust, turn the sexual thing into friendship. You just say to yourself, if I carry on like I'm doing at the moment, I'm going to cause misery. So I'll stop doing it and make this woman a friend.'

'What? You just say it and it happens?'

'It might be hard,' Blackburn said. 'Take a long time. But you draw on will-power. Make it work.'

'Jesus,' said Geordie. 'I'll try that.'

'Thought you said it was hypothetical.'

'It is,' said Geordie. 'I mean I'll try it *if* it ever happens to me.'

'Then there's sublimation,' Blackburn said.

'Sublim- Jesus! I never heard anyone talk like you.'

'That's when you take this energy I mentioned, this sexual energy, and instead of using it for sex, you use it for something else.'

217

'Like learning words, say, or being a detective?'

'Yeah, could be anything. You might be a doctor, say, and because you choose to be celibate, you use the sexual energy on your work, then you might discover a cure for AIDS, something like that.'

'Celibate?'

'It means you don't have sex.'

'Never?'

'That's right. Some people choose to be celibate.'

'Christ,' said Geordie. 'Talking to you, all these words, same with Sam and Celia, I realize I don't know fuck.'

Chapter 56

Frances parked at the end of the street. She could see Sam Turner's house quite clearly. There didn't seem to be anyone in, but she sat there for an hour anyway, waiting. Get some idea about the place.

Then the kid came out, a kid in a baseball cap. Frances nearly smiled. That's exactly what the policeman had said. A kid in a baseball cap. So Sam Turner *had* been at the bottom of it. He hadn't had the guts to do it himself, got a child to do it instead. That was typical of him, his sort.

Frances wondered if Sam Turner was alone in the house now. She was itching to get it over with, just go in there and kill him. But she had to be sure.

Some time later the kid in the baseball cap came back, knocked on the door. Frances only caught a glimpse of the figure who opened the door. It wasn't Sam Turner, someone much taller than him. Someone at least as tall as Bob Blackburn.

Yes, why not? It probably was Bob Blackburn. So, they were all here together, Turner and the kid in the baseball cap, and Bob Blackburn. If it was possible to get in there, Frances could finish the job altogether. Except she wouldn't stand a chance with three of them. She'd have to wait, make sure only one of them was in there, then go in. She hoped it was Sam Turner. She'd really like to get him first.

Frances sat in the car the rest of the afternoon, but no one else came out of the house, no one else went in. Towards early evening she saw Sam Turner come down the street, hands in his pockets. That kind of swagger he had. Just to watch him made Frances angry.

He took a key out of his pocket and let himself in.

Frances thought maybe she could set fire to the house, burn them all. But it was only speculation. She knew what she would have to do. Knew she would have to be patient. And she knew she could be patient, too. Wait for ever if necessary, if that's what it took to do the right thing.

She started the car and drove home. She *could* wait for ever, but she was getting weary of it all now. She wanted it to be finished so that she could rejoin Graham. So that they could be together again. His voice was some comfort, but it wasn't enough. She wanted to be *with* him.

She went to bed early, got down under the covers but didn't go right to sleep. All the time she had this picture of Sam Turner in front of her. In her imagination she stabbed him with the knife, but he didn't bleed. The knife went in and came out again, but it didn't leave a mark. He was just as sound after the stabbing as before.

Frances tried harder, taking the knife across his throat, twisting it, then trying to decapitate him, cut him into pieces. None of it worked. He just stood there with his hands in his pockets, a little smile on his face, mocking her.

In the kitchen she boiled a pan of milk, made herself a drink with honey, and took it back to bed with her. Had she been dreaming? She couldn't remember if she had been asleep or not. Or was this terrible vision of Sam Turner some kind of sign?

She tried to ask Graham about it, but he wasn't talking. Frances sipped the drink but the vision of Sam Turner kept coming back. Every time she tried to kill him he smiled.

None of the others had been like this. They hadn't given her any trouble at all. Most of them had just laid down and died. Been so surprised they hadn't even had time to say anything.

Frances didn't sleep all night. She got out of bed twice more, even tried making herself some toast. But nothing worked. In the morning light she was still awake. Exhausted, and unable to sleep.

Chapter 57

Sam walked to Jane's house. It was a heavy night and there were few people on the streets. One of those nights when your head feels like it might burst. He knew it was going to happen now and thought it strange that it should be the night he intended to dig up Graham East. Because that's whose body it would be in the cellar. Frances was the killer and the body would provide the proof.

What he had not been able to figure was why Delany had not arrested her already. Surely the police were not that dumb? He had talked it over on the telephone with Clive Desmond, the Calendar reporter, and it turned out that she had been a main suspect at one time, as had Sam himself, but they had discounted Frances because she didn't have a passport.

What had probably happened was that Graham had killed the women in New Zealand and Sweden, then he had died or Frances had killed him, and she'd taken over the task. That would explain it. It was neat. It was worth twelve grand.

So why didn't it feel like it was worth twelve grand? When you're walking through the town to sleep with Jane Deacon twelve grand doesn't seem like much. *She's* coming out of it with a stretch of white beach and a bikini for life, spelling out something in the region of a million quid if you count the insurance money. She wears black for a couple a days but doesn't grieve, she lies, and she comes on at Sam like he doesn't remember a woman coming on, ever.

That's why he doesn't tell her anything. Somehow she's got to be implicated. She's clever, and even without the information Sam could give her she remains in control. What's she gonna be like if she ever feels she doesn't have control?

Don't tell her anything yet, Sam told himself. First make sure it's Graham East in the cellar. Don't give her anything until then. Ride it out. Don't make puns.

He let himself into the house and did his usual checks before she came home from work. She was all smiles. 'I've got the money,' she said. 'Final transfer went through today.'

'So when do you go?'

'A few days,' she said. 'I've got to pack, make arrangements about the house. Then I'll be off.'

'You know where?'

'Spain first. I've got some friends there, well, acquaintances really. Then Italy.' She shrugged her shoulders. 'Just travel for a while. I'll think about it tomorrow.'

'Mañana?'

'Yes.' She gave him the look, said, 'I'm going to have a bath, get changed.'

She doesn't mention it, Sam thought. She knows exactly how to do it. Pretend like it's an ordinary evening. Not say a word. No words necessary when it's inevitable. Sam sat down at the kitchen table, thought he might kill for a small scotch.

★

She lingered in the bath longer than usual, wondering if he'd come up while she was still in there. Open the door and walk over, pull her out of the tub through the bubbles. Do it hard. She didn't really want that, wanted it to last longer. If she was honest, she wanted both, wanted more than both. A surprise of any kind would be nice.

He didn't come. She dried herself and put a white dress on, knee-length, silly little puff sleeves, the kind of thing men like. She squatted to fix the diaphragm and had the same thought again, that he would come in now, catch her squatting on the floor. She stayed down there a few moments longer than necessary, but didn't hear his footstep on the stair.

He was going to make her go downstairs and tell him, 'I'm ready.' Jane thought she had made the running up till now, it would be nice for him to take over. But maybe he needed to be led all the way. Whatever, she was committed to it now.

He came in when she was brushing her teeth.

Sam waited until it was a question of Jane Deacon or her drinks cabinet. He walked up the stairs and opened the bathroom door. She was stood over the wash-basin wearing something loose and white. Bare legs and feet. As he walked over to her she said something through her toothbrush, but he couldn't make out what it was. He stood close behind her, feeling the warmth of her through the stuff of her dress. Some kind of perfume, or maybe it was soap. He didn't know. She carried on brushing as he put his hands on her hips.

The motion of the toothbrush carried right down so that her butt and thighs moved as well, tight now against his own stir-ring body. He ran his hands down over her hips and then up again beneath her arms. There was nothing under the dress but her.

He took her by the hips again and pulled her towards him. She responded by arching her back, bringing her head close to him and turning it a little, brushing his face with her wet lips. Sam ran

222

his lips along the line of her neck, took a bite of skin between his teeth, dropped it and carried on.

When his hands brushed her breasts she arched a little more and took a quick intake of breath. But his hands were already elsewhere, running down her sides, over her belly and thighs. He pushed her shoulders gently forward and she leaned down over the basin. There was a clink as the toothbrush hit the porcelain and she gave up the idea of a final rinse. She gripped the sides of the bowl and pushed her butt into him, Sam's erection fitting in there, hard now, still through both sets of clothes. Sam ran his hands up her thighs and eased the cheeks open a little. Her head went forward and there was the faintest sigh. Now for a moment she seemed to move every muscle in her body, slowly, like a stretching yawn, though there was nothing tired about it.

He moved his hands forward now, to her breasts, cupping one in each hand, lightly brushing the hard nipples with his thumbs. There was that sigh again and Jane moved her position, placing her arms over the basin and laying her head on them. Her butt came back again, moving even closer into him.

Sam pulled her skirt now, high up to her waist, and she spread her legs in anticipation of his touch. He backed away a little, ran one hand down over her hip while the other travelled up her thigh, both of them coming together between her thighs, just short. She was breathing faster. He eased the lips of her vagina apart with the back of his thumbs and she came in a sudden gush, gagging slightly, her head rolling from side to side on her arms. She seemed as though she might straighten up for a moment, but changed her mind and pushed back against him again as his hands went under the body of her dress and found her nipples.

He got the condom out of his pocket and tore it open between his teeth with one hand, still caressing her with the other. Then he stepped back a little to unzip his fly and fit it in place. Jane didn't move. When he was ready he touched her again, firmly now, his whole hand covering the bush of wet hair. 'D'you want it?' he said.

'Yeah,' she said, barely audible, her face in her hands.

'Now,' he said, placing the tip of his penis just there.

'Yeah,' she said, louder this time. Then she said, 'Agh,' and a moment later, 'Ugh,' words she didn't use every day, and she pushed back with all her strength as he entered and went deep inside her.

Chapter 58

In the morning she lay in his arms. Neither of them had slept during the night. Occasionally one or the other would drift off, but then suddenly they would be awake again, reaching out for each other. She said she would have to get up, she had a meeting at the office, sort out the final details of the handover. Sam would have liked to stay in her bed, with her or without her now, he didn't mind. But he got up all the same, sat on the side of the bed naked and watched her dress. She looked bloody good. Tired in her face, around the eyes, and the pallor of fatigue draped about her, but every garment she put on, she looked just as good as she did without it.

When she was ready she came over and kissed him. She put her forehead next to his and said, 'What about tonight?'

'I don't know,' he told her. 'I've got something to do with Gus. Geordie might be here when you get home.'

She pouted. Trying to look like a little girl, but looking like herself pouting.

'I'll try,' he said, meaning it. 'If I can, I will.'

'I'm looking forward,' she said, and left.

Sam got in the shower and washed the night away. A hard day coming up. He realized he hadn't thought about her all night. So close to her that it wasn't necessary to think. First time she'd been out of his mind for a long time. It seemed like every day, every night had been full of her since the day he'd met Deacon in Betty's Every one except last night.

Now with the water cascading over his body he had to return reluctantly to the thought that she might be implicated in the murders. What the fuck, he thought, she would always seem good for those few hours. If they never touched again, the memory, for that was what it was already, would still be a good one.

He used Jane's telephone to ring Gus. Marie answered the phone and Sam said, 'How're you doing?'

'Sam?' she said. 'I'm fine. Working too hard. How about you?'

'I'm OK,' he told her. 'Was wondering if Gus is getting out of bed today?'

'He's up already,' she said. 'Looks terrible, but he's on his feet.'

'Ask him what time he wants to start,' Sam said.

'Just a minute.'

Sam hung on to the phone, picturing Marie going to look for Gus. He had witnessed their relationship for years, sat with each of them in the early days, when they fought all the time. They'd somehow got it together so they didn't crowd each other any more, come to terms with the fact that each of them needed a separate existence as well as the one they shared. But they were together. Sam often told Gus how lucky he was, but Gus, he knew already.

'Sam? He said around one. That OK?'

'Yeah. I'll be ready. Hey, Marie, when you coming to work with us?'

She laughed down the line. 'I'm keeping the option open,' she said. 'What they're doing to the Health Service.'

He hung up and rang Celia, find out where he was supposed to be. Talking to a woman at Betty's, name of Fletcher, thought her husband was trying to poison her so he could marry his floozie. Life sometimes must get lonely.

★

After the interview with Mrs Fletcher Sam had time to get back home for a bite to eat and change before Gus picked him up. He found Geordie's 'poem' on his pillow and carried it back into the sitting room. 'Does this mean you're going away again?' he asked.

'No,' Geordie said. 'It's just a present. Is it right? The spelling and everything?'

'Some of it's OK,' Sam said. He read through it again. Some of the words were misspelled: *agen/again, frend/friends, plees/please, wen/when, werld/world*. 'And some of it's in fuckin' Chinese.'

'I'm multi-lingual,' Geordie said.

Sam looked at him, watched him go to the sink and rinse a cup out, said nothing. Then Geordie started laughing. 'You know what it means?' he asked.

'Yeah. I know, but where did *you* get it from?'

'It's Bob,' Geordie said. 'He knows loads of fuckin' words, Sam. You listen to him, after a while you get bells ringing in your head. Multi-this, subjugate-the-other, hypo-fuckin' poly-bleedin'-morpheus. They come out one after the other. You close your eyes, you might think he's making sense but really you're punch drunk. It does your head in.'

Chapter 59

Gus and Sam started work in the cellar just after two. By three-thirty they still hadn't got the first brick out. 'Christ,' Gus said, 'I think this was a mistake, Sam.'

'You got a temperature?' Sam asked.

'It's so fuckin' cold down here. Yeah, I'm sweating, but I'm freezing cold.'

'Put my coat on,' Sam said. 'Sit on the chair. It's coming loose now.'

Gus put Sam's coat over his head, held it tight together under his chin. Sam went back to working on the wall. They had chipped out most of the cement around one brick but it still wouldn't come out. Now Sam was using the cold chisel and hammer to split the brick. 'Once I get this out, it should be easy,' he said.

Gus stood and paced up and down the tiny room. 'Tell you what, Sam,' he said. 'D'you mind if I wait in the car? I'm gonna have to lay down.'

Sam walked to the car with him, got him bedded down on the back seat. 'I'm sorry,' Gus said. 'I just feel like shit.'

Sam rolled himself a cigarette, lit it and walked back to the house, down to the cellar. It was weird being there alone. He went back upstairs again and bolted the door so no mad bastard would come in and knife him. Too many killings in this case already, he thought. When Deacon had bought it Sam'd already found himself hoping it wasn't contagious. Since then they'd been going down like flies.

He hit his thumb with the hammer and threw it across the cellar. 'Jesus, Frances,' he said, 'if you put this wall up, you should be working in the fuckin' construction industry.'

Eventually the brick came out and he got the lump hammer to try take the rest of the wall down. It was more difficult than he thought, though, and before it got easier he had to loose a whole row of bricks, stacking them on the other side of the room in a puddle of water.

There was a smell now. Best way to describe it would be like rotten meat. That together with the brick dust and cement in the confined space made him feel like retching. He worked for about ten minutes at a time, spaced with trips upstairs where he opened one of the windows and took in gulps of fresh air. Should have brought some kind of mask to work down there.

What he eventually unearthed was a tomb. The false wall

227

concealed a space only about thirty inches wide, The real wall beyond it was covered in piping, gas and water mains, and on a shelf about four feet off the ground was something the size of a body wrapped in black polythene. Sam could tell from feeling the outside that it was a body, he didn't need to unwrap it. Placed on top of the body were the dead remains of a bunch of flowers, and with them a postcard, something written on it.

Sam took the card and walked over the rubble to the candle. He wiped it on his overalls, get the surface dust off. It was a photograph of Michelangelo's Virgin. On the back in a tiny script, blue ink, were the words, *To My Darling Graham. Rest in Peace Until We Meet Again. Love Frances.*

He took the card back to the body and placed it on what might have been the guy's chest. Then he had to get out of there, the stench was overwhelming, making his eyes water.

Gus was sleeping on the back seat of the Volvo, but when Sam told him what he'd found he wanted to go back to the house, see it for himself.

'Christ, Gus,' said Sam, 'there's nothing to see. It's just a plastic bag.'

They walked back to the house together, and Gus went into the cellar by himself. 'I don't ever want to go down there again,' Sam told him. Gus was a few minutes down there, then he came back up with the hammers and cold chisels and spewed on the floor.

Sam took the tools from him, said, 'I told you so.'

'So what we got?' Gus said on the way back to York.

'About twelve grand,' Sam told him. 'Frances even signed the postcard. Graham either died or she killed him, and since then she's been killing everyone who ever had anything to do with him.'

'But why?' said Gus.

'We'll ask her,' said Sam. 'Now.'

'What about the killing in New Zealand, the woman in Sweden? She doesn't even have a passport.'

'Maybe they're down to someone else,' Sam said. 'But I'd like to bet we can pin all the other killings on her.'

Sam drove to Frances's house and parked outside. They knocked on her door but there was no answer. 'No car here, either,' said Gus.

'She won't be far away,' said Sam. 'We could leave it, come back later. I wouldn't mind a wash.'

'OK. I'll drop you at home, pick you up again in an hour.'

Chapter 60

Geordie had already left for the cul-de-sac, and Bob Blackburn was sat in Sam's chair gripping the arm rests with both hands. He jumped out of the chair as Sam came through the door, sat down, then got out of the chair again. He wasn't shaking, but looked like he had been. 'Frances is here,' he said. 'All afternoon, sat outside in her car, watching the house.'

Sam went outside but there was no black Panda in the street. 'She's not here now,' he said. 'How the hell did she know you were here?'

'I don't know,' Blackburn said. 'Geordie noticed the car about an hour after you left.'

'Well, she's gone. I'm gonna go see her with Gus soon, drop her off at the police station.'

He went in the bathroom and washed the smell away, changed his clothes. Twenty minutes before Gus was due to pick him up he rang Jane's number.

'We cracked it,' Sam told her when she picked up the phone.

'Graham East's body is in Frances's old house in Leeds. She must have done the other killings as well.'

'Sam, are you sure?'

'I'm telling you,' he said. 'We just got back.'

'Are you coming over?'

'No, we're gonna get Frances. I'll come over later.'

Jane started shouting. 'Oh, God! Sam, Oh, God!'

'What's going on?' he said. 'Something happened?'

'He's here,' she said urgently, hysteria in her voice. 'Sam, Graham's here. He's in the house.'

'He can't be, we just . . .'

Jane's voice was rising to a scream. 'Sam, what shall I do? He's in the house.'

'OK. Jesus, just get the fuck out of there.' The phone went dead and Sam ran out of the house. No car, he ran back into the house and rang Gus.

'Get round to the cul-de-sac,' he said. 'Fuckin' fast. Graham East's there.'

'Sam, we just found the guy's body.'

'Just go,' Sam told him. 'Don't do anything else, don't talk, just get in the fuckin' car.'

'OK, I'm on my way.'

Sam put the phone down, said to Blackburn, 'Lock the door, don't let anyone in.' Then he left the house and ran through the town towards Bishophill. How *could* Graham be there? Jane must have got it wrong. He knew it wasn't Graham. There would be a rational explanation.

Geordie was on a stretcher being loaded into an ambulance, there were tubes coming out of him, and the ambulance driver was holding some kind of bottle above the kid's head.

'They think he'll be OK,' Gus said.

Sam looked at the kid's face, small and white, his eyes closed. 'What happened?'

'He's been shot,' the ambulance driver said. 'That's what it looks like. Shot in the back.'

'Is he gonna live?'

'He might be OK,' the driver said. 'If I can get him to the hospital.'

'I'll go with him,' Gus said.

'OK. Christ, Gus. Was he conscious? Did he say anything? What about Jane?'

'He was face-down in the front room,' Gus told him, getting into the ambulance. 'I just rang emergency. No sign of Jane.'

The ambulance moved off, lights flashing. Sam went to the door of the house where a policeman tried to stop him. He brushed past. 'I work here,' he told the guy.

Delany, his sergeant, and two other cops were in the front room. 'I'm glad you people aren't looking after me,' Delany said when Sam entered the room.

'Shit, I'm not a fuckin' zoo keeper,' Sam told him. 'What happened here?'

'Your friend Graham East came here to get Mrs Deacon,' Delany said. 'Shot your assistant. Mrs Deacon must have run out the house, and Graham took off after her. He won't get far.'

'Graham's dead,' Sam told him. 'This's something different. They never used a gun before.'

'Guns, knives, what's the difference?' Delany said. 'The man's a psycho, he'll use anything he gets his hands on.'

'I just told you he's dead,' said Sam. 'You don't listen.'

'OK, I'm listening. What you telling me?'

Sam told him about the Leeds house, the cellar, the body, everything. Delany told his sergeant to have Frances picked up, then, 'I'll come with you,' he said. 'We can't do anything here.' He turned to Sam and said, 'You better be on the level. You've been a thorn in my side ever since this case began.'

'You're kidding me,' Sam said.

★

231

When they'd left Sam did his usual checks of the house, out of habit, he supposed. He took the Walther and put it in his pocket. If other people had guns, it might even up the odds a little.

The telephone was on the floor in Jane's room, must have been where she answered it when Sam rang. He used it to ring the hospital, check how Geordie was doing. They would only tell him that the kid was in the operating theatre.

Deacon's wardrobe was open. Maybe she was getting more things ready for Geordie? There were two suitcases by her dressing table, getting ready to leave for the sun.

Sam went into the next room and sat down at the large antique desk. Yeah, passport, personal papers on there. Christ, Delany said she got out of the house and whoever shot Geordie was out after her. What was she doing, just legging it through the town?

He picked up the passport and opened it from the back, take a look at the photograph. Yeah, that was her, the little mouth, eyes staring out. A face from another time and place.

He thumbed through the stamped pages and stopped at one with a green stamp, said *Inrest Sverige Passkontrollen Göteborg*. There was a date as well, the date was the day before Lotta Jensen was killed.

'You're kidding me,' Sam said.

The previous page showed she had been to New Zealand as well. Entered a couple of days before Sarah Dunn died, left a week later. Must have taken a few days to see the sights. Jesus, what a nerve.

Sam leafed through the other documents on the desk. The most interesting one was Jane's birth certificate. Sam had seen the record in the public library, but this was the original document. She had been born in Leeds and named Jane Debra. Under the heading Name and Surname of Father the registrar had written in, David Golding.

He folded the birth certificate and put it in his inside pocket with the passport. 'You'll have to come back to collect these,' he said. 'And I'm gonna be waiting for you.'

There was a hammering on the door then, and he went down to answer it.

'You lock yourself in for?' Delany said, walking past him.

'Habit,' Sam said.

'Your theory doesn't work,' Delany told him. 'Frances was dead when we got there. Shot in the head.'

'But there was no note,' Sam said.

'No. Nothing. I want you down at the station.'

'I'm not coming,' Sam told him. 'I'm staying here till the blonde gets back.'

'I could arrest you.'

'You could,' Sam told him. 'But you don't want to fuck up any more. Might lose your job.'

Chapter 61

Sam sat looking at the phone until it rang. Jane Deacon's voice said, 'Sam? Thank God it's you. Is it all right? Can I come back?'

'Where are you?' he asked. 'I was worried.'

'I don't know. In a phone box.'

'Yeah,' he said. 'Come back now.'

Fifteen minutes later she let herself in. She walked into the front room wearing that little blue cashmere suit, just like the first time he saw her. Bit more worn maybe.

'Where's Geordie?' she said. 'Is he all right?'

'In the hospital,' Sam told her. 'He's gonna survive.'

'Oh!' That was a surprise for her. She must have thought he was dead.

'Tell me what happened?' Sam said.

'Geordie let a man into the house,' she said. 'I thought it was Graham. He shot Geordie. Then I ran out of the house.'

'Graham's dead,' Sam said. 'I told you. I saw his body this afternoon.'

'Sam, I *thought* it was him. I didn't have time to think. Whoever it was, he shot Geordie. I just ran.'

'Frances is dead,' Sam said.

'Oh, when? Oh, no.'

'That's ham acting, Jane,' said Sam. 'Your little sister, wasn't she?'

'Sister? No. What do you mean?'

'I mean you're a fuckin' bad actress,' Sam said. 'And an even worse liar.' He took the birth certificate and passport out of his pocket and threw them at her.

She picked the passport up, left the birth certificate by her feet. Sam watched her expression change as the implications dawned on her. It happened like a slide show, her shoulders slowly dropping, her mouth opening and closing again. She glanced at the passport, put it in her pocket. She looked at the birth certificate on the floor, and for a moment she thought of picking it up. Then she looked back at Sam as she realized there was no way out. Except one.

Now she had a gun in her hand.

'You gonna shoot *me* as well?' he said. 'Then you'll have to go round the hospital and shoot Geordie again. Put the gun away, Jane, it's all over.'

The gun was shaking in her hand, but not so much that she would miss him if the thing went off. It was pointed mainly at his head, occasionally going down to his chest, but then she would raise it again.

'Sit down,' she said. 'Over there.' Motioning to the easy chair.

Sam did what she said.

'And put your hands in your pockets. I need to think.' She held the gun with both hands now, steadying it.

'Fuckin' late in the day,' Sam said, putting his hands in his

234

pockets, feeling the Walther there, cold against his hand, next to a pack of tobacco.

'No one knows I've come back here,' she said. 'Anyone could have shot you. By the time Geordie comes round, *if* he comes round, I could be out of the country.'

'So you *are* gonna shoot me?'

She hadn't made her mind up about that. But she was getting closer to a decision every moment that passed. She nodded her head slowly.

'Without telling me what happened?'

'You've guessed it already,' she said. 'Frances was my sister.'

'I know that. I read your birth certificate.'

'Frances had the idea Graham wanted her to kill all the people in the communal house. I saw it as an easy way of getting rid of Terry. She'd kill him, I'd have you as an alibi.'

'But you killed the two women,' Sam said. 'Lotta Jensen, and the other one, the New Zealander.'

The blonde shook her head. Something like a smile creased her face. 'No,' she said. 'Frances borrowed my passport. She had a blonde wig, looked just like her sister.'

'The executioner's face . . .' Sam said. 'So, tonight you panicked when I said I was going to Frances's house. You shot Geordie, then went round and shot Frances.'

'It's a pity you know everything,' said Jane. 'We were getting on so well. Now you leave me no choice.' Thinking she was bullet-proof.

'Last cigarette?' he said. 'For old time's sake?'

'Move very slowly,' she said.

Sam took the pack of tobacco and papers from his pocket, carefully rolled a cigarette and put it to his mouth. He found a box of matches and struck one, lit the cigarette. Blew out a stream of smoke, but not enough to hide behind. The blonde with the gun was still there when it cleared.

'One hand back in your pocket,' she said.

'You're so considerate, Jane.'

She shook her head. Somewhere inside must have been the ghost of a smile, but it didn't show. 'You're a funny man, Sam,' she said, 'but this's not a time for jokes.'

He had managed to grip the Walther and had it pointed towards her. There was a moment when he thought he might not have to use it, when she faltered, flickered her eyes a couple of times, and the gun in her hand wavered away from him. But a second later it was pointed at his head. Sam looking straight into the barrel. He refocused and saw her eyes then, and knew she was going to do it.

'You're not even gonna let me finish the cigarette?' he said. Her finger began closing on the trigger. She was going to do it now. She'd run out of words.

Sam shot her through his pocket. He thought it would get her somewhere in the upper leg, but the gun bucked when he pulled the trigger. Bucked! Christ, it almost did a somersault. And the noise, Jesus! It was bad enough outside, when he shot it through the car window, but inside it sounded more like a train crash. She dropped her own gun and they both watched it bounce on the carpet. That went off as well, the bullet hitting the piano and setting up a whole sequence of reverberations. Jane clutched her lower chest. She didn't say anything, just looked real surprised like something had happened she hadn't even thought of.

She went down on her knees first then toppled over and laid on her back, just about the same position her husband had ended up in. Sam glanced at the photograph of Deacon on top of the piano, nodded at the image, then got out of the chair and looked at her. She'd passed out but was still breathing. She'd live, but the blue cashmere suit was a total write-off. Pity about that, Sam thought, real nice suit.

Then he killed his cigarette.

Chapter 62

Sam took Wanda back to their table and held the chair for her while she sat down. 'Would *you* like to dance, Celia?' he said.

'Oh, Sam, you don't want to dance with an old girl like me,' she said.

He walked around the table and took her by the hand. Led her on to the small dance floor. 'They're playing our tune,' he said.

Gus and Marie waltzed past as Sam placed his hand on Celia's hip. 'I'll try not to step on your toes,' he said.

'Gus said you went to see Jane Deacon?' Celia said.

'She wouldn't see me,' Sam told her. 'I spoke to her shrink. A woman doctor, even looks a bit like her. She said Jane is a control freak. She controlled Frances, almost completely, could get her to do anything she wanted. We'll never know if the killings were Frances's idea or Jane's. But Jane was behind it all the way. She knew Frances would be a suspect, so lending her her own passport was a stroke of genius. No one was going to suspect Jane.' He swung Celia round. 'Apparently it was Jane who introduced Graham to Frances in the first place,' he said. 'At one of the Chapeltown Carnivals.'

'Why did you want to see her, Sam?'

'Dunno,' he said. 'We got pretty close over the last weeks. Maybe I needed to see if she was still there.'

'It doesn't sound as though she is.'

'Or ever was, really,' Sam said. 'That one keeps coming up all the time for me. You think you know somebody, talk the same language. Then you find out they were somebody else.'

'That doesn't happen so much with me,' Celia said. 'I think it's the company you keep.'

'Yeah,' he said. 'Homeless drop-outs, old Quaker ladies feeding me ginger biscuit powder, getting me hooked.'

She looked up into his eyes. 'There you go again,' he said. 'Twinkling those eyes at me.'

Celia's peel of laughter came and she hung on to him tightly as he swung her round the floor. 'So, you're very pleased with yourself?' she said.

'Hell, I'm pleased with all of us,' said Sam. 'We kept it together. We're a real team.'

'So Sam said Gus could buy a car,' Geordie said to Wanda at the table. 'Then when I've finished learning words I'm gonna have driving lessons, and when that's over we'll get another car, and I'll be able to use it.'

'I could give you some driving lessons, if you like,' said Wanda. 'Make it happen faster.'

'OK,' Geordie said. 'Celia's giving me some as well. So I should be good.' He watched Sam and Celia as they danced past the table. 'What do you think about Sam?' he asked. 'You think he's a good dancer?'

'Yes,' Wanda told him. 'He surprises you.'

'I surprised him as well,' said Geordie. 'Moved up to my own flat. I'm sleeping there all the time now. Playing sounds, reading books, listening to quiz shows on the radio. I'm learning loads. You wanna teach me to dance?'

Wanda smiled. 'OK,' she said. She stood and walked on to the floor, Geordie following her. 'Have you ever tried before?'

'No,' Geordie confessed. 'But I'm celibate, so it should be fairly easy.'